Death and Wine

Also by Paul Breen

Death and Wine

A Cy and Liz Bartholomew Mystery

Paul Breen

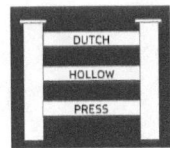

Dutch Hollow Press

ISBN 979-8-9996612-1-0 (paperback)

ISBN 979-8-9996612-0-3 (ebook)

ISBN 979-8-9996612-2-7 (hardcover)

Book Cover Design by ebooklaunch.com

Author photo by Dave Greenwell

For my parents, John and Loretta Breen

Chapter 1

I placed my hand on Liz's forearm as the gate lifted. A black SUV pulled in front of us, its left blinker flashing as it exited the parking structure. My hand relaxed, and we walked down the hill. Dirty clouds dominated the sky, but I could see the blue of Lake Monona through the trees.

"It feels odd to be toting luggage in our hometown," Liz said. "How far to the hotel?"

It was a B&B and not a hotel, but she knew that, so I didn't correct her. "We'll go down a block to that five-point intersection. Then we turn up Wilson Street, and it's on the right."

If it were my decision, we would have slept at home and driven in each day rather than sleeping in a strange bed. But Liz felt that staying overnight gave her valuable networking opportunities. She was the one breaking into a career in wine, so I agreed.

I took her hand at the intersection. When the "Walk" sign turned, I tugged her forward.

"I can see the sign," she said. "I may be *legally blind*, but I'm not *blind*."

After three crosswalks, we approached The Larson Place Bed & Breakfast. The renovations I had heard about were apparent, as the wood façade was ivy free and painted light blue. The porch looked pristine, and the front door was new. There was also a manicured lawn instead of a well-worn miniature parking lot.

"Looks good," I said. "Last time I was here, it looked like student housing."

"It's big." Her nose scrunched up. "Three stories, like you said, but I don't see the second-floor door or porch you talked about."

She was referring to a door that once led out onto a tiny second-story metal porch. About ten years ago, the building housed apartments and my locksmith company got a call about a room which the manager couldn't enter. I picked the lock, entered, and found a dead body.

"When they remodeled, they must have taken away the second-floor porch and door," I said as we stopped in front of the building.

"Let's hope they don't put us in that room." Her thick auburn hair bounced as her head turned. "Who wants to sleep in a room where someone died?"

"The guy had a heart attack," I said with a chuckle. "Nothing to worry about."

"It's still creepy."

We crossed in front of the house where we would sleep the next three nights. Liz was joining five other experts to rate wines from Wisconsin vineyards for an upcoming book on Midwestern wines. The house had plenty of room for the critics and their support staff.

The newly installed walkway was red brick, and the lawn looked healthy. Evenly trimmed bushes edged the front yard.

Everything seemed perfectly green compared to neighboring properties.

"Ambrose told me the back of the building is only two stories. The new owners knocked down the back half and replaced it with a large event room. That room has a high ceiling, so it takes up both stories. Plus, he said they combined a few rooms to make larger bedrooms."

"Who is Ambrose?" I asked. "Is he running this shindig?"

"Yes, Ambrose Houser. He's a critic who is trying to be the pied piper for non-Vitis vinifera wines."

I didn't remember what a non-Vitis vinifera wine was and didn't want to know, so I just nodded.

Nodding was one thing I was good at.

Stepping onto the porch, I paused, touched the red brick steps, and peered at the pristine smart lock on the wooden door. Liz pulled out her phone, and the lock clicked. Before I could grasp the handle, the door opened, revealing a mustached man who looked straight out of the early nineteen seventies. He was about my height, and I guessed him to be in his late thirties, which meant he was more than ten years younger than my fifty-one years. He wore a charcoal sport coat, yellow turtleneck, gray pants, and black shoes. Curly brown hair covered his head and most of his ears.

"Good morning," mustache man said. "Might you be Elizabeth? Elizabeth and Silas?" His arms and upper body moved, but his legs were stationary.

Liz blinked a few times, which is what she did when her eyes struggled to focus. "Yes." She elbowed in front of me and stuck out a hand. I had worried that she had overdressed, but the man's outfit eliminated any concern. "Call me Liz and call him

Cy. We have been married for twenty-five years and I've never even heard his mom call him Silas."

"Well, I'm Ambrose Houser." His low, melodious voice fit his look. If we were going to do karaoke, I'd want him to take the lead. "It's good to meet both of you. I'm in charge of the tasting." He glanced at the Apple Watch on his wrist. "You're the last to arrive. A few of us pulled in yesterday evening and the rest this morning. You should have time to get settled in your room."

The foyer was impressive. A six-foot wide staircase, which looked original, dominated the area. A beige and burgundy rug was affixed to the wooden steps, giving them a warm, classic appearance. Hallways sat on each side of the stairs, and a doorless room was to our right populated by two empty chairs, a brown rug, and a brick fireplace. To our left was a closed door.

Pushing down the extension on Liz's suitcase, I grabbed the handle, pausing at the sight of a woman coming down the hallway. Stopping next to Ambrose, she brushed back wavy blonde hair. She was a few inches taller than Liz and was dressed casually in shorts and a tank top which revealed her bare midriff. When she smiled, her eyebrows jumped up and down and dimples punctured her cheeks. Not surprisingly, her teeth were perfectly white. She even smelled good.

"Who do we have here?" The woman's hand rested on Ambrose's shoulder, but her blue eyes locked onto mine. She leaned forward and took my hand. I felt like I should drop to one knee, but I knew better.

"Hello, I'm Cy." Motioning toward my wife, I released the woman's grip. "Guess you could say I'm Mrs. Bartholomew's assistant."

"And my husband." Liz offered her hand as she stepped on the staircase's first step. "Call me Liz."

"Oh, you're the *local* critic that Josh suggested. I'm Carpenter Dalbesio."

She looked more like a model or a social media influencer than a wine critic. Her voice was earthy. I guessed she was a Midwesterner like Liz and me. "Carpenter?" I said. "That's an unusual name. What was the last name again?"

Her smile widened and I swear her teeth glittered. "Dalbesio. It starts with D-A and not D-E."

"Good to know."

"The last name is one of only two good things I got from my ex-husband." Her gaze bounced between Ambrose and me. "The other, of course, is my daughter." Reaching up, she nearly touched Liz's hair. "What beautiful hair; it's so full and voluptuous. Is it your natural color?"

"Thank you," Liz said. "Yes, it is my natural color."

That wasn't quite true as she had recently started dyeing her hair, eliminating some gray. Any change in color was slight, though I thought it was more reddish than it had been.

"Oh," Carpenter said, taking Liz's hand. "There is one thing. Are you superstitious?"

Liz's eyes locked onto the woman. "Superstitious?"

Ambrose laughed and his arms flailed about like a marionette. "Carpenter got in last night and, well, I let her switch rooms with you."

"A good night's sleep is important for tasting." She looked at Ambrose, who nodded his agreement. "I thought it might freak me out a bit knowing a death occurred in the room. Ambrose thought it would be okay to switch, since the one you moved to is bigger."

"There should be a notification on your phone. Your room number and access code have changed," he said.

Liz did not look pleased. "Let me guess. You put us on the second floor."

Chapter 2

We were relieved they hadn't moved us to the room where I had found a dead man ten years earlier. Our relief vanished when instead, they put us on the third floor in a room where, according to Ambrose, someone was murdered nearly a century ago.

"Are you okay with staying in this room?" I asked as we reached the top of the staircase. Two closed doors sat on one side of the hall. One room was marked 3A and the other 3B. At the end of the hall was a bathroom, its door partially open. I glanced out one of the hallway windows.

"Yes," Liz said. "I'm not about to create a fuss. It might be different if you weren't with me." She pulled out her phone, and soon the door clicked. "Are these decent locks?" She usually asked about security since she knew I'd tell her anyway.

"They're good. I don't know how easy it would be to hack in. If it were me, I'd pick the key lock." Liz swung the door open, revealing a canopied king-size bed. The bedspread was white and blue with a pattern of flowers lining the edging.

"This is huge," she said as we stepped inside. "It's a little warm and stuffy. Luckily, they left a window open. This must be a room where they combined two, since we've got two large windows."

"There's only two bedrooms on this floor and a bathroom. The guy with the mustache said his room is up here, so there's just three of us on this level."

She kneeled on the bed and lifted one of the room's two window shades. "Beautiful view. We can see Lake Monona, though the roof blocks some of it."

I crouched next to her, placing a hand around her waist. Having been in security for thirty years meant that, rather than seeing a beautiful lake, I saw a point of access which was approachable from the roof. I closed and locked the window.

"If you close it up, it will get stifling up here. Leave at least this one open since it's got a screen."

"Okay." I lifted the window, then made sure the screen was secure.

She turned, gave me a peck on the lips, and pointed at the luggage. "Put the bag on the bed. I want to brush my hair and then we can go downstairs. You shouldn't be late for your first official job as a wine critic."

She was making fun of me as I was not a wine critic and this was not my job.

Instead of standing around until she was ready, I walked down the hall to the bathroom. Unlike the other doors, it had a lever lock. I closed it, pushed the interior button, and rattled the door, making sure it stayed shut. Looking out the shoulder-level window, I expected a view but got only the side of the adjacent office building.

When I opened the bathroom door, Liz was waiting. I led her down the staircase and followed her through the foyer and into the hallway. We came to a large kitchen with two tables. The first was white and encircled by eight chairs, and the second was cherry red. The acrylic flooring at the room's edge clashed with the wood floors in the older part of the house.

We walked through the kitchen, drawn by the voices. Entering the event room, my gaze rose to the windows, which surrounded an enormous flat-screen television. The back of the building faced southeast, but the neighboring apartments blocked much of the morning sun. Mechanical blinds, which I expected would be closed as the sun approached its zenith, topped each window.

Ambrose Houser stood behind a lectern near the back windows, and two women in black and white server outfits stood behind a bar counter. Six small, round, high-top tables were dispersed throughout the room, a single person occupying all but one.

Ambrose motioned us to sit at the empty table. Liz didn't seem to notice, so I put an arm around her shoulder and guided her to the spot. Stools awaited us, but, like the others, we just leaned against our table.

Moments later, Ambrose tapped an empty glass with his butter knife. "We're going to start," he said. "We'll begin with introductions, then I'll lay out how the event will unfold. Hopefully, we'll have time for questions."

Liz and the others in the room clapped. I didn't want to, but I joined in.

"Well, you'll be relieved to hear that my introduction will be brief. My name is Ambrose Houser. I've met all of you before today except, well, Liz and her husband Silas...er, Cy. Most of you have already attended my tasting sessions, so this is old hat for you. As for my background, well, I'll start by saying I've been a sommelier and a critic since joining my parents' wine import business in suburban Minneapolis as a twenty-one-year-old. I won't bore you with a listing of certifications or publications, other than to mention that a few years ago, I published a book on east coast wines, imaginatively titled *Wines and Wineries of New England*."

Laughter spattered through the room, including from Liz. I wanted to pull out my phone and play solitaire, but that wasn't an option.

"The New England book and the one I'm currently working on differ from most wine criticism," he continued. "Instead of another tome on West Coast or European wines made from Vitas vinifera grapes, these books focus on wine made from grapes that grow throughout North America. Growing and buying locally is important but doesn't preclude the inclusion of Old-World grapes. Blind tasting is a pillar of my approach. The testing will be by you, a panel of connoisseurs under conditions which few wine experts, well, adhere to. We will limit blind tasting to twenty-five entries per day. Okay. Now I'll turn things over to *The Boss*."

Everyone clapped as Ambrose left the lectern and was replaced by an attractive young woman. Her black hair was in a bun and she wore a white shirt, black pants, and fiery red lipstick. "First off," she said. "No one calls me *The Boss* except for Ambrose. He gets away with it because he is *my* boss."

There was more laughing, and I looked around the room. Half the people were young enough to be my children, including the current speaker. I thought it odd that she wore lipstick. Liz claimed lipstick was a no-no for wine tasting. She told me lots of wine-tasting no-nos. Surprisingly, I remembered that one.

"My name is Boston Cruz," the woman at the podium said. "I'll be managing the operation of this event. Those who haven't been to one of Ambrose's tastings might wonder where the first flight is. We'll set it out as soon as introductions are done. For subsequent sessions, flights will be ready prior to your arrival."

"What's a flight?" I whispered to Liz.

"Shush," she mouthed.

"You'll see we've got me and two other staff." Boston motioned toward the two women behind the bar counter. "Renee, Abby, and I will take glasses and bottles from refrigeration or the cellar. We will open, unbind, decant as necessary, pour, and bring the glasses to you. Each of you will judge four to eight wines per hour in three separate sessions. Vintners sent two bottles of each entry and all six of you will judge the same flight of wines at the same time. You will provide a numerical rating for each wine. I will compile the ratings, and we will try to come to an agreement on the rating to be included in Ambrose's book. We will also collect your notes, as Ambrose will incorporate many of them into the textual description of the entries."

Boston talked more about the testing process and wine tasting issues of which I had no interest. A notebook and a pamphlet on the table caught my attention. I took the notebook, but Liz grabbed it from my hands, telling me it was for her notes. She let me look at the pamphlet, which included pictures and biographies of everyone in the room. Everyone except me.

"One last note," Boston said. "You may have noticed that Elizabeth Bartholomew has an assistant. His name is Silas Bartholomew, and he's Elizabeth's husband."

"Call me Cy!" I called out. Everyone looked at us.

"Cy," she said. "Call him Cy. He is here because Elizabeth is visually challenged and has requested his assistance in evaluating color, hue, and viscosity. Ambrose reviewed this with various experts in the field and they thought it appropriate. Silas—Cy that is, won't taste. The only glass he'll have will be for water."

People asked a few questions, though none of them made sense to me other than one about how and where they were storing bottles, and which would be decanted.

The next speaker was Carpenter Dalbesio, the attractive woman who had moved us from the *heart attack room* to the *murder room*. She introduced herself and pointed out again that the second letter in her last name was an "a" and not an "e." She then pulled out her phone and held it out in front of her. "Hello, this is Carpenter Dalbesio from *The Wine Carpenter,* and I'm in Madison, Wisconsin, for a tasting for Ambrose Houser's upcoming book on Midwestern wines." Turning the phone toward the audience, she asked us to say hello to her "followers."

I am good at non-compliance, so I said nothing.

When she finished her media moment, Ambrose got to his feet and noted that Carpenter would not be recording or streaming during tasting sessions. He sat back down and Carpenter introduced the short, red-headed man at the table next to us as Josh Peterson. She gave him a kiss on the cheek and ceded the lectern.

Josh talked in spurts, and people laughed at his comments. Rather than listening to his spiel, I read the biography included in the pamphlet. The write-up said he was from New England but lived in Madison. He wrote for a variety of national magazines, but I had never heard of him. Katie

Coolidge followed. Like Carpenter, she was a skinny blonde. A Californian, she wrote for a San Francisco newspaper and a west-coast-based website.

After her introduction, Katie turned toward Ambrose. "Who do you want next?"

"Well," he said. "How about the Bartholomews?"

Liz and I glanced at each other as the wine critics provided a light round of applause.

Chapter 3

When we got to the lectern, I was tempted to crack a joke, but the audience wanted to hear from Liz, so I waited for her to speak. Staring at the people in the room, their youth struck me again. My guess was that Ambrose was the oldest person besides Liz and me. And every woman, including Liz, Boston, the servers, and the critics, was attractive. I wondered if this was how the wine world was, or just how Ambrose Houser's world was.

"Hello, I'm Liz Bartholomew and, as Ambrose mentioned, this is my husband, Cy. Unlike most of you, I only recently got into the wine industry. For the first twenty-five years of my professional career, I worked for the Madison Public Library." She paused, as if letting the comment sink in. "While working, I got involved in wine, earning multiple certifications. The list is in my biography, but I want to point out that, besides being a sommelier, I'm a certified bourbon and Scotch expert, and I've also judged several cheese competitions. My husband says that's appropriate for a Wisconsin native." A few chuckles came from the audience, and she turned to me. "Do you want to say anything, Dear?"

She never called me "Dear," so the question caught me by surprise. Perhaps she was nervous. I leaned forward, as if there was a microphone. "I'm Cy, and I can't tell a seven-dollar wine from a seventy-dollar one. In case you're wondering about my background, I was a long-time partner in Madison's largest private security company, MB Lock & Security. It was something I started with friends when I was just twenty. I oversaw the locksmith division. Should any of you get locked out of your room, I'm the one to call."

There were a few smiles. "Who's next?" Liz asked.

A brunette with lengthy, straight hair raised her hand. "I'm Missy LeBrun."

"Missy is the other local critic," Ambrose said in a booming voice.

"That other guy was from Madison, too," I told Liz as we got back to our table. I flipped through the pamphlet, pointing at the picture and biography of Josh Peterson.

Arriving at the lectern, Missy cleared her throat. "Hello." Attractive but awkward, she had long, angular features and her monotone voice was lower than I expected. "I'm Missy LeBrun and I'm...uh...excited to welcome everyone to Wisconsin. My name is Missy LeBrun." She paused, as if realizing she had repeated herself. Then she forced out a smile. "I'm a Wisconsin native and a graduate of the University of Nevada-Las Vegas and their Sommelier Academy." Her voice cracked, and she cleared her throat. "Sorry about that. I'm a writer and not a public speaker, so I'm nervous. I am, however, excited to be part of this event and to share the Wisconsin wine experience with such a talented group."

She stopped talking and stood silently. Finally, Ambrose got to his feet and clapped. The rest of us joined in, and Missy almost curtsied as she left the lectern.

Ambrose announced that Boston and her team would prepare for the first flight while he commented on the event. "Before we do our first tasting, which, as you might expect, is sparkling wine, I want to touch on a few rules. Prior to each flight, your server will provide details on the entries. Entry numbers are marked on the base of the glasses. Your notebooks have room for notations, grades, and notes for each entry. We prohibit cell phone use during sessions. Keep in mind that this is not a competition, and we are not giving medals. We are simply grading using a hundred-point scale. Forty minutes after the session begins, your server will summarize your grades and give them to Boston. She will compile them, and we will discuss."

As he finished, a server approached our table holding a circular tray filled with eight glasses of sparkling wine. She placed the tray on the table and returned with a carafe of water, a trio of glasses, and a plastic cup for Liz to spit into. The woman's nametag said "Renee," and she smelled like wine. She scooted away, returning with a pile of napkins.

Renee tossed back her long, curly black hair and introduced herself. She appeared to be about my twenty-two-year-old daughter's age. "I'm Renee Curry, a Hospitality Management student at Madison College. I'll be graduating in May, and I plan for a career in the wine industry. Though it's not my first tasting, this one is different because it gives me an opportunity to meet experts and understand how wine fits within the hospitality industry." She smiled at the end and let out a breath, as if she had practiced the line.

"Interesting," I lied.

She smiled and her gaze fell on Liz. "Getting back to business, I want to point out that at least ninety percent of the grapes used in all the wines you will sample were grown in the Midwest. The pamphlet details which American Viticultural Areas, or AVAs, we included in that definition. Mr. Houser's official grading scale is also listed. The sparkling wines you were just served were stored at forty-two degrees. We opened the bottles ten minutes ago and filled the glasses five minutes ago."

"How much is in each sample?" I asked.

"Two ounces," Liz said, without looking at me. "It's always two ounces."

"Yes, she's right. Oh, and before I go. Mr. Houser wanted to be clear about you, Mr. Bartholomew. You're not to taste or smell the wines."

"I can already smell them," I said, motioning to the sparkling wine swishing in my wife's glass.

She tossed her hair to one side. "Just don't provide feedback on aroma perceptions to Mrs. Bartholomew."

Liz wouldn't care what I thought anyway, so I nodded my agreement.

"Finally, note the timer at the podium." Renee looked at the clock, which showed just over two minutes. "At forty minutes, I'll collect scores. I'll check in with you in a few moments."

Liz sniffed the wine as the liquid swished within the glass. "I don't like flute glasses," she muttered, her nose dipping in. She turned toward me and returned the sample to the table. "What do you think about color? I'm thinking deep straw for one and six. Pale yellow for five and eight. Medium yellow on two, and maybe pale gold on three, four, and seven. Though seven might be a deep yellow."

This was the part of wine tasting I understood. Liz had a chart at home that showed about forty different colors for wine. At one point, she feared she would completely lose her eyesight, so she forced me to judge color with her. She'd pour a glass of wine, and we would note the color.

Earlier this year, she brought a fellow sommelier to the house, and the three of us judged the color of six red wines. We had identical ratings when judging in a well-lit room. When we did it in a dark area of the house, Liz struggled. But this room was well lit, so she would do fine with or without my help.

I put the pamphlet behind the glasses, and Liz got out of her chair. Picking up each glass briefly, I listed the entries in order of darkness. "Six is the lightest. Followed by one. Five and eight are about the same, then seven. Three and four are about the same."

We went through the details, and she noted the color of each entry. The only change she made was to agree with my read that both three and four were pale gold.

"There's sediment and cloudiness in number three," she said, picking up the entry again. "Pét-nat, I assume. A bit of legs on three, four, and eight."

I had no idea what Pét-nat meant and didn't ask. But I knew legs were portions of the liquid that clung to the sides of the glass. "Yeah, that's what I see too."

Taking her first sip, her tongue pushed out, then slid along her lips. She took another taste and repeated. It was going to be a long day.

"Semi-dry," she said, writing in her notes. "La Crescent. There's another grape as well, probably frontenac blanc."

She continued to mutter and write, but I didn't care what grapes were in the wine. My job for this flight was done, so I leaned back and stared at the wine geeks around the room. Carpenter, the blonde with followers, sipped from a glass. The woman was ridiculously attractive, but much less so when spitting into a cup. That's when I heard my wife spit into hers.

Oh, yes. The beautiful sound of a wine tasting.

Chapter 4

Liz spent about five minutes on each wine, writing notes and scoring. Our server, Renee, stopped by as Liz started on her fifth entry. They talked about entry number three, which Liz thought was so different from the rest that it made it difficult to judge. When the timer chimed, Renee returned.

Liz flipped her notebook around and opened it to the sheet for the first session. The server wrote the numbers on a sheet of paper that included Liz's and Josh's names.

Boston placed a whiteboard behind the lectern and detailed the ratings. After five minutes, they were complete, with entry number four receiving the highest rating: a ninety-one. The consistency of the scores between reviewers surprised me. Liz and Katie provided identical scores on seven of the eight entries. Katie's average score was the lowest of the six. Liz's was the second lowest.

The discussion was as boring as I expected, with Ambrose, Josh, and Missy blabbering on for long spouts about scents they detected in each wine. Missy identified peaches and apricots in several entries. All I smelled was wine.

The critics eventually agreed on a rating for seven of the eight wines. Opinions on entry three, however, were strong, with Ambrose, Katie, and Liz providing low scores, while

Carpenter, Josh, and Missy graded higher. Boston ended the conversation by determining the median and mean grades for the entry, saying Ambrose would use one of the two figures. She then unveiled the bottles they had tasted.

Everyone but me oohed as each bottle was revealed, followed by mutterings. Carpenter commented a few times that she "just knew it." After Boston finished, Katie meandered to our table. She and Liz complained about the grade for entry three. At another table, Josh was leaning into Carpenter's ear with a hand resting on her shoulder.

"It is now, um, eleven forty-five," Ambrose said, clearing his throat. "That was a good first session. The second will begin at one-thirty sharp. I know that at least Boston, Josh, Carpenter, and I are going to meet Josh's wife and Caleb and Jenn Iacomini, owners of Fierce Heart Winery, at a nearby establishment for a light lunch. Josh says the restaurant is a hometown favorite. He says it's, well, nothing fancy, so casual dress is fine. Regardless, you are welcome to join us. We'll be heading over after a bio break."

Our destination was on the opposite side of the Wisconsin State Capitol building and about a ten-minute walk. Liz and I walked with Katie while the rest of the group was far ahead. When we entered the three-story building which housed the restaurant, Ambrose waved us over, and we passed between a large cheese poster and the wooden bar counter.

To my surprise, no one ordered wine. When drinks arrived, I counted two mixed drinks, at least one cola, and two tap beers, including mine. There were no spit cups.

As I took my first sip, Carpenter pulled out her iPhone. "Hello, this is Carpenter Dalbesio, from *The Wine Carpenter*. I'm here for lunch at The Old Fashion in Madison, Wisconsin."

It was The Old *Fashioned*, but I didn't correct her.

"We just finished our first session at our event in Madison. This week's tasting is for Wisconsin wineries and includes eighty entries." She turned the camera toward the rest of the table and away from me. Stepping back, she panned across the group. Then she moved in closer, focusing on Josh, who was next to her. His response was tentative and reserved. I waited nervously until Carpenter got to our side of the table.

As Liz and Katie talked, I perused the menu. Though I wasn't overly hungry, I wanted something that wasn't bland, since it would annoy everyone. The chili looked good, as did the spicy burger. But I decided a burger would be too much.

"What are you getting?" Liz asked.

"Chili."

"No, you won't." She hit my shoulder. "I'll smell your breath all afternoon. Get something that's not gonna mess with my nose."

I turned my attention to the menu as Carpenter's camera aimed at Katie. "Ms. Coolidge, do you want to say anything to my followers?"

Katie smiled and said, "Hello." Her teeth were almost as white as Carpenter's.

Carpenter put a hand on my shoulder, as if stopping me from leaning into the shot. "This," she said, "is Katie Coolidge, from Monterey. She's our lone California girl. How are you liking it here in Wisconsin?"

"It's beautiful," she said. "The lakes are magnificent, and the State Capitol looks like the one in DC. This evening, we're going for a boat ride and a swim. I'm looking forward to it."

"You know there's no surfing, right?" Carpenter said with a giggle.

When the camera turned to Liz, she gave a fake smile and introduced herself. I knew her smile was fake because her natural smile was crooked, pulling up higher on her left side. It was because of a childhood injury to her cheek. She was very conscious of the resulting scar and how it affected her appearance. Once, before we were married, she got teary-eyed recounting how a boy named Stevie Schaffer called her "frozen face" and "scar face." It happened forty years ago, but if I ever saw the kid, I'd leave him with a crooked nose.

"Like Missy, Liz is a local critic," Carpenter said. "She used to be a librarian, isn't that right?"

Liz looked like she had been caught stealing from a cookie jar. "Yes, I was a librarian."

"How is your room? I hear there was a murder in it a hundred years ago." She paused and aimed the camera at herself. "Full disclosure: I arrived in Madison last night, and Ambrose told me the story of the killing, so I changed rooms with Liz and Cy. I didn't want to sleep alone in the room." The phone flipped around, aiming at Liz. "Hope there are no hard feelings."

"Not at all. Actually, I was relieved since my husband found a dead man on the second floor a few years ago. I didn't want to be on the second floor."

"Oh, really," Carpenter said. "Maybe that's me getting my comeuppance." The camera aimed at me. "This is Elizabeth's husband, Cy. What's your role?"

"I'm Liz's *plus one*," I said, not wanting to say more for someone's TikTok or YouTube video.

"You first heard it here," Carpenter said. "He's the *plus one*." She went into some concluding remarks, finally putting the phone away as the server returned. "Hope you don't mind the videos," she said after the server took our orders. "YouTube and TikTok are my angle as a wine critic. It's how I differentiate myself from the crowd, though I try not to be too intrusive. For instance, I wanted to ask about you being retired, but I don't cross certain lines in the videos. You seem way too young to be retired. Are you even fifty?"

"Fifty-one," I said, feeling good that she at least pretended to think I was under fifty. "But I'm only semi-retired. I still work part-time as a locksmith."

Carpenter looked at Liz, then returned her gaze to me. "Is what she said true?"

"Is what true?" I asked.

"Did you really find someone dead on the second floor? Any chance it's haunted? My followers love hauntings."

I decided to only answer the first question.

Chapter 5

The server handed out bills as we finished our meals. After a few moments of chaos, we exited the building and stood in the sunlight. Liz muttered something, then approached a woman I had not yet met.

"Hello, I'm Liz Bartholomew. I think I recognize you. Are you one of the winery owners?"

The woman had olive skin, black hair, and a strong jawline. "No, I'm Amanda Peterson." A smile slid onto her face. "Josh Peterson's wife."

"Oh, don't you shop at Dawsons?" Liz replied. "It's a liquor store on the west side where I work."

"Yes, that's me," Amanda said, her smile widening. "I'm usually in on Tuesdays, and you're often working. My husband tells me to rely on your advice for wine and spirits. I may be married to a wine critic, but you're my go-to."

Liz grabbed my elbow and introduced me to the woman. After small talk, we parted from the group. Pulling out my phone, I checked the time. We had forty-five minutes before the next session, so we aimed for a twenty-minute walk.

"I didn't know you knew Josh's wife."

Liz glanced at the others before replying. "I recognized her as a regular at Dawsons. Think I've mentioned her to you before.

Remember, I said there was a woman who likes zinfandel and expensive bourbon. One time, she told the owner about how helpful I was. She's been at the restaurant a few times too, but I don't think she was with her husband."

The restaurant Liz referred to was Premier. Liz worked two days a week as Premier's sommelier.

As we walked, sweat formed on my forehead. A breeze blew off the lake, providing relief. "Were you glad to see the Iacominis?" Liz asked.

"Who are the Iacominis?"

She chuckled and held four of my fingers in her left hand, the way she often did. "They own Fierce Heart Winery. It's north of Madison. We've been there several times."

We've been to lots of wineries and lots of fancy tasting rooms. Usually, I can't differentiate one from another. "Think I remember it, but it's a little vague."

"Caleb looks to be about our age, maybe a few years older. He's a big guy, but a little frumpy."

"And her?"

"Early forties, I'd say. Not frumpy. Thought you'd be glad there are a few people who are more our age."

We stopped at an intersection. I glanced behind us to make sure none of the critics were within earshot, which was unlikely since we had been walking for several minutes. "Happy to hear that not everyone in the wine industry is young and attractive. All these young women. It surprises me. I thought, from what you said, that wine critics were old white guys."

"Katie told me that Ambrose wants to be relevant to a young audience." The light turned. "She also implied that he's got an eye for the ladies, so our group is not a representative sample of American wine critics."

"Makes sense," I said. "I'll have to keep him away from you."

She hit my shoulder. "He's got a lot of younger and better targets than me." Liz was more attractive than she realized, but I understood her point. "I just hope the Iacominis come on the boat outing," she said. "They'll keep us from looking too wrinkly and old."

While I thought we looked good for our age, there's enormous pressure on women to look good in a swimsuit, and this was not a group any woman would want to compete with. "You don't look wrinkly and old," I finally said.

"If I do, Carpenter's followers will know." She ran a hand through her thick auburn hair. "I should have worked to lose five pounds before this. Oh, well. I'll make sure Carpenter doesn't have videos of her standing next to me. She could be a model. So could Boston. At least you got Josh. He's not overweight, but he doesn't look like a model. Ambrose, on the other hand, looks a little like Tom Selleck. Did you see his photo in the brochure? There's chest hair sticking out the top of his shirt."

"Isn't chest hair out of fashion?"

"I don't mind it," she said. "Back hair is another matter."

"You're making me jealous."

"Oh, don't be. Katie said Ambrose and Boston are a thing. She said Ambrose was newly divorced when they met while doing tastings for his first book. The one on New England wines."

"Boston?" That was surprising, since she must be ten to fifteen years younger than him. We were approaching The Larson Place, and I spotted Carpenter, her phone aimed at the house. I gave Liz a warning, and as we got to the property's edge, the phone turned toward us.

"Here they are," Carpenter said, a gleaming smile on her face. "Liz and Cy Bartholomew. Can you give a wave to my followers?"

We waved, though I would have preferred giving her the finger.

"We're here at the Larson Place Bed & Breakfast, in downtown Madison, Wisconsin," she continued. "Cy, can you tell us about the body you found in the B&B? Whose room is it now?"

I didn't know whose room it was. Throwing a look at my wife as the camera recorded, she said the app only told her which room she was in. It didn't spell out who was in the other rooms. After a few comments, we stepped inside and walked up the stairs. I pointed to the room, marked 2B. "It was this one."

"Phew!" Carpenter said. "That isn't my room. I think I saw Katie come out earlier. It must be hers." She stepped up to the door and knocked. After a brief wait, she turned off the camera. "Let's return after Katie's back so you can show me where you found the body. Right now, we should head downstairs. The second round starts soon."

Chapter 6

The afternoon sessions were as dull as I expected. Seven white wines comprised the first flight, and the final included five port wines, which left the room smelling of the fortified wine. Once again, ninety-one was the top score, and Liz's ratings aligned closely with Katie's. After finishing the day's grading, Ambrose rushed to the lectern and announced plans for dinner and a boat outing. The trip included a nautical tour of nearby Lake Monona and a twilight swim. Caleb and Jenn Iacomini from Fierce Heart Winery would join us. Apparently, they were more than vintners, as they were bringing liquor from their distillery.

The idea of a planned swim surprised and annoyed me. When Liz first told me about it, I was sure she would opt out. While Ambrose claimed it was a tradition at his tastings, she would never get into a lake at night. And even if she wanted to, I would do my best to talk her out of it.

When we arrived at the restaurant, they sat our group at three separate but adjacent tables. Ambrose assigned our seats, which further irritated me. But as a *plus one*, I couldn't complain.

Liz was at his table, along with Boston and Caleb Iacomini. The other Iacomini sat at the next table, with Carpenter, Katie, and the two servers. I slid in next to Missy LeBrun, across from Josh and Amanda Peterson.

"I'm surprised he separated Liz and me, but didn't separate you two," I said.

Josh was the first to respond. "He wants Liz with him and Caleb. He is just getting Fierce Distillery rolling, and Ambrose knows your wife is a whiskey expert." For the first time, I detected a New England accent. "Caleb may be the most influential vintner in the state, and Ambrose wants to entertain him."

"There's a reason for everything Ambrose does," Amanda said.

"He sounds calculating," Missy said in her low, monotone voice. Her eyes widened and her lips curled inward. "I didn't have that impression."

A server interrupted. Josh and Missy followed my lead by ordering beer while Amanda stayed with water.

After the server drifted to the next table, Carpenter arrived, holding her iPhone. "We've got Josh and Amanda Peterson on this side." The couple waved. "And on this side, we've got Cy Bartholomew and Missy LeBrun. That makes this an all-Wisconsin table. Wow!"

We waved and told Carpenter's followers about our drink orders. Missy sounded even less enthusiastic than me.

Missy shook her head after Carpenter moved to another table. "I was looking forward to the swim until I thought about Carpenter and her camera. Until I jump into the water, I'm going to have a sweatshirt around my waist, and I'll wear a T-shirt. Anything to hide my pasty skin." She looked at Amanda. "You're going, aren't you? I bet you'd look great in a swimsuit."

"Thanks." Her gaze dropped. "But no. I've got to work tomorrow. Besides, something's bothering my stomach." She turned toward her husband. "I'm just going to eat something light, then head home."

He patted her shoulder. "Okay. Hopefully, you'll feel better."

"Is something going around?" Missy asked. "Sorry to sound the alarm, but I catch, like, everything."

Amanda said it was probably nothing and Josh changed the subject, telling us about the upcoming excursion. The boat was a twenty-four-foot tri-toon. Hearing it was a pontoon boat was a letdown for a vessel called *Eloquence*. I had imagined a sleek sailboat or a haughty yacht, though I don't know if I've ever seen anything all that fancy on Lake Monona.

He claimed toons were ideal for the lake. It was news to me as I didn't even know that the long tubes on the bottom were called "toons."

Josh asked me to help him set sail from the dock. He had parked the *Eloquence* on its trailer at a yacht club near the Yahara River. We'd launch and enter the lake on its southeastern side, far from where we were eating dinner. The plan was to sail two miles to a launch near The Larson Place B&B, where we would pick up the rest of the entourage. I enjoyed being on the water, so I agreed, though I made sure Liz would join us.

Amanda left when we finished eating. The rest of us settled the bill and returned to the B&B. Though we were going to stay on the boat, we put on swimsuits and Liz tied a sweatshirt around her waist. She covered her top with a Wisconsin Badgers T-shirt, and I supplemented my boxer-style swimsuit with a BN Security shirt.

With sneakers on, we hurried outside, finding Josh leaning against his Ford F-150. Soon we were on the road, crossing between Lake Monona and Monona Bay. Five minutes later, the truck exited the highway and pulled up to a keypad entry that included an intercom. Josh entered four digits. The first was a nine and the last two were six and three. I wasn't sure about the second digit.

He parked in front of a covered pontoon boat. Like a dozen others, it sat on a trailer. Hopping out, we peeled the cover off, revealing the *Eloquence*. "Amanda helped me get ready," he said, "but there are things that can't be done until launch." The three of us folded the cover, then he opened a bin inside the boat and stuck it inside. He took a few minutes counting lifejackets, some stored near the back and the rest in a compartment in the middle of the boat.

As we waited, Liz and I circled the boat so we could see the name written on its backside. As we stood near a fence, I thought about the code Josh had used when coming into the marina. I entered the numbers I had seen him enter, "9-?-6-3," as a note on my phone. Looking at my keyboard, I figured it out within a few seconds. "Wine," I said. That was his entry code.

Liz gave me a puzzled look.

"I'll tell you later."

Josh put on a captain's hat and smiled as he hooked the trailer to the truck. Liz and I moved to the side as he backed the trailer to the edge of the landing.

I mentioned that I once owned an F-150, so he handed me a key from his bulky key ring. "Back the truck up about twenty feet while I'm in the boat. We want to get to where the trailer's wheel well is mostly in the water. Wait until I give you the okay. Once you stop, put it in park. Are you okay with that?"

I nodded and Liz stayed far from the truck as I got inside. The locked gate was in front of me, and the landing was behind. The trailer tilted as he climbed onto the pontoon boat. Once he gave me the okay, I backed up slowly. Looking at the side mirror, I watched the trailer's tires descend into the water, stopping while the wheel well was still visible.

Stepping out of the vehicle, I nodded to my wife and met Josh crouched at the edge of the boat. He had me unhook and unstrap the boat from the trailer. Then he had me crank the strap tight and back up further.

I got behind the wheel, shifted into reverse, and backed the truck down the launch and into the river. The boat's engine purred, and I felt it slide into the water. Putting the truck into drive, it lurched forward until all four wheels were out of the water.

Josh pulled the *Eloquence* to the edge of the dock that sat beside the landing. "Jump aboard," he said, tossing me a rope. "Tie that to the end. Any knot will do."

After tying the boat to the dock, I called Liz over. Holding her waist, I lifted as she jumped onto the front of the boat. I followed, and Josh pointed out two lifejackets. He re-did the knot before returning to the dock and asking us to wait as he parked the pickup and the trailer.

Liz struggled to find a strap on her life vest, so I grabbed it and handed it to her. The sound of his truck made me turn away from the water. I watched as the pickup disappeared behind the building.

Liz blinked several times. "I don't like going out this late."

"It's a pontoon boat." I patted the boat's blue fender, which encased the seats. "What could go wrong?"

"You're not the blind one going onto a lake at sunset."

Once I had my vest on, I put my arm around her as Josh turned the corner. She was right that I wasn't the blind one. But it wasn't much better being the plus one who was worried about the blind one.

Chapter 7

Sofa-like benches were on both sides of the boat's front. Each gray bench was roughly eight feet long and sat four. An L-shaped bench sat toward the rear and to the left, or port, side of the captain's chair. Liz and I added up who we expected on board. It came to twelve, which meant things would be tight.

Josh undid the rope and jumped aboard. Turning the boat toward the lake, he took off at high speed. He called Ambrose as we entered Lake Monona, telling him we'd be at the Law Park launch in ten minutes. Liz and I sat across from the captain's chair. Taking her glasses off, she squinted into the horizon.

"How late will we be out?" I asked.

"Maybe nine thirty. We'll be back by ten."

"When does it get dark?"

"Maybe nine," he said.

Liz clutched my hand.

"I was going to tour the shoreline before the swim," Josh said, "but I'll cut things short."

It was a two-mile ride to the launch, with the lighted Wisconsin State Capitol in front of us the entire trip. After five or six minutes, I spotted a pair of launches and made out a group waiting between the two. Josh brought the boat alongside, then maneuvered so the group could climb from the nearby dock onto the front, or bow, of the boat.

Josh stayed at the controls and asked me to help people board. Liz and I went to the bow, and she sat on a bench. I tossed the rope to Ambrose, and he pulled it tight to his chest.

At the dock's edge, Carpenter stood, wearing sunglasses for no good reason and a string bikini, which looked like it might slip off if I pulled her up too quickly. She held her phone in one hand, so I grabbed the other. She introduced me again to her followers as I lifted her aboard and continued entertaining them as she walked toward the back of the boat.

The winery owners were next, so I introduced myself as they boarded. Caleb Iacomini was at least six-foot one and well over two hundred pounds. A prominent nose marked his face, and dark spots anchored deep-set eyes. He was balding and wore a Hawaiian shirt and blue swimming trunks, while his wife, Jenn, looked elegant in a blue one-piece. Ambrose handed me a cooler. I passed it to Caleb, and he followed his wife to the back of the boat. Katie boarded afterward and sat beside Liz.

Our servers, Renee and Abby, were next, followed by Boston and Missy. All wore bikinis, except for Missy who wore a T-shirt and shorts.

Ambrose was last, and as he came aboard, he handed me the rope.

"How many we got?" Josh asked, looking at me.

I realized I was the de facto first mate, so I counted the passengers and yelled, "Twelve! Including us!"

The boat pulled away from the launch, settling into a southwesterly route that ran parallel to the shoreline.

Once I closed the gate, Katie and Missy slid over, leaving space for me to sit next to Liz. Squeezing in, I nodded at Renee and Abby, who were talking to Jenn. It was a struggle to not stare at the scantily clad women who surrounded me.

"Cy!" Josh called. "Pull out the rest of the vests and hand them out. They're stowed beneath."

There was a compartment near the middle of the deck, so I walked over and opened it. Carpenter was in front of me putting a vest on, while Ambrose strapped an orange lifejacket over his hairy chest. I handed a clump to Renee, telling her to keep one and pass on the rest. Double checking my strap, I walked to the back of the boat with a lifejacket in hand.

"There's an extra," Josh said.

As I stowed the vest, Caleb waved me over. The orange vest covering his Hawaiian shirt made him look even bigger. He kneeled and gave me a plastic cup filled with amber liquid. "At dinner, your wife told me she wanted to try the rye. This is it."

The aroma cleared my sinuses.

"You want rye, bourbon, or brandy?" he asked.

Looking back, I spotted bottles sticking out of the open cooler. "What do you suggest?"

He smiled. "I'm a brandy man, amongst other things."

"Brandy it is."

As he reached into the cooler, I closed the cover to the underdeck compartment. When I turned around, another plastic cup was in front of me. I took it and thanked him before passing one to Liz and squeezing in between her and Katie.

"I hope you enjoy the rye," Caleb said to Liz.

Realizing she probably didn't know he was speaking to her, I elbowed her side. She called out, "Thanks." Caleb stood in the middle of the boat, taking drink orders from the other women.

Liz looked at me after smelling the liquor. "This isn't rye; it's brandy."

We exchanged cups. After smelling the brandy, I took a sip and swished it in my mouth. While I took a second gulp, she was holding the cup in front of her free hand, apparently trying to get a sense of the liquid's color despite the darkness around us.

Caleb returned with three more cups of brandy.

"Abby and I are both trying the bourbon," Renee said, as if explaining why Caleb wasn't serving them.

"The bourbon is good, of course," Jenn said. Though she smiled, I thought she looked sad, as if something weighed on her mind. "But I'm a wine person, so I favor brandy."

"What do you think about the rye?" I whispered to Liz. "No comments on whether it's peppery or malty or smoky or whatever. Just good or bad."

"It's good. Very good, actually."

Caleb returned, handing cups to Renee and Abby. He asked Liz what she thought of the rye. I knew it would be a whiskey geek answer, so I tried not to listen. He seemed pleased by her reply, and he provided details on how the liquor was distilled and aged.

"What are you drinking?" I asked Caleb once he finished his spiel.

He nodded at the cup in his hand. "Rye, like your wife. But I brought a bottle of brandy for people on the foredeck." He pulled a bottle from inside his vest and set it next to his wife. "If anyone wants more bourbon or rye, the bottles are aft." Running a hand over his wife's shoulder, he walked to the back of the boat.

The vessel slowed, and Josh announced we were at the entrance to Monona Bay. Pointing out several landmarks, he explained how the road and railroad tracks separating the lake from the bay were constructed in the eighteen fifties. The boat headed southeast, and he noted the nearby Olin Park. The *Eloquence* turned northeasterly as we passed Turville Point, and Josh motioned toward Wiicawak Bay and the Yahara River in the distance.

"Now we are heading toward the Monona shoreline. If you, like me, are a fan of sixties soul music, this is an important, though tragic, area. It is where Otis Redding's plane crashed in nineteen sixty-nine, killing the singer and six others."

"Was he the guy in the band in *Animal House*?" Abby asked me.

"No," I said, holding back an eye roll. "That's not him. You ever heard of '(Sittin' on) the Dock of the Bay'?"

From the back of the boat, Caleb, Ambrose, and Josh started humming and then singing the song's chorus. A few people nodded. Finally, Josh announced we were turning toward the Capitol. Minutes later, we would anchor near the middle of the lake for a swim.

My glass was empty, so I kneeled next to Jenn and filled it. She asked me for a top-up, and soon I refilled everyone sitting in the group, except Liz, who wanted a clean glass. As I returned from the back, Missy peeled off her shorts, revealing the bottom of a two-piece suit.

"What about your shirt?" Katie asked. "You don't want to get that wet, do you?"

"It's just a cheap shirt. Let it get wet." Missy's gaze passed amongst her co-passengers. "I can't compete with you and this group."

"Oh, don't be silly," Katie said. "You look great."

I was not about to get involved in the discussion, so I stared ahead as the boat headed toward the Wisconsin State Capitol. "You doing okay?" I asked Liz.

"Yes, I guess." She took a sip of brandy. "While everyone swims, I'll stay in this exact spot."

"You'll be fine."

She straightened up and took in the cool air. "I hope so."

Chapter 8

It was after nine when Josh called me to the back of the boat. Carpenter filmed as he announced we were dropping anchor. He said we were clear of algae blooms and far enough from shore for privacy. The passengers refilled their cups, took off their shoes, and moved about the crowded deck.

Josh pulled me close. "I know your wife isn't going in. Are you?"

"No. She shouldn't be by herself on the lake."

"Great. I mean. Not great that she can't be alone, but great that you'll be onboard. Would you mind taking the helm? It would allow me to jump in."

Being in charge of the *Eloquence* was unnerving, but I agreed. Glimpsing Carpenter, I imagined the video she was showing her followers. "One question, though," I asked. "Don't I need a boat license to be in charge?"

He plopped his smartphone into a cupholder. "You were born before nineteen eighty-nine, right? State law only requires you to have a valid driver's license to captain a boat."

Unfortunately, I was born well before then. "I'm good on that."

"Then you're good to be captain."

Kind of frightening, I thought.

"Once everyone's off, I'll run through a few things with you," he said. "Take the captain's chair while I drop anchor, okay?"

It hadn't even occurred to me that pontoon boats had anchors, but I was glad they did since I didn't want to float away from the swimmers and leave them floundering in the growing darkness.

After anchoring the boat, Josh stood at the bow. "If you go in the water," he announced, "you have to wear a vest. No exceptions." His gaze slid amongst the passengers. "Got it?"

"Yes, sir!" Ambrose said with a laugh.

"Stay between the shore and the boat." He checked his watch. "It's nine minutes after nine. We've got half an hour of reasonable light. We'll limit the swim to probably twenty-five minutes. I'll go in the water last and come out first. And everyone exits and returns to the boat at the bow. While I'm in the lake, Cy is the captain. Questions?"

"Can we bring drinks?" Boston asked.

"Sure. If you have an empty, don't just leave the plastic cup in the lake. Bring it to the bow and Cy or Liz will put it in the trash."

There was nodding and a few more questions before Ambrose led the passengers to the bow, opened the gate, and eased into the lake while holding a half-full plastic cup.

"Will you record while I jump in and get a little of me in the water?" Carpenter asked, handing me her drink before I could reply. "Let's turn my phone on, so you get me going in. If it locks you out, the password is M-A-D-D-I-E." She put her finger on the screen and the video camera turned on. After saying a few words to her followers, she handed the phone to me and jumped off the bow.

I wanted to tell her to stick it, but nothing came out. She reached out of the water, so I gave her the plastic cup.

The two servers jumped off next. Missy then eased into the lake, her hair tied up to keep it out of the water. As the women exited the boat, Jenn took off Caleb's vest. He then unbuttoned his Hawaiian shirt, and she folded it and placed it on her chair.

"The navigation lights are on." Josh started toward the captain's chair while I trailed, filming the whole time. Reaching up, he tapped the awning, and a light turned on. "This is the Bimini light. It's just a touch thing. There is also a spotlight, and we even have underwater lights which I sometimes use for fishing, but we'll leave those off."

A splash of water came over the side, followed by laughs. I ignored it and nodded my agreement.

"Otherwise, encourage people to stay port-side. That's the left of the boat. It keeps people on the side where light comes from downtown." He looked about the deck. "That's about it. My watch is waterproof. I've got my alarm set. Once it goes off, we'll come aboard. I'll come out first and I'm guessing Carpenter will be out last."

I followed Josh to the bow, and he placed the white captain's hat on my head. It felt heavy.

He dove head-first into the water, and I took Liz's hand. "Come with me and sit near the captain's chair."

"I bet you say that to all the girls."

It dawned on me that she didn't realize I was filming, so I turned the video off as she got to her feet. The boat rocked, and I pulled her close. She sat near the corner on the L-shaped bench, which was surrounded by lighted cup holders, two of which held smartphones and watches.

"You're the bartender," I said. "Undoubtedly, we'll have orders. If you can't read the labels, you can tell which bottle is which by the smell. Carpenter suckered me into filming some of the chaos, but it won't stop me from helping with the drinks. If someone asks, you fill and I'll deliver. Don't get out of your chair."

After entering M-A-D-D-I-E into Carpenter's phone, I turned the camera back on and filmed the downtown Madison skyline as voices clamored from below and water splashed. Caleb and Jenn were on their backs, their feet resting against the port-side toon. Carpenter called to me from behind the boat. Josh was next to her, and she dunked his head briefly underwater. He came back up, then dunked her. I didn't know if her followers would find their antics interesting, but I didn't.

I filmed as everyone drank and splashed. The swimmers eventually requested refills, so I stuck Carpenter's phone in a cupholder. Kneeling next to Liz, the boat lurched to one side, and I looked to the right, or starboard side, and spotted a motorboat coming toward us. It turned as it came close, leaving a wake which caused the *Eloquence* to tilt side-to-side.

Carrying five drinks, I walked gingerly, kneeling at the bow. Josh came from underwater and grabbed the gate. I wondered how he would carry the cups, but noticed Renee beside him, navigation lights glistening off her curly black hair.

"What was that noise?" Liz asked as I sat in the captain's chair.

"What noise?"

"Like a snake hitting and licking the boat."

"A snake?" I said. "Licking?"

"Uh-huh. Like something slurping as it ran into the side of the boat."

"The waves probably knocked the boat against Caleb or Jenn." I peered over the side, but the two had moved away from the toons. "Is everyone okay? Did anyone bang into the boat?"

Everyone seemed indifferent, and the winery owners talked amongst themselves. Pulling out my phone, I flipped on the flashlight. Waves punched the *Eloquence*, and the motorboat's lights were in the distance. When I turned the flashlight off, I noticed stars in the sky.

"Probably a branch or something." I put the phone back into my pocket. "Nothing's there now."

Katie caught my attention, so I walked to the bow. "We're racing," she said, pointing at Missy. "Can you be the judge and let us know who wins? It's once around the boat."

I nodded. "To your marks. Get set. Go!"

The two women started on the port side. They used a freestyle stroke, but the lifejackets made racing difficult. Katie had a lead as they circled *Eloquence's* stern. The darkness on the starboard side made it challenging to see them, but I heard splashing and laughing. I walked to the bow as Katie finished two lengths ahead.

I thought that was it, but the two servers soon challenged them to a relay race. This time, I hardly paid attention as they circled the boat. At the end, the servers finished a full five lengths ahead.

"Cy," Liz said, as I clapped for the winners. "The motorboat's coming close again."

The engine was getting louder. I stared at it, then rushed to the port side. "Josh, is this motorboat a problem? Is he being a dick or is this just something that happens?"

"People are idiots," he said from the darkness. "He thinks he's far enough from us, but he probably doesn't know we're swimming." There was splashing as Josh approached. I felt the boat move as he rubbed against the port-side toon. He emerged at the bow and lifted himself aboard. I walked toward him as he looked at the motorboat. "It's turning, but its wake will hit us."

The alarm on Josh's wrist went off. He pulled up a cushion from the bench. Inside was a stack of towels, which he laid on another cushion.

"Time to get out of the water!" He rubbed a towel against his face before wrapping it around his neck. "Everyone out," he repeated as the wake rocked the boat. "Remember to bring your cups. A trash can is beside the cushion. Put empties inside."

The boat lurched as Caleb grabbed the bow. He helped his wife aboard, then pulled himself up. Josh headed to the captain's chair, so I stayed at the bow as Abby and Renee boarded. Katie started to board next, but jumped back in.

"Wardrobe issue," Missy said with a laugh.

"Nearly lost my bottoms," Katie said as I pulled her onto the boat. Taking a towel, she sat in the spot where she had been earlier.

Missy followed, muttering something about how her hair wouldn't recover from the lake water. I helped Boston and Ambrose aboard next.

"That's nine," I said to myself.

"Nothing like a good night swim." Ambrose used his towel to dry Boston's face.

Counting those on board, I came to eleven, including me. I got out my phone and turned on the flashlight. Aiming it toward the port side, I saw no one.

We were one short.

Chapter 9

A trio of women stood on the deck, towels around their shoulders, while others made their way to the back of the boat. Josh stood beside the captain's chair, drying his legs while Liz stared blankly forward, the cooler between her feet. I slipped past Missy as she drained water from her shirt and bumped into Boston as she tied a towel around her waist.

"Josh," I said as I closed in. "You said Carpenter might be in last, right?"

He nodded.

"We're one short and I don't see her."

His red eyebrows scrunched together as he surveyed the deck. After a few moments, he stepped over the cooler and peered over the boat's edge. "Carpenter? Time to come in! Carpenter?"

Ambrose repeated the call, then Boston joined in. Soon, most everyone was staring into the lake, calling her name. Picking up Carpenter's phone, I tapped on its light. Josh returned to the captain's chair and flipped on the underwater lights.

"She probably went..." he said.

I aimed the camera at the nearest boat launch and hit the record button. "Might she have swum ashore?"

Josh pulled what appeared to be a large flashlight from beneath the deck. He flipped it on, and I realized it was the boat's spotlight. He aimed the beam thirty or forty feet from the boat. The light went toward the front of the boat, then toward the middle of the lake.

"Carpenter!" Ambrose yelled. "This isn't funny!"

Grabbing my lifejacket, Josh pulled me closer. "Keep shining this; I'm going in." I stuck Carpenter's phone into my pocket and took the flashlight as he rushed ahead. The gate opened, and I heard a splash as he jumped in.

Within seconds, Ambrose, Boston, and Katie followed him in. People were no longer yelling that it wasn't funny. Instead, they just called her name.

Moving the beam back and forth, the light aimed at an imaginary path that led to the launch. Boston and Ambrose were swimming away from the boat on the port side, while Katie and Josh were behind the boat, heading to the deeper part of the lake. As I moved the spotlight to the starboard side, I realized Liz and I were the only ones aboard.

The spotlight beam started near the boat, and with each pass, I brought it further out. On the third pass, I paused and retraced the spotlight's path. Something was far aft on the starboard side. I called out to Josh and Katie, since I'd seen them heading in that direction.

"You see her?" Josh yelled.

"No." I looked at Liz, who was staring forward, not even looking at the spotlight. "Something's floating."

"Put the spotlight on it," Katie said. I heard splashing and spotted Josh approaching the spot where the beam hit the water. She was several lengths behind him.

A few swimmers called out questions, but there was nothing to say until Josh arrived at the spot. I glanced at Liz. Her eyes were closed. I assumed she was listening.

"It's...it's a lifejacket," he said.

He lifted the jacket into the air. Once Katie arrived, he handed it to her. They had a brief conversation, then she yelled something and started for the boat, carrying the lifejacket. After briefly following her, I turned the light to where Josh was heading.

Renee, Abby, and Jenn met Katie about thirty feet from the boat. Jenn took the vest and swam to the bow. I tried to ignore her and focused on the light in front of me.

Jenn pulled herself aboard, holding the orange vest. "Josh wants us to call 911." She dropped the lifejacket onto the deck. "You're to man the light."

"Yes. Definitely." I considered grabbing my phone, but I was trying to keep the beam steady. Multiple people were swimming further from the boat and I wanted to provide whatever light I could.

Before Jenn found her phone, Liz had called 911. Jenn knelt next to her as she explained the situation.

"Tell them we're about half a mile out." I continued to stare into the lake as Missy pulled herself aboard. "If we went northwest, we'd hit shore between Brittingham Dog Park and Monona Terrace."

Missy rolled onto her back, puffing and wheezing. Then she turned over and spit out water. "Should have...brought...my...inhaler."

The captain's hat was still on my head. I wanted to throw it next to the captain's chair or toss it at Josh, who was the true captain of the *Eloquence*. What were the chances that a stand-in was in charge when someone disappeared? Almost everyone was in the lake. Some weren't wearing lifejackets. I was in charge of chaos.

"911 wants everyone out of the water," Liz said to me. "They'll be here in a few minutes, and they don't want to risk running into anyone."

I sent Jenn to the bow to let people know. She was shaking as she walked past Missy, but soon Caleb and Boston were aboard. After spotting Ambrose in the spotlight beam, I yelled out about the rescue crew being on its way. Nodding, he started toward the boat.

Jenn sat on one of the front benches, holding the retrieved lifejacket. "Why would she have taken this off?" she said to herself. "Maybe she wanted to make a grand entrance onto the boat."

Renee crawled aboard next. She remained on all fours between the two benches and beside a prostrate Missy LeBrun.

Caleb stepped closer, the boat shaking with each step. He held the lifejacket in the air. Like most of the other vests, it was orange with a single strap that would go around the wearer's chest, but the clip was undone and the strap hung down, dragging on the deck. Falling into the captain's chair, he held the lifejacket in both hands.

Liz grabbed my wrist. "What the hell was she thinking?"

Chapter 10

J osh and Katie were the last to return. Both laid on the deck, sucking air and spitting water. Liz announced that a City of Madison Lake Rescue Team was approaching. I turned off the searchlight and heard the rescue boat's motor. Josh stumbled to the captain's chair and called to the rescue boat. Within a few minutes, it was on our port side, its searchlight pointing forward.

Two scuba divers and staff from the City of Madison Fire Department were on the vessel, one holding a bullhorn. The rescue crew told us to aim our spotlight at the location where we thought the missing swimmer went down. Josh nodded to me, so I returned to the perch and aimed the beam past the back of the boat to the starboard side. It was where I had seen the lifejacket, but it was not where I'd last seen Carpenter.

Two divers fell backwards out of the boat simultaneously, causing a splash which rocked their boat. Switching hands, I tried to hold the light steady. Eventually, the divers arrived at the spot and went underwater, so I flipped the light off.

We sat in silence as waves slapped against the toons and Missy wept. The captain of the rescue boat asked about the missing woman's swimming ability and whether she had been drinking. Josh said she was an average swimmer who had had four or five drinks that evening.

The rescue boat's engine started, and the vessel began a loosening circular pattern around the *Eloquence*. It seemed a necessary but futile effort, since I assumed she had headed for land.

"Why don't they let us go?" Ambrose asked. "She might have swum to the beach and could be waiting for us at the B&B."

Picking up Carpenter's phone, I held it at eye level. "She doesn't have this. She won't be able to get into the house or her room. If she gets ashore, she'll contact the police or wait at the launch."

Josh snatched the captain's hat from my head, then leaned back in his chair. "They want our boat to stay here since it's anchored. I'm sure they've recorded the GPS location, but they probably won't let us go until a second boat arrives."

Ambrose rested a hand on the back of the captain's chair. "Could she make it ashore? Is she a good enough swimmer?"

"Maybe." Josh straightened up and looked toward the shoreline. "We're probably half a mile out. I could do it in under thirty minutes. I think she could make it in thirty-five."

"What time did your alarm go off?" Liz asked. "Soon afterwards was when we realized she was missing."

Josh punched a button on his watch. "The alarm was set for nine forty."

I checked my phone, which read, "10:29 PM." Unless she made it ashore, she'd have been in the lake without a vest for nearly an hour. Brushing a hand through my hair, I glimpsed the hat, which was now on Josh's head. He was now responsible, but whatever happened occurred when the hat was on my head.

Minutes later, a boat from the Dane County Sheriff's Marine Enforcement unit pulled in front of the other rescue vessel. The deputy yelled questions rather than using a bullhorn. After a few minutes, they told us to dock. Josh explained that most of the passengers were staying downtown and he had picked them up at the Law Park ramp, but the boat would dock at the yacht club on the Yahara River. The sheriff's office told us a police officer would meet with people at Law Park and a deputy would meet the captain at the yacht club.

"Thank God," Ambrose said as Josh pulled up the anchor.

Caleb laid the half-full bottles of liquor on their sides, his deep-set eyes looking weary, and he closed the cooler. The twin engines started, so I walked to the bow, aiming the spotlight forward in the faint hope we'd see Carpenter ahead of us as we headed to the launch.

The *Eloquence* approached shore in near silence. Josh pulled us to the dock that skirted the launch. Hopping off, I tied the boat to a wooden post. A flashing police light caught my attention, and I spotted two officers. Behind them was an ambulance with its back doors open.

Missy got off first. She was no longer crying, but her body was shaking and her skin was damp and cold. Drool was on her chin, and I wondered if she was in shock. She still had her lifejacket on, so I undid the clasp and slid it off. The shirt should come off too, but a police officer was at the end of the dock and EMTs were nearby. First responders would handle her better than an underemployed locksmith.

As the others climbed down, I asked if they had left phones or anything else onboard. Caleb was holding his cooler but had forgotten his phone. His wife, however, was still on the boat and she found it and brought it to him.

Before Ambrose got off, I had him check for Missy's phone, since I assumed it was still aboard. He found it, as well as Carpenter's. I told him to leave Carpenter's, as I knew the password and would give it to the police when we docked.

"Make sure the EMTs look at Missy," I said, as Ambrose stepped ashore. He nodded and slapped my shoulder. I climbed aboard, joining Liz and Josh. Once Ambrose undid the knot, the engines started and we pulled away from the shore.

"Keep the spotlight ahead," Josh said. "I have a fear that we'll run into poor Carpenter."

Before turning the light on, I grabbed Carpenter's phone and stuck it into my pocket. Minutes passed, and I wedged the spotlight handle between my chest and a cushion, freeing my hand to open Carpenter's phone. I entered the password, then clicked on photos. The last four were videos I had taken.

With the sound down, I watched the first, which included Carpenter jumping into the water and Josh telling me about the boat's lights. She showed up a few times in the second video. Early on, she dunked Josh's head underwater, and he responded in-kind. The third video showed Josh giving her his drink. They were aft of the boat on the port side, and I saw she was wearing her life vest. Unfortunately, the camera followed Josh swimming toward the bow. Soon after, it turned off.

The footage didn't show her going to the starboard side, nor did it imply she was in distress. I watched the last video, which I'd shot after we realized she was missing. Then I closed the device and focused on the spotlight as we stayed tight to the shoreline. The boat went around Turville Point and pulled into the river that drained into Lake Wingra. Ahead of us, on the starboard side, I saw docks and flashing police lights. I didn't know if Josh wanted the spotlight for docking, so I approached the captain's chair. He said nothing, but his eyes were red and filled with tears.

Chapter 11

Two deputies from the Dane County Sheriff's Marine Enforcement Unit were waiting for us. They were both in their forties, but I didn't recognize either. The taller of the two asked who had been captaining the boat when the incident occurred. Josh started raising his hand, but I stopped him and lifted mine. Following a brief explanation, I handed them Carpenter's phone and told them I had recorded a few videos while people were swimming, and one while we searched. I gave the deputies her access code, so they entered it and watched two videos.

Josh nudged in between us and noted when he saw Carpenter. They went back further in her photos, and he showed them a recent picture of them together at the dock next to the *Eloquence*. Liz held my hand, her eyes staring forward.

Josh and I talked to the deputies for several minutes, telling them about where we had last seen Carpenter and when. After taking statements and collecting contact information, the police staked tape around the boat. It seemed unnecessary, but the deputy explained it was only a precaution, saying they would not search the boat unless the circumstances of Carpenter's disappearance were deemed suspicious.

Josh, apparently unconcerned, took a key from his key ring and handed it to the deputy. The three of us then walked through the lighted parking lot to Josh's Ford pickup.

It was nearly midnight when he dropped us outside The Larson Place B&B, saying he would park and join us in a few minutes.

Crossing the street, I pointed at the house. "It looks like every light is on, so they're up. How do I explain what happened?"

Liz batted her eyes and squinted. "Explain what? They know as much as we do."

"It happened under my watch," I said. "Someone disappeared and may have drowned."

She released my hand and thrust her arm around my waist. "There wasn't a shipwreck, and you weren't really in charge. They were adults swimming in a lake. This was Josh's event; not yours. You're no more at fault than anyone else."

She was right, but it didn't feel that way. Ten people went for a swim along the boat, when I was supposedly in charge. Maybe it shouldn't weigh on my mind, but I knew it would. The only thing I thought of was locating her and finding out what happened. It was the least I could do for Carpenter.

"It's reminiscent of Ben," I said.

She stopped in front of the B&B and put a hand on my cheek. "Cy. This is nothing like Ben. He was doing his job and ran into some thug. He knew the risk of working in the middle of the night. God knows you and I knew the risks. As to this? This was an accident."

My chest tightened as I remembered a night twenty years ago. It was a Friday, and I had a cold which I had picked up from our baby daughter. It was back in the days when many of our locksmith calls were people locked out of their cars. Like most nights, I was finishing my shift and the new kid, Ben Petersik, was on call. I was heading home when a call came in from a stranded motorist at an eastside mall. There was something fishy about a three in the morning call from the mall, but I was bushed and Ben lived nearby.

He was only twenty-two and hadn't been with us for more than a month. I thought he would be a good locksmith someday, but I'll never know. When he arrived, someone hit him on the back of the head with a heavy object. They robbed him, taking cash, a credit card, and locksmith equipment from the van. The police estimated the value of the haul at four hundred dollars.

Undoubtedly, the attacker only intended to knock him out, but that's not how things turned out. When he was overdue on checking in, I headed to the location. When I arrived, I saw flashing lights and an ambulance. Ben was dead.

It was not my fault, but I was in charge. He was my responsibility, and since that day I carried a burden. Now it happened again.

The thing that made it worse was that Carpenter had a daughter. She'd mentioned her when we first met in the Larson Place's foyer. I didn't know how old she was or what sort of relationship she had with her mother.

Ben also had a daughter. She was two weeks younger than our middle child. Every year or two, I would run into Ben's widow, Tara. Sometimes, their daughter was with her. One time, Tara asked whether I thought the police were still investigating. She was frustrated since they had not caught the man who had killed her husband. I told her that MB Lock

& Security was encouraging the police to keep the case active. When I close my eyes, I still see the look she gave me.

The last time I saw them, Tara was polite, but the daughter seemed to glare at me. I suspect she knew I was the person who sent her father out that night. I suspect she held it against me. And I understood.

I tugged Liz forward as she pulled out her phone. Once the lock turned, I opened the door and, like the last time, Ambrose greeted us. He was wearing a baby blue robe that barely went below his knees, revealing black sandals. A white towel was wrapped around his neck.

"Well?" he said as Boston and Katie joined him. "Have you heard anything?"

Ushering Liz inside, I shook my head. "We gave them our contact information, but we have heard nothing new."

"How about Josh?" Boston asked. "Where's he?"

"Parking the truck. He should be here in a few minutes. We're all in the dark as to what will happen next."

"The police will contact Josh." Ambrose glanced back at Boston. "I told them he is closest to her."

I wasn't surprised, as I had sensed a closeness between them. Boston suggested we go back to the kitchen.

"None of us can sleep," Katie said after hugging Liz. "Do you guys want something to drink? We are finishing a couple of bottles of port from the tasting."

Port wine was an odd choice, since we'd spent the last few hours talking about a woman who had disappeared while swimming off the boat's port side, but no one else seemed to connect the two.

The room was dimly lit. Katie slid her half-filled glass to the end of the table, allowing Liz to sit in the middle and me at the other end. Ambrose sighed as he eased into the spot opposite Liz. Boston set empty glasses in front of us. I expected her to pour the wine herself, but she rounded the table, settling next to Ambrose and across from Katie. Liz filled our glasses halfway and the scent of warm berries filled the air.

Ambrose cleared his throat. "They are keeping Missy overnight. The ambulance guy said she was in shock."

"Not surprised," I replied. "Also, she said something about an inhaler. Maybe she has asthma."

Boston leaned forward. She was in a gray sweatshirt that was at least two sizes too big. "I told them the same thing. Ambrose tried to get into her room to check if there's any medicine, but he needs a code from the owner, and they haven't answered his text."

"Do you want me to break in?" I asked.

Boston straightened up. "Could you do that? These are brand-new locks."

"No problem. Five minutes at most."

Liz tapped my arm. "The people at the hospital will figure out that she has asthma. They're not stupid, you know? Besides, you might ruin the lock, and we can't be paying to fix it."

There was no way I'd ruin the lock, so it was tempting to argue, but I held off. "Okay, but if the police direct me to break in, it's not a problem."

Liz looked Boston in the eye, which is something she rarely does anymore, especially in poor light. "She'll be fine. Being in the hospital is best for her. My guess is she'll be back by lunchtime tomorrow. If necessary, we'll send Cy to pick her up."

Everyone looked at me. I was fine with picking her up, but it was a reminder that I was the one who wasn't necessary. And the one time I had been necessary, something went wrong. Terribly wrong.

"Speaking of, well, tomorrow," Ambrose said, clearing his throat. I was struggling to take him seriously since he was wearing what I decided was a woman's robe. "It seems callous to even bring this up, but we need to decide whether to move forward or whether we, well, cancel tomorrow's tastings or even the entire event."

Boston set her glass on the table. "Renee and Abby will be here as planned in the morning. They're picking up bagels and cake donuts. Sparkling wine will be available as well. If there's a change of plans, I should let them know."

There was a long silence.

"Can you continue without Carpenter and Missy?" I asked. "Are there rules about how many critics you got tasting the wine?" Liz's expression told me it was a stupid question. It seemed I asked a lot of stupid questions. All I could do was wait for an answer.

"No." Ambrose sounded defeated. "A section in the book will describe the testing. If we have fewer testers tomorrow or even for the rest of the week, I'll disclose it. The goal is transparency. If people want to argue that four or five are not enough, that's fine, but I doubt anyone will. Most wine criticism is the opinion of a single critic. Using four judges in a competition is, well, the norm. I like six because it gives us the opportunity to include critics from the home state, while not giving those home-grown critics too much sway over the ratings. Some think..." Ambrose's brow scrunched together, and he got to his feet. "What's that?"

"It's Josh," Liz said, without looking toward the porch.

Though I had heard nothing, Ambrose and Boston went into the hallway. Murmurs came from the foyer, and I inferred hugs were being shared. Katie stood and walked to the edge of the kitchen. Ambrose and Boston returned, along with Josh. Katie gave him a hug without saying a word.

Boston offered him a glass, but he said he needed to call his wife. We all nodded our approval.

Josh left the kitchen, then quickly returned. "Are we still on for tomorrow?"

"If we are, are you okay with it?" Ambrose asked.

"Yes, that's what Carpenter would want us to do. Though if we hear she's in the hospital, I'll go to her, regardless of the time."

Ambrose looked at Boston. "Agreed."

Josh turned away, and we sat in silence.

Liz finished her port and put a hand on my knee. "We have a big day tomorrow. We should go to bed."

Several heads nodded. "Refer to the flyer for the schedule," Boston announced. "If you don't have a hard copy, there's a pdf in your email."

"There is?" I said.

"Well. There's a schedule in everyone's email except yours."

I should have known.

Chapter 12

Liz and I were tired and sweaty, but since we didn't go into the lake, we skipped showers and climbed into shorts and T-shirts. Ambrose was still downstairs, so we rushed to the bathroom to wash up. Finishing first, I took Liz's phone and let myself into our room. Leaving the lights off, I started a check for cameras and listening devices.

Years in the security business had left me safety conscious. Liz called it paranoid. I aimed my camera around the room, focusing on obvious places such as the smoke alarm, the outlets, decorations, and the room's lone mirror. Anything near a power source got extra attention.

I'd seen too many hidden cameras and listening devices in hotels and in B&Bs. First, I looked for them by trying to identify infrared lights. Noting nothing, I flipped the lights back on. After closing and locking the window we had left open, I walked through the room, looking for holes in the walls and running my fingers along decorations and fixtures. The only thing I found was a sticky spot on top of the mirror. Nothing was attached to it, but the adhesive felt fresh.

Moving on, I put our phones into airplane mode and pulled out my RF detector. The device searched for wireless signals emitted by surveillance equipment. As I moved around the room holding the detector, I heard the restroom door open. I hurried to the door and called to Liz.

"Cy?" she said. The only light came through the windows.

"Yeah, I'm here. Stay to your right, away from the windows. At the corner to your left is one of those automatic or robotic vacuums and, going further, past the windows are the stairs. Just stay along the wall to your right."

"I know." Walking toward me, her hand ran along the wall. "It's not like I'm blind."

When she got close, I grabbed her hand and guided her to our room. After the deadbolt slammed shut, I whispered into her ear, telling her I was doing the nighttime security check. This was done whenever we stayed away from home, so she knew the drill and waited quietly until I finished.

Opening our suitcase, I pulled out our portable door jammer and set it on the nightstand. "Do you think it's a good idea that they are continuing the tasting?" I asked in a quiet voice.

She sat on the bed and slipped off her shoes. "Hard to say. At least half the cost of this event relates to travel and this place. If he cancels, he'll have to pay for another tasting. No idea if he's rich or something, but that's got to be a good chunk of money."

"It just seems cold. I mean, we don't even know if she's alive."

Liz nodded. "It sounds like Josh was closest to her. He said she'd want it to go on. So that's what we should do."

"You think they can still make it work?"

"Yes. I agree with his comment about only needing four tasters. The number of critics for this thing surprised me. When I worked at that competition in St. Louis, they had forty tasters, but we were in pods. So only four people tasted each wine."

Liz was referring to a competition she had judged in the spring. It was her first wine festival, and she did not ask for accommodations for her sight. All went well until she fell down a stairway while trying to find a bathroom. She told me the stairwell was dark, and it didn't help that she had sampled sixty wines.

I was in a nearby bar watching the Brewers-Cardinals game when she called me for help. They had blocked off the area, but I snuck up the stairs, distracting a security guard by throwing a quarter down a hallway. When I found her, she was sitting on the darkened staircase. While she was only bruised, she was afraid to climb the stairs alone.

The St. Louis competition convinced her she needed to be forthcoming about her eyesight. She was concerned it would prevent her from being selected for competitions and events, so it was a pleasant surprise when Ambrose contacted her about this tasting. She signed a contract he had sent via email, but included a note saying I would accompany her to the tasting. Three days later, he responded, saying I could attend the event as her assistant. She jumped around our living room in excitement like a ten-year-old.

"Why does Ambrose use so many wine tasters?" I asked. "Why not just save money and have four?"

"He includes people from the state that is being tested, but he wants to minimize our influence. That's because he doesn't necessarily know or trust the local tasters. For this event, that's Missy and me. It's about managing public relations while maintaining control."

"How about Josh and Carpenter?" I asked, searching for something to talk about as we got ready for bed. "Is something going on between them?"

"Duh," she said with a laugh. "It's obvious. At first, I didn't get what she saw in him since she's the classic blonde bombshell, while he's just there." Pulling back the bedsheets, she crawled inside. "But out on the boat, you could see he's got things together. He's also got a bit of the upper-crust sense about him. He said he was raised out in Nantucket, didn't he? Katie told me that his family has a ton of money. So, he's got the money and the breeding."

"And she's got the looks."

"Exactly."

"Okay. The next question is whether his wife knows. If it's obvious that he's having an affair, you'd think she'd know."

Liz patted my side of the bed, which told me she wanted me to join her. "She must know. Maybe that's why she didn't go on the boat and why she stayed home. I wouldn't want to watch my husband flirting with his mistress."

"That means we've got Ambrose and Boston fooling around, and Josh and Carpenter. How about Katie? She's the only one of the regular wine tasters we haven't mentioned. She's cute. Who's she sleeping with?"

"Oh, shut up. She doesn't have to be cute to be sleeping with someone. Lots of homely people get some."

"Yeah," I said with a nod. "Didn't mean it that way. All I meant was that she probably gets attention from plenty of men."

"She told me she's been divorced for three years. No kids. She dates but isn't seeing anyone right now. Getting back to

Ambrose, I heard him come upstairs, but he headed back down."

"Maybe he's with Boston, like you had suggested. Can't blame him, though he's a little old for her." I moved the luggage to the closet so Liz wouldn't trip on it. "I'll set the door jammer in place so we can get to sleep."

Her eyes were closed, and her glasses were on the side table. I crouched in front of the door, pushed one edge of the door jammer beneath it, and twisted the device until its leg pushed hard against the floor. No one would get into the room, even if they picked the lock or stole the access code.

Flipping off one light, I verified that the window toward the foot of the bed was locked. The other was still open, though the screen was in place. I hated leaving it unlocked, but it was a warm evening, and I knew Liz wanted it open. Slipping into bed, I saw her eyes flutter, and she crunched her lips together. I leaned over, gave her a kiss, and said goodnight. Her lips moved, but no sound came out, so I turned off the other light, leaving the room pitch dark.

⚜

A nudge against my shoulder interrupted a dream. I opened my eyes. Liz was perched on her left elbow, looking toward my ringing phone, which was on the nightstand. My first thought was that it would be one of our daughters, but why would they call me and not Liz? My eyes focused on the display, which said, "MB Security." I let out a breath of relief. "It's only work. What the hell are they calling for? They know I'm unavailable." Twisting into a sitting position, I picked up the phone. "Cy Bartholomew."

"Cy. Pete. Sorry to bother you, but we've got a priority one call from Madison PD requesting someone to access a room in downtown Madison."

Pete Chase was an owner of MB Lock & Security and a good friend. But I instantly regretted telling him I was staying downtown. "I'm not taking anything this week, since I'm helping my wife with this wine tasting thing. We talked about it. Remember?"

"I know," he said. "But MPD wants to get into a room inside the place you're staying."

"What do you mean? The place I'm staying?"

He read the address on Wilson Street. "That's the location you gave for your wife's event. The Larson Place Bed & Breakfast."

"Why do the cops want in here?" Even as the words came out, I knew the answer related to Carpenter, and I knew it wasn't good.

Chapter 13

For more than twenty-five years, MB Lock & Security had contracts with multiple law enforcement agencies in Dane County. Because of this, I knew many officers by name and even more by sight. But the name on the notification Pete sent was unfamiliar.

The note said the building owners had not responded to requests for access and the Madison Police Department would be onsite at five o'clock. I assumed the B&B was owned by a small-time landlord who didn't monitor phone and text traffic sent to the number associated with the property. The police would arrive momentarily.

After a bathroom break, I propped goggles atop my head and grabbed my kit, leaving Liz in bed. Ambrose's room was quiet, and no light shone under the door. I knocked twice, but there was no answer, so I pulled out one of my kit's flashlights and proceeded down the staircase. A gentle humming surprised me, and a light shone from below. At first, I thought I heard snoring, but as I descended the staircase, I realized the sound was from the first floor's robotic vacuum cleaner. The illumination came from a night light in the foyer.

Liz had mentioned that Boston's room was on the first floor, so I walked through the kitchen past the humming vacuum and flipped on the event room's lights. It was empty as expected, so I continued to my left, until I found a room with a smart lock. A faint light shone under the door. I leaned against it and knocked with the butt of the flashlight.

A woman's voice muttered something. Then a male voice said, "Maybe there's news...news about Carpenter."

I stepped back and dropped the flashlight beam so it aimed downward. "Boston," I said. "It's Cy. The police are on their way. They want to get inside Carpenter's room."

The familiar sound of a retreating deadbolt preceded the opening of the door. Ambrose stepped out, closing the door behind him. He was barefoot but wearing a different robe. This one could have belonged to Hugh Hefner or Liberace. Creases crossed the left side of his face, and he looked ridiculous. "Have they found her? Is Carpenter okay?"

"Don't know," I said. "The police want to look in her room."

"Why?" He stepped toward me, and I smelled liquor on his breath. "What are they thinking?"

I waved him into the kitchen and told the truth. "They could be checking for a suicide note."

Ambrose's eyes widened. "Suicide? Carpenter? Why would they think that?"

He knew everything about the disappearance that I did, but I knew how cops thought, and they'd have to consider suicide. Yet he knew her much better than I did. "Do you think it's something she would do? Kill herself, I mean?"

"Carpenter!" He looked past me and seemed to realize he was talking too loudly. "She would never kill herself. She would never do that to Maddie."

My mind's eye saw the password on her phone shining at me after I entered the digits in. "Is Maddie her daughter?"

"Yes. The little girl starts kindergarten this fall. Carpenter just, well, adores her."

"Okay," I said. "Hopefully that's not it, but the cops only know what we told them about her disappearance. They know she had a lifejacket but took it off. They are covering their bases."

"Do you think they found her body?" He put his hands over his face. "Why else would they think suicide?"

I considered the situation before responding. "They likely switched from a rescue to a recovery mission after an hour, but they know she could have swum ashore. Any intense lake search will wait until morning while hoping they find her on a beach or she shows up at a police station or something. If they don't find a note, they'll ramp up searching within the city. There's always the chance she came ashore, and someone is taking care of her without knowing she's missing."

Ambrose took one hand from his face and leaned against the kitchen wall. "What can I do to help? Will they want to talk to us again?"

"As far as I know, they just want to get into her room. Does your Bluetooth access get you into all areas, or can you change things so you can get into hers?"

He shook his head. "I don't think I can get into anyone's room but mine."

I wanted to comment about him coming out of Boston's room but held off. "You switched Liz and Carpenter's rooms on Monday night. Right? How'd you do that?"

"I submitted a request through the app to the site manager on Monday night. He or she approved it almost right away.

They updated access and sent a text or maybe an email to Carpenter and to your wife. I submitted a request on the app and sent a text last night asking for access to Carpenter's room. They haven't responded."

"Okay, fine. I'll break in. What room is it?"

"2D." He pulled his robe tight. "Can I come along?"

"Unless there's a safe in the room or something, the cops won't even want me inside. You're better off just going to bed. Also, I like it quiet when I work. I don't want everyone standing around in the hallway. Either way, I'll let you know if there's news."

Ambrose walked theatrically into the kitchen, as he seemed to mull over what I had said. Taking a glass from a cupboard, he turned in a circle and pulled on the faucet. "Well, you're probably right." He took a gulp of water. "I'll go back to bed, though I doubt I'll be able to get back to sleep. Let me know if there's, um, anything new."

He knocked on Boston's door. Within a few seconds, it opened and he slipped inside.

Standing near the door, I examined the lock, verifying it was the same model that was on Liz's and my room. Then I went outside the house, figuring it would be better if the police didn't ring the bell or pound on the door.

After propping the front door open with the flashlight, I sat on the top porch step. If I had downloaded the app and entered the security code, my phone would have given me access, but I had not downloaded it, so I kept the door ajar.

The porch faced the southwest, so the only sign of the coming sunrise was a lightness in the sky. At nine minutes after five, a police cruiser approached. No street parking spots were available, so it pulled into the driveway.

It took a minute for the officer to exit the car. She looked suspiciously at me, so I told her I was with MB Lock & Security.

"Thank you for being responsive," she said. "I'm Officer Hansen." She was powerfully built and older than I expected. A mole was on one side of her chin and, though she wore a hat, her hair appeared to be shorter than mine. She had the demeanor of a veteran, but I didn't recognize her. Perhaps she was a transfer.

We shook hands. "Are you trying to get into Carpenter's room?" I asked. "Afraid I don't remember her last name. Del something I think."

She glanced at a small notepad. "Carpenter Dalbesio."

"That's it. She disappeared last night while swimming in Lake Monona. Any news?"

"Not that I am aware of. I need to look in her room. The property owners have been unresponsive, which is why we called for your assistance."

It was the answer I expected but didn't want. As we stood on the porch's bottom step, I told her about the situation. I wanted to make sure she knew I was staying in the same B&B. She nodded as I spoke. Before going inside, I suggested we avoid waking the other guests.

"Affirmative," she said.

Cops who said "affirmative" made me nervous.

"It won't take long," she continued, "though I'll also tape off the room. Hopefully you can relock the room after I leave."

While locksmiths sometimes broke the locks they picked, I rarely did. It was something I prided myself on. If it didn't lock automatically, I would figure something out.

"Before I pick her, keep in mind these are smart locks which can be opened via Bluetooth from a smartphone. Last night, I gave Carpenter's phone to a Dane County deputy. If you had that, you could get in by holding the phone near the door."

She shook her head as she stared at the ground. "I would need permission to request evidence from the sheriff's office. It would be more efficient if you got me in. That way I don't have to have dispatch wake someone else."

"Sure. The room's on the second floor."

The officer followed me inside. I closed the door and walked up the steps, taking two at a time. Flipping on a light, I pointed at the room with a gold "2D" on its face.

Dropping to one knee, I rolled open my kit and flipped on my headlamp. Then I cleaned a small flashlight with a wipe and slid it into my mouth. I didn't know anyone else who did this routine, but it worked for me. Liz still couldn't believe I regularly put flashlights in my mouth.

The physical lock was a pin tumbler, the same as the ones on the other doors. I placed my ear against the wooden door and asked Officer Hansen to knock. After counting to ten, I inserted a hook pick and a tension wrench into the keyhole.

As always, I felt the interior of the mechanism in my mind and in my body. For me, lock picking is a holistic process. Once I could feel and see it, I knew how its pieces interacted and how the mechanism worked. It wasn't long before I felt and heard the pins. There were sounds and feedback from every movement. The first pin was the hardest and took several minutes. When I ushered the pin to the shear line, where the lock's plug and cylinder met, I adjusted the tension. It was mine now. I knew and understood her. The rest of the pins came quickly, the tumbler turned, and the deadbolt dropped.

I looked up at Hansen, smiling at the easy conquest. Then I remembered what might be inside, and the smile disappeared.

Chapter 14

Officer Hansen stepped inside Carpenter's room, partially closing the door. Sitting on the hallway floor, I stared at a painting of a feather that hung on the wall. After five minutes, Hansen was done and her hands were empty. If she had found a note, she would have bagged it. I wanted to ask to be sure, but I didn't know her and it seemed unprofessional. The officer closed the door and asked me to relock it. Before I could reply, the door automatically locked.

She jiggled the handle, then put police tape across the door. Two tacks held each piece in place. It was for show, but I thought it a good idea since the property owner might contact Ambrose and re-set the code so his phone could open the door. This clarified that no one should enter the room.

Josh peeked out his door, apparently wondering about the noise. Hansen and I walked down the hallway, and I nodded to him and followed the officer out of the building. When I returned, he was waiting. I told him there was no news. We talked about being eager for information, but eventually went back to our rooms.

I flipped on the light. Liz was sleeping on her side, her ample auburn hair facing me. Slipping off my shoes and socks, I turned the light off and crawled into bed without re-setting the door jamb. The only noise came from Liz's breathing. The next thing I remembered was her alarm going off. She climbed over me and hurried to the bathroom. I fell into semi-consciousness, thinking about the lock I had picked hours earlier. In my dream, I was part of it. The pin tumblers, the cylinder cam, the springs. We were all one.

Years ago, I told Liz about my lock dreams. She thought it was weird, and it probably was, so I stopped telling her about them. Last year, she asked about my lock dreams. I lied and told her I didn't have them anymore. It was one thing I no longer shared. It was just between me and the locks.

The thump of the deadbolt woke me. I sat up as Liz rushed inside and flipped on the light. She said it was ten minutes until breakfast, so I stumbled down the hall, relieved to see the bathroom door open. I was out of the shower in less than five minutes. She waited on the bed while I finished getting ready. As I led her down the stairs, the smell of bagels caught my attention.

We sat at the kitchen table, joining Ambrose, Katie, Josh and his wife, Amanda. The servers placed glasses of water and sparkling wine beside our plates. I wanted a sesame seed bagel but was told they only had plain. The only variety was in the donuts, which included powdered and glazed. Renee said it was a taster thing, but I couldn't understand how sesame seeds would affect the taste of wine.

Liz ordered one bagel, while I took three. Katie asked about the police visit, and Amanda told us about a story on the local morning news about Carpenter's disappearance. As we spoke, Ambrose announced that several national outlets had picked up the story. He showed me an article on his phone, which included a picture of her. The article's title was, "Popular wine vlogger feared drowned in Wisconsin lake."

"I stopped by," Amanda said, "to support Josh and to see if there's anything I could do." Her gaze jumped to me and then to Ambrose. "Any chance the press will show up here? Is that a concern?"

We all looked at Ambrose. For a moment, I saw panic in his face, but then his eyes widened as if a thought had come into his mind. "They can't come inside, even if they want to," he said. "Perhaps, however, I will provide a statement. That might get them off our backs."

Boston leaned over his shoulder. "Are you going to send something out via social media?"

"That would be easiest," he replied.

"Is it necessary?" Josh asked. "Can't you wait until you actually know something? If they show up at the door, that's another matter."

Ambrose pushed his lips together, then finally agreed to wait.

"What if they ring the doorbell while we're testing?" Boston asked.

"I could man the door and get rid of them," Amanda replied. "Though I need to leave for work before ten."

I cleared my throat. "Guess I can man it after that. I'm not all that necessary, anyway."

Liz elbowed my ribs, mouthing, "Of course you're necessary."

I wasn't, but didn't argue. "If the doorbell rings after Amanda leaves, I'll answer it."

We all nodded our agreement. As we ate, Boston and her team focused on the event room. I took one sip of the sparkling wine and turned the bottle toward me. It was from a winery in Door County. The selection was probably leftover from the prior morning's testing.

While I was not in the mood for sparkling wine, I commented that the "Champagne" tasted good. I only did it to see who would scold me first. The wine didn't come from the Champagne region of France, so wine people would never call it Champagne.

Rather than getting a verbal response, they looked knowingly at me, then at each other, and finally at Liz.

"Cy is pulling our legs," Liz said. "He thinks he's being smart."

"No more food for him," Ambrose said, and everyone chuckled.

At five minutes after nine, Boston told us we needed to move to the main room. Amanda announced she'd be by the fireplace until nine forty-five, then she'd take off. She gave her husband a hug and started down the hall.

The other tasters entered the event room before we did. Eight white wines sat in an oval on four of the six tables accompanied by a water glass, a notebook, and the ever-present red spit cup. Two corner tables were empty.

Once again, Renee was responsible for our table and Josh's. Ripping off a single sheet from Liz's notebook, I made initial grades on each entry's color, but struggled to ignore the first entry's distinctive floral aroma. They were very light wines, and I graded six of them as medium straw and two as pale straw, the latter being the lightest color in the chart Liz had trained me on.

Liz and I agreed on all but one. After a second look, I decided she was right, and she recorded five medium straws and three pale straws. The disagreement felt strange, particularly when I glimpsed Carpenter's and Missy's empty tables. The event was to continue for three more days, and I wondered if the number of wine tasters would change again.

Out of the corner of my eye, I spotted Amanda trying to get my attention. My part of this flight was done, so I told Liz I would be back.

Amanda motioned me forward, so I joined her in the fireplace room. "A TV station truck is out there," she said, pointing at a van parked about a block away. "It's been there for about ten minutes. Can't tell if they're here for us or something at the courthouse."

"Got it," I said. "I'll handle it."

"Sorry to leave, but I got to get to work, and it looked like you weren't doing anything."

That summed things up. "Appreciate you watching," I said.

"Let's hope they don't create a scene. Josh is already upset."

"I take it he is close to Carpenter."

She gave me a weary look as she stuck her phone into her pocket. "The two of them are more than close. Don't you already know that?"

"Yes. Guess I suspected." While I wanted to do or say something comforting, nothing seemed appropriate. "Didn't want to make assumptions."

A frown slid onto her face, and she looked away and wiped her eyes. "Josh and I are separating. I'm trying not to judge him or Carpenter. But it's hard, you know, since I still care about him. Even if we divorce, we'll stay friends. I just know it."

I struggled to find magical words that would make everything seem alright. "The way you feel is normal. All you can do is to be supportive of a person you care about. That's okay." It wasn't magical, but it was what I came up with.

"Thanks." She nodded, saluted, and turned around. Something told me her salutes were usually crisp and professional, but this one was playful or half-hearted.

I peered out the window as she walked toward the parking ramp. A few minutes later, I returned to the event room. Almost immediately, the doorbell rang. Liz was sipping her fourth entry, so I touched her knee and told her I would be right back. Before I left the room, Ambrose hopped out of his chair and chased me down.

"Let me know if it's the press," he said. "If so, I'll take care of them. Most likely, I'll just express our concern for Carpenter."

Someone spit in a red cup as I hurried past the dishes on the kitchen table. After opening the heavy door, I stepped outside. A cool morning breeze blew across the porch and a young, fair-haired woman stood in front of me with a microphone. Behind her hovered a burly man with a video camera. The woman looked familiar. If I remembered correctly, I'd seen her on a morning newscast, though usually she was standing in front of the courthouse, the police station, or a burning building.

The reporter identified herself, but I didn't catch her name. She asked who I was and whether I had a statement about the disappearance of Carpenter Dalbesio. My initial thought was to just say I knew nothing and had no comment, but as the camera stared at me and the microphone closed in, I realized it wasn't my decision. The press wanted a statement and this was Ambrose's event, so I told them I would return with him. Perhaps he would give them what they wanted.

Ambrose met me in the hallway. Adjusting his pale-yellow sweater, he cleared his throat and walked to the door. I followed, telling him I would be just inside and would help if he needed to make a quick exit. He nodded and cleared his throat again. For a moment, I thought he was going to break into a song. Instead, he opened the door, slipped outside, and shut it behind him. After four minutes, he returned, looking pleased. My guess was that he had nailed the statement. Maybe it would help him sell a few books.

The rest of the flight went well, considering the circumstances. Katie and Liz were aligned again in their scores, though all four critics had different ratings on one entry. When they finally worked through the difficult one, Boston announced they would take a break until the ten-thirty session.

We walked back into the kitchen. Breakfast had been cleaned up, presumably by the servers, but there were leftover donuts, so I took a powdered one and a napkin. After biting into its fluffiness, the doorbell rang again. I hurried into the foyer, leaving Liz in the kitchen. Fully expecting another television camera, I put the donut and the napkin on the first step of the staircase and opened the door.

But there was no attractive young reporter and no camera. Instead, I saw the familiar face of Detective Byron Knutsen, wearing plain clothes and a thin tie. His balding head was shaved, but a thin red beard hid part of his face. A woman in plain clothes, who I assumed was also a detective, stood next to him. Two uniformed City of Madison police officers, both of whom I recognized, flanked them, and a Dane County Sheriff's Deputy waited on the walkway.

"Cy?" Knutsen said. "What the hell are you doing here?"

I was as surprised to see him as he was to see me. But there was only one reason a detective from the Madison Police Department's Investigative Services Unit would be at The Larson Place.

Chapter 15

I t was a sunny July day, but the police presence told me it wouldn't be an enjoyable one. Knutsen introduced the blonde woman at his side as Detective Alexis Bailey with the Dane County Sheriff's Office. She nodded and handed me a warrant to search portions of the property. She told me in a squeaky voice that she wanted to speak to Josh Peterson, as she had a warrant to search his boat, the *Eloquence*.

"Do you have news about Carpenter?" I asked as I shook Bailey's warm and damp hand.

"I'm afraid so," she said, her voice cracking. "Early this morning, the Sheriff's Office Dive Team recovered her body."

Cars continued down Wilson Street, but for a moment, they seemed to slow. I looked at Bailey, then pointed at Knutsen. "If you're here, her death must be suspicious. There's no other reason you'd be involved."

"Cy," Knutsen said. "What are you doing here? Do you know Miss Dalbesio?"

"She's a wine critic." I glanced back at the Larson Place. "My wife and a half-dozen others are doing a wine tasting thing here. As for me, I'm a kind of hanger-on."

"I knew your wife worked weekends at a liquor store, but I didn't know she was into wine," he said. "How is Liz? Is she still working at the Sequoia branch?"

I was surprised he remembered her name and the library branch where she had last worked. "She's fine, but she had some vision issues which forced her into a career change. Now she does critic stuff like this. She's inside right now. We were on the boat last night when Carpenter disappeared."

Bailey seemed anxious, so I opened the door and ushered them inside. Ambrose joined us in the foyer, shaking Knutsen's and Bailey's hands. Boston was soon behind him.

"Have you found Carpenter?" Ambrose asked. He reached for Boston and clasped her hand. A tear threatened to roll down his cheek. "I fear the worst."

Bailey looked up at him. "How well did you know her?"

"Well. I've known her for four or five years. She collaborated on my book about New England wines and is helping on my upcoming one as well."

I pointed at Josh as he came down the stairs and gave a brief introduction. Bailey pulled out a sheet of paper and held it in front of him. "Mr. Peterson, you're going to need to come with me to the dock where your boat is kept. As you can see, we have a warrant to search a boat called *Eloquence*."

"Is she okay?" Josh's face was flat and blotchy. "Is Carpenter alright?"

"No." Bailey took back her warrant and tucked it inside her jacket pocket. "This morning, at about six-fifteen, the Dane County Sheriff's Office Dive Team located Carpenter Dalbesio's body."

Josh dropped as if collapsing and sat on the bottom step, right next to my donut. He covered his face with his hands and sobbed.

Ambrose stepped closer to Bailey. "Have you notified her parents? They're divorced but live in the Chicago area. I think her mom's in Naperville and her father's in Aurora. Or maybe vice versa."

"I talked to her mother this morning, who then contacted the father. They're coming up and should be here within hours." She turned toward me. "Can you show Detective Knutsen her room? It's upstairs, I believe. Then I want you, your wife, and Mr. Peterson to go to the Public Safety Building for statements."

She was referring to the building that housed the Dane County Sheriff's Office. It was only two blocks away. I hadn't been inside for a few years, but remembered it being a dump.

Knutsen extended his arm and read from a notepad in his left hand. "The rest of you will stay with me for statements. I'm looking for five people: Ambrose Houser," he motioned toward him, "as well as Katie Coolidge, Boston Cruz, Renee Curry, and Abby Johnson."

I led Knutsen and one of the uniformed officers past my donut and up the staircase. Discussion continued between Bailey and the group. "Carpenter's room is pretty obvious," I said, pointing at the door plastered with police tape. "An Officer Hansen came over this morning."

"Yes. That was before we found the body."

I paused as they approached Carpenter's door. "I picked the lock, but it reset when she closed the door. Do you want me to break in again?"

"No. The owner finally got back to us." Knutsen pointed at the officer. "Benny downloaded the lock's app and can get us inside. Forensics should be here soon. At that point, he'll open it and let them in."

"Okay. Makes sense." I leaned forward and lowered my voice. "They want Liz and me to go down to the Public Safety Building for a statement. Can you guys just interview us here? Isn't that what you're doing for everyone else? The county offices are depressing."

I preferred Knutsen interviewing us. Despite continually dealing with criminals and filling out reports, he oozed a quiet confidence and maintained an even keel. People liked him, and I trusted him.

He looked at the stairway before responding. "MPD is cooperating with the sheriff's office on this investigation, but the lake is their jurisdiction, not ours, so they are driving things. Deputies did the initial interviews for you two and for the guy who owns the boat. We took statements from everyone else. Bailey wants to be consistent and keep your statements with the county. Meanwhile, we'll take the rest. If Bailey wants to talk with you at the Public Safety Building, then that's what you need to do."

This was an example of the politics between police organizations. They helped each other but understood turf. This was a Dane County Sheriff's Office case. Deciding who takes statements was their decision and not his. I nodded and followed him down the stairs.

The front door was open, and the deputy had joined the others in the foyer. I waited as Bailey led Josh onto the porch, closing the door behind her. Knutsen leaned toward the deputy. The detective then put his hands in the air and announced that he and his officer would take statements one at a time, except for me and Liz, who were going to the Public Safety Building.

The deputy introduced himself and I ignored my now squished donut and followed him into the kitchen, where we found Liz, Renee, and Abby washing wine glasses.

He led Liz and me out of the building, and we started on the five-minute walk to the Public Safety Building, which housed the Dane County Sheriff's Office. When we arrived, the deputy passed Liz to a colleague and took me into a nine-by-nine interview room. A table sat in the middle of the space with two chairs on each side. While there was not a mirror on the wall, a small camera in a corner was aimed at me.

The deputy brought me two Styrofoam cups, one filled with awful coffee, the other with lukewarm water. I sipped at both for fifteen minutes before a plainclothes detective arrived. She was in her early thirties and slightly built. She had a scar on her left cheek. It was less pronounced than Liz's but was the only thing that differentiated her from a timid housewife. I wondered if the injury impacted her smile like it did for Liz.

"Silas Bartholomew," she said as she sat across from me.

"Call me Cy."

"Detective Cam Schuster." She smiled, and the crease on her cheek deepened. I realized her scar was not as long as Liz's. "I think you know my father, Tom Schuster. He was a detective with the Madison Police Department. He retired in May."

"Sure, I know Tom. Good guy." Looking at her, I saw his freckled skin, light brown hair, and reserved manner. Tom Schuster was smart and tougher than he looked. I pondered whether the same was true of her. "How's your dad doing?"

"He's fine, thanks." She smiled. "Right now, he's up north fishing. On Rice Lake."

I told her a quick story about him. She laughed, and I realized she had gotten me to relax. That was fine, but I wondered about her motivation.

"My understanding," she said, "is that you were on an outing on Lake Monona with Miss Carpenter Dalbesio." I nodded and wondered if she was recording the conversation. "Is that correct?"

"Yeah. Unfortunately, I was the captain when everyone went swimming and Carpenter...disappeared. I feel kind of responsible, you know?"

"You were the boat captain? I thought it was Josh Peterson's boat?"

I told her Josh had put me in charge while people went swimming. She didn't seem to dwell on it. "Can you start by telling me about what led to the outing?" Her head bopped side-to-side. "From the beginning."

I gave her a long explanation of how Liz became a late recruit for the wine tasting. I told her about my wife's vision problems and my limited involvement in the tasting. Then I detailed the boat trip and recounted Josh asking me to help launch the boat. We talked about Liz, and I explained that the outing was something she wanted to do, even though she worried about being on the lake at night. Next, I recounted launching the *Eloquence* on the Yahara River and picking up the rest of the people, including the Iacominis. Finally, I went through the swim and the search for Carpenter.

"The victim and the others were in the water for approximately twenty-five minutes?" she said.

I nodded.

"Neither you nor your wife got into the lake?"

"Correct. Like I mentioned, Josh put me in charge of the boat. Besides, I couldn't leave Liz alone. She was kind of freaking out since she struggles to see in the dark. I think she was worried about falling into the water. Like I said, my wife is legally blind."

"Oh, okay. I understand."

She had me go through everything I remembered from the swim. I told her about Carpenter's phone and about me recording the activity for a few minutes. Then I recounted the motorboat that had created waves, the women racing around the boat, Josh's alarm going off, and him calling people in.

Schuster dug into the motorboat, which had come close to us during the outing. That made sense and I wondered whether she might have swum away from the *Eloquence* and gotten hit by the motorboat. I finally asked if that was a possibility, but she shook her head and said it wasn't.

"What do you know about Ms. Dalbesio?" she asked.

"Not much. She was attractive." I paused, realizing it was a stupid comment. "She had worked with Ambrose Houser on his book on the wines of New England, so she must know him, Josh, and Katie pretty well. The three of them worked on that book and were doing tastings for one on Midwestern wines. I don't know if Boston was involved in both books. Someone mentioned that Carpenter has a daughter named Maddie. Her daughter's name was the password for her phone, so I assume she was important to her."

"Do you know if the victim had a sexual or romantic relationship with anyone who was aboard the boat?"

"I don't *know* anything," I replied.

"Do you *suspect* something?"

"Josh's wife, Amanda, told me that Josh and Carpenter were close, and she mentioned that her and Josh were separating. The implication was that Josh and Carpenter were having an affair, but I know nothing for sure. Perhaps they were just platonic friends."

"Or maybe not?"

I shrugged my shoulders. "Josh seems like a nice guy, so I'm trying to give him the benefit of the doubt."

Schuster turned a page in her notebook. "Amanda was not on the boat. Correct?"

"Correct. Amanda ate with us prior to the excursion, but she mentioned something about working the next day, so she headed home. Plus, she wasn't feeling well."

"We'll certainly be talking to her," Schuster said as she jotted down a note. After a few more questions, we were done. Before exiting the room, she said she'd check if Liz was free to go.

Schuster returned with a transcription of my statement. The conversation had obviously been recorded, so I skimmed and signed it.

She then asked if they could access my phone records for Tuesday. I nodded, so she slipped an additional form in front of me, which I signed. It was tempting to ask about Carpenter's death. I was curious because I didn't understand why they seemed to think her death was not an accident. Perhaps someone had drugged her? All they needed to do was undo her lifejacket's strap and pull it off. Then her body would probably sink to the bottom of Lake Monona.

"Are my wife and I free to go?"

"Yes," she said with a smile.

"Can I ask you one question? Why do you think her death is suspicious? Couldn't she have just taken off her vest because she wanted to dive under the boat or something and she hit her head or got into trouble?"

Schuster looked to the side for a moment, as if deciding how to respond. "No," she said. "Someone murdered her. Someone who was in the water."

"You're sure about that?"

"One hundred percent." She leaned her fists against the top of the table. "Someone slit her throat with a knife."

"Holy shit." I hadn't expected that. "In the water?"

"Yes. In the water."

Chapter 16

When Liz started at the liquor store, it was just a summer job and she was always home by ten at night. After she lost her driver's license and retired from the library, she increased her hours at the store. By then, her role had expanded, and she became responsible for all their wine and liquor purchases.

One of our daughters or I would drive her to and from work. When none of us were available, she took a cab or an Uber. It was about this time that she started her wine and whiskey website. I tried to dissuade her from doing it, since I thought a website made her a more public figure, which brought risks which I thought exceeded any potential benefit. She disagreed, arguing I was being my normally paranoid self.

When she got a second job at a downtown restaurant, we had similar discussions. Meanwhile, I struggled. My role as an owner of MB Lock & Security took sixty to seventy hours per week, and all three of our daughters were busy with school. After several months, the other owners of MB Lock & Security knew I was drowning. They encouraged me to pull back from work and took steps to minimize my workload.

Four months ago, Jeff Brown pulled me into his office. He was the company's president and, like me, a twenty percent owner. He was the only one of us who wore a suit, and his office was on the third floor. It was a change from the early days when he wore a security guard uniform and worked out of a corner in his parents' garage. As I sat across from him, he told me I was the best locksmith he ever knew, and my skill had been important to the growth of MB Lock & Security. However, he didn't think those skills were important for the company's future. He said I had to decide whether I had the time and the drive to help them grow the company into a twenty-first century powerhouse. If I wanted to be an integral part of the company's future, I needed to update my skill set. If not, I risked becoming obsolete.

Jeff was probably worried about how I would react, but I understood. While I was a crack locksmith, I was running the division because I was an owner. I thought I was a good manager, but my energy and commitment were waning. The company could get by cheaper if they brought in someone else to run the division. The manager didn't have to be a top locksmith. They only needed to be competent and understand the industry.

While I still loved being a locksmith, I hated meetings and almost everything else about the job. Training was the worst, as there were technological innovations I had to learn. As I sat in Jeff's office, I realized that thirty years was enough. The business no longer needed me, and I no longer needed the business. We talked for ten minutes, and I mentioned a willingness to sell my share of MB Lock & Security.

The hard part was that I was only fifty, and we had three daughters in college. Few wives would have accepted the idea, but Liz had just been through her own changes. Money would be tight, so we went through the numbers. She was working about forty hours per week between her two jobs, and I would still work twenty as a locksmith. Neither of us would make nearly as much as we had been, but we had her pension and the money from selling my share of the business. We decided it could work.

Our daughters were relieved, since they were as worried about their mother's safety as I was. Our oldest daughter, Kayla, told me that my role was to keep her mother safe while allowing her to pursue her fledgling career. We joked I was her mom's *plus one*, which became a standard line within the family. Helping Liz succeed wasn't exciting or sexy, but those were the cards I was dealt. And it was better than going to another three-day security and risk management summit.

Liz's safety wasn't an issue while she was inside the Public Safety Building, but I was concerned about her police interview. Detective Schuster led me down a staircase and through a long hallway. She opened the lobby door, and a sense of relief overcame me when I heard Liz's laugh.

The detective stopped and nodded as she held the door. Liz was sitting next to a young woman in a light blue polo shirt with the Dane County logo. The woman was not a deputy, but I assumed she was a county employee. Another loud laugh came out, this time from both women.

"Liz," I said as the lobby door closed. "How are you?"

"See!" Liz said.

The woman laughed. "Miss Liz said you'd say just that."

"Actually, I thought you'd say, 'How are you doing?'"

The woman continued laughing. "Close enough."

Liz stood and pulled the woman up with her left hand. "This is Tiff Jones. She used to be a regular at my branch when she was in middle school."

"Nice to meet you," I said as we shook hands. It wasn't unusual for my wife to run into people she knew from her days as a librarian. Many were young adults who remembered her from visiting the library as children. It often led to me standing and nodding in the middle of a grocery store while she and some stranger laughed. Nodding was one of my strengths.

"Miss Liz was my favorite unofficial babysitter," the woman said. "She let me and my friends get away with a few things, but if we went too far, watch out!"

There was more laughing, and finally, they hugged and we exited the building. The fresh air was warm and the scent of the lake, which was only five or six hundred feet away, was unmistakable. Taking Liz's elbow, I maneuvered so I was on her left.

"Did they tell you about Carpenter?" she asked. "Someone cut her throat."

"I'm surprised they told you."

"Didn't they tell you?"

"Yeah, they did. But I knew the father of the woman who interviewed me."

She guffawed. "So what? I knew Tiff and Deputy Frederick."

"Guess they're not keeping the fact to themselves." I glanced to the side as a blue pickup pulled into an open spot along the sidewalk. The man in the passenger seat stared me down, so I looked away and waited until we were far past the vehicle before speaking. "How the hell could have someone cut her throat? We were there the whole time and heard nothing. No screams. No splashing. At least no splashing that stood out."

"Did you tell your interviewer about Josh and Carpenter?" she asked.

"I told them I suspected something was going on between them based on what Amanda said. How about you? What did you tell them?"

"Carpenter and Josh seemed close; that's what I said." She looked at me as if her admission was better than mine. "Would you want to go somewhere for a few minutes? It's already too late for the ten-thirty tasting. If they re-schedule, they'll text me. I don't want to go back to the B&B while the police are there."

"The cops shouldn't make you nervous. We were both in the boat the whole time. They can't suspect us."

Her eyes widened, and she pulled me closer. "That raises another issue. Do we want to be inside that old house while speculating about which one of them is a murderer?"

It was a good point. "Let's take a right here and relax in the vacant lot where the old St. Ray's was." The area had been the site of a cathedral which burned down twenty years earlier. There was talk of rebuilding, but nothing came of it. The spot was now an unofficial park. It was closer than walking to the lake, and it was usually quiet.

She pulled my arm tight, implying her agreement. "None of those people seem like killers." She paused, and we waited at a crosswalk. The lot where we parked the day before was across the street. "Ambrose may be a little self-centered, but everyone seems nice."

"Even Josh?"

She nodded. "Something was going on between him and Carpenter. Obviously, I think low of him for fooling around on his wife, but who knows the background? And she doesn't seem crushed by it, does she? I'll try not to judge until I know everything."

"Who benefits from Carpenter's death?" I asked. "Is she rich?"

"I don't think so." Liz's brow scrunched together. "Katie said Carpenter and her ex share custody of a daughter. She does all that YouTube and TikTok stuff to make her wine criticism a full-time job. The feeling I got was that she was getting by while building her brand. Nothing more. If anything, Katie suspects that part of Carpenter's interest in Josh related to his money. She said Josh isn't rich, but his family is loaded."

"What did you hear about Carpenter's ex?" I asked. "He's got to be suspect number one."

"Seriously?" She flashed her crooked smile.

"Yeah. They got to consider an ex-spouse and any boyfriends and ex-boyfriends."

"How could her ex-husband have done it? Doesn't it have to be someone who was on the boat? No one else was near her, right?"

I thought back to the swim in Lake Monona and about the dimming light. "Do you remember the motorboat that came close?"

"It wasn't that close."

"Suppose someone jumped off," I said. "Someone who could swim well or with scuba gear. They could come up quietly."

"That seems unlikely. If he had scuba gear, he might as well have just swum from the shore. Why bother with a boat?"

She was right, but I didn't want to admit it. "If the ex doesn't have an alibi, the cops will dig into him. Otherwise, they'll focus on the people who were with us on the boat. At certain times, Josh was swimming with her. He was the one who had the best opportunity to do something, but we didn't hear a yell or a splash when she was attacked."

"How about Amanda as a suspect?" Liz asked. "She's fit, and Katie told me she had gone swimming with them at some of the earlier events. Jealousy is an awfully good motive."

"It is," I said as I considered the suggestion. "If she doesn't have an alibi, then she might as well have been on the boat. Same with Carpenter's ex."

Arriving at the park, I spotted a shaded bench, and we sat on a part that was devoid of bird poop. The area included several paths surrounded by grass, a few clumps of flowers, and about two dozen trees. The paths were composed of a mix of red gravel and cement, the latter of which formed the shape of crosses. A woman with two small black dogs was nearby, but the three of them ignored us.

For several minutes, Liz updated me on our daughter's latest text messages. Most of them focused on roommate and boyfriend troubles. As the conversation waned, we pulled out our phones. After losing what seemed like eight straight games of solitaire, I leaned my head on Liz's lap and closed my eyes, thinking about the boat ride. I remembered Carpenter descending into the water and recalled the weight of the captain's hat on my head.

"We're on for a four o'clock tasting," Liz said.

I opened my eyes, feeling slightly confused. "What? The tasting?" I sat up. "They're going to keep going?"

"Uh-huh. Ambrose sent a text asking me and Josh to read our email. The email says the police are just about finished and Missy's back. She's resting in her room, but she will be ready for the session."

"How about Josh?" I stretched my arms. "Is he back?"

"Ambrose's text and email is to me and him, so probably not." There was silence as she replied to the note. "He wants to do two tastings starting at four. We'll cram both into an hour and a half. He wants to make sure Josh and I can make it. Are you okay with our going?"

I nodded, seeing she was ready to tell him we would be there.

"Do you think Josh killed her?" she asked as she hit send.

"It's possible, as he had the best opportunity. It's just he doesn't seem like a killer. Then again, none of them do."

We started back to the sidewalk. "Do we need to worry about our safety?" she asked. "Should we go home tonight and come back in the morning?"

For once, I was less worried than my wife. "I don't see any reason the killer would come after us, unless they think we have information for the cops that would implicate them. Which we don't. At least, not yet. Though I want to make sure the cops figure out what happened to Carpenter. I owe it to her. I was in charge when it happened. It's my responsibility."

"Don't be silly. You weren't responsible for Carpenter. Josh put you in charge of the boat, but you weren't her lifeguard."

"I know," I said. "I just think back to Ben and to his daughter. Maybe this is an opportunity for me to make up for that. Perhaps I can help her daughter in a way I couldn't help Ben's. Maybe I can provide some closure for her."

"Okay, but don't go down a rabbit hole. I understand your desire to help, but it's not your responsibility, so don't overdo it. Be safe. Try not to talk about the murder around them or in the B&B. Okay?"

"Sure. But I'll be curious to hear the conversations people have. They'll all be wondering who killed her. People may talk about issues others have had with her or about professional rivalries. Someone might come right out and talk about Josh and Carpenter. Maybe someone will point out that Josh benefits from her death, or maybe she had something on him."

"Do you think Carpenter had an affair with anyone else in the group?" Liz asked.

The thought hadn't even occurred to me. "Not me," I said with a chuckle as I wrapped my hand around her waist.

"She had an affair with Ambrose."

"Ambrose? How do you figure?"

"Katie told me."

I nodded slowly. "Okay then. Let's see what dirt we hear while you taste expensive wine and spit into a plastic cup."

Chapter 17

When The Larson Place came into view, I felt a chill. The murder did not occur in the building, so the feeling of dread puzzled me. Before I dwelt on it, Liz's phone rang. It was Ambrose. He told her the police needed me to open a shed at the B&B. The road's walk sign turned, and she said we would be there momentarily. An unmarked Ford Interceptor was in the driveway, and I debated whether it was Bailey's or Knutsen's vehicle. Then I spotted a bald head in the driver's seat.

The car door opened as we walked up the pathway and Knutsen stepped out wearing black sunglasses. "Cy! Liz!" he yelled louder than necessary. "Been waiting for you."

"I hear you need me to break into the shed." I motioned toward the back lot.

"Yep. It's probably a waste of time, but..." he paused as we approached. "We're looking to see if we can find the source of the weapon. I would have called it in, but the guy with the mustache told me you'd be here any minute."

We shook hands. "Does that mean you found the knife?"

Knutsen nodded and his jaw slid from side-to-side. For a moment, I thought he was chewing gum, but I realized he had a cough drop or hard candy in his mouth. "It's a common kitchen knife which is sometimes sold as part of a set. The knife doesn't match the set that's inside the house, but the owner says there's kitchenware in the shed."

We followed him down the driveway. Once behind the house, the shed came into view. I remembered it from ten years earlier when the manager had opened it to pull out a ladder. The building could hold a compact car, but it was far from the driveway, so it was not used to house a vehicle.

"Will you need your kit?"

"Let's see what it is," I said as we crossed the small backyard. "Always got the basics on me and I can't imagine it being anything difficult."

"The owner says it's a Yale padlock. There are two keys, but they accidentally took both with them on vacation. It was tempting to just saw the damn thing off, but we don't have a replacement lock, and I didn't want to leave the shed unsecured. Plus, I figure you could get it open in a jiffy."

The shed was light blue. It had been painted recently, but unlike the house, it hadn't been restored. The doorway was about six feet high, and the roof was black with only a slight pitch. Unlike the front yard, the back had not been re-sodded and the grass around the shed was unkempt. Knutsen stopped a few feet from the building and let me pass.

"The owner was mistaken," I said as I touched the black, blue and silver device. "It's not a Yale, but rather a Master Lock. They have some buggers, but this is just a general security lock, the sort of thing you put on your locker at school. Four-pin cylinder, dual lever. Looks brand new." I pulled out my mobile kit, aiming the light at the keyhole. No scratches were on the entryway. I was sure no one had ever picked this lock before. "I'll have her in just a moment."

"You'll have her?" Liz said. I felt her eyes rolling.

"It's just a lock, Hun." I held it and the tension wrench in my left hand, then slid the rake into the plug.

"What sort of knife was it?" Liz asked Knutsen.

I was about to ask her to be quiet but decided against it. This would be easy enough. I could open this lock during a thunderstorm on a sinking boat. A little noise wouldn't matter.

"It's an eight-inch Japanese-style chef's knife. Very common," he replied. "They're sold in sets, but also individually, so we may be on a fool's errand."

The first pin moved, so I strengthened the tension. Liz and Knutsen talked about kitchen knives while I focused on the pin chambers and the feel of the pins as they moved ever so slightly. Then I had it; the mechanism turned, the spring engaged, and I pulled the shackle from the padlock's body.

"That was quick," Knutsen said.

"I'll put it in as six minutes on your bill." The kit slid into my pocket, and I backed away while examining the keyhole for marks or damage. "Six minutes is our lowest billing increment."

We waited as Knutsen searched for a light switch inside the shed. He flipped on a small flashlight, and its beam shone against a wall, pausing on an orange extension ladder and an aluminum canoe. He mumbled a few words, and the overhead light turned on revealing a bicycle and boxes of materials.

"Do you have to go through all those?" I asked, pointing at the boxes.

"No. A uniform needs to go through them. I got an interview to go to." Stepping outside, he pulled out his phone.

Moments later, he hung up and said someone would arrive within minutes. "Thanks for your help, Cy."

"Were there prints on the knife?" I asked.

"Don't know, but I'll be surprised if there are. Last I heard, they were processing it."

"Where'd they find it?"

He stepped back into the shed and waved us closer. "Bottom of the lake. Roughly thirty feet from the body."

"That close." I glanced at Liz, who was still outside. "Whoever killed her must have dropped the knife right afterward."

Knutsen nodded in agreement. "The press already know we have it, but we won't detail where we found it until a press conference later today, so don't share. I'm only telling you because our friends in the sheriff's office tell me you and Liz are officially cleared. Detective Bailey says you two never got into the water. Every witness verified your story."

"Glad you don't think we're killers."

Knutsen smiled and slapped my shoulder. "I knew you had nothing to do with it. I hear you never even met our victim before yesterday."

"Yeah. That's what I told Detective Schuster."

"You met Cam?" He rested his hands on his waist. "Did you know she's Tom Schuster's kid?"

I nodded, and we talked for a few minutes as we exited the shed and walked along the driveway. As we got to the steps, I spotted a female police officer approaching us on the sidewalk. The officer undoubtedly walked from the Madison Police Department office, which was only a block further away than the Dane County Sheriff's office. Knutsen greeted her on the driveway. The woman looked like she could be one of my nineteen-year-old daughter's friends. We waved goodbye as Knutsen led her to the shed.

Liz and I stepped inside and walked into the kitchen. The same group from the previous night was at the table. It was as if they had never left. The only difference was they had glasses of water in front of them instead of port wine.

Katie waved Liz over, and we listened to a rundown of the police interviews they had gone through. She said Knutsen talked with her, Ambrose, and Boston, while a uniformed officer spoke with Renee and Abby. Afterward, Boston gave the two servers a break until later when they would prepare for the afternoon session.

"That Detective Knutsen views us as suspects," Boston said as she looked at Ambrose. "We weren't even near Carpenter when we were in the water. There's no way either of us could have done anything without the other seeing."

"At least you two were never in the lake," Katie said, pointing at Liz and then at me. "They got to know you are innocent."

I nodded in agreement. "Have you heard from Josh? Is he still with Detective Bailey?"

"He hasn't responded to my email or to my text," Ambrose said. "My guess is they're still interviewing him. I'm sure they know he was with Carpenter for part of the swim."

I leaned forward. "Why would they think he'd want to kill her? Josh and Carpenter were close."

Boston, Ambrose, and Katie exchanged glances. "That's just the thing," Boston said. "They may have been a little *too* close."

Ambrose was nodding. "They were seeing each other. It was common knowledge, at least with the rest of the base crew."

"What do you mean by the *base crew*?"

He pointed at Boston and at Katie. "Us three. The ones who do all the tasting events. We've known something was going on for a while."

"Plus," Katie said, "Carpenter and Josh knew each other from way back. They both worked on the Jersey Shore one summer before or during college. They had something going and apparently it revived."

Ambrose nodded approvingly before draining the last of his water. "One thing I admitted to was that Carpenter was pulling back on their relationship."

Boston tugged him closer. "No way. You're kidding?"

"No, I'm not!" His voice was raspy but loud. It was almost a roar. "On Monday night, she told me she gave him an ultimatum. Either he file for divorce or it was over. She was tired of waiting."

"Wow," Boston said. "Why didn't you tell me?"

"She asked me not to, and she wasn't dumping him. It was maneuvering. She didn't want to continue until he at least filed for divorce."

There was a long silence. "That could change things," Boston said. "Do you think they'll let him go?" Her gaze jumped between us. "None of us saw him do anything. Do they have enough evidence to arrest him?"

Liz's back straightened. "Do you really think Josh is a killer? A murderer?"

"Well," Ambrose said. "Normally, I wouldn't. But I've been thinking things through, and I can't imagine any other..." He paused at the sound of footsteps on the porch.

All five of us froze as we listened to the lock thump. I stood and walked to the edge of the hallway as the door opened.

Entering the foyer, I saw Josh closing the door. He looked at me and swallowed hard.

"Welcome back," I said. "Glad to see Bailey finally finished with you."

"Me too." Holding a hand in front of his face, he left a gap of an inch between his thumb and index finger. "I was this close to calling my lawyer. Unfortunately, I don't think they're finished with me. They think I had something to do with Carp...something to do with Carp's death. I swear, I didn't."

"Everyone will be happy to see you," I lied and patted his shoulder. "Come join us in the kitchen."

Chapter 18

All eyes were on Josh as he followed me into the kitchen. Even Liz looked him over as he slouched in from the semi-lit hallway. Ambrose stood, approached, and hugged him. The moment felt laughable. Minutes before he had laid Carpenter's death at Josh's feet and now they were hugging. Liz and I looked at each other and I tried not to shake my head.

Ambrose guided him to a chair, while Boston put a fresh glass of water on the table. We repeated stories about our police interviews and statements. Josh said Detective Bailey didn't say a word as they drove to the yacht club.

A squad car was waiting for them. Josh said he let them inside the gates and walked them to the *Eloquence*, which was still docked. She wrote his access code in her notepad, ripped it out, and handed it, along with the boat's keys, to the deputy who had met them outside. The deputy told Bailey that forensics would arrive within the hour.

Bailey drove him to the Public Safety Building for an interview and a statement. He said she and another Dane County Sheriff's detective conducted the interview. They went through the entire boat excursion multiple times, he explained, with a focus on the swim.

"Obviously, they see me as their number one suspect." He shook his head from side to side. "That Detective Bailey has a voice like…"

"A fifteen-year-old?" I suggested. I thought fifteen sounded better than thirteen.

"Yes. A fifteen-year-old. The whole thing felt surreal. They had me describe the swim over and over and over. It was ridiculous. If I said something different from what I said the previous time, they jumped all over me." He rubbed his eyes with the palms of his hands. "They backed off when I said I was not talking anymore without my lawyer. Luckily, they didn't push me, because the one I have isn't a defense lawyer. If I called him, I suppose he would have sent one over, rather than coming himself."

"That was all they asked you about?" Ambrose asked.

"They asked about me and Carpenter, of course." His hands retreated to his sides, and he stared at the wooden table. "I admitted everything. I told them we were involved, and that I love her. Or rather, that I loved her, and she loved me. Finally, I admitted that Carp was pushing me to divorce Amanda. Guess she was tired of me dragging my feet. While I had hired a lawyer and filed for a formal separation, that was not enough for her."

"You filed for separation?" Ambrose asked.

He nodded and the two men's eyes locked. "I also brought up you and Carpenter, but I was clear that you were with Boston the entire time you were in the water. At least I think you were." He motioned toward Boston. "I told them to check with you to be sure, but I was pretty confident about you two being together the whole time we were in the lake."

Liz pointed at Ambrose. "Is he saying that you and Carpenter used to be a thing?"

The room was silent. Then Ambrose's eyes widened, and his chin dropped. "Carpenter and I, um, yes. For a short time, we had more than just a professional relationship." He didn't look at Boston, who was at his side, and his head leaned forward. "This was before me and Boston started...well, dating."

"I also told him about Carpenter's review of Fusion Rock." Josh took a drink from his glass, letting out a satisfied gasp as he finished. "And I told them about Caleb's reaction."

"Fusion Rock?" I asked. "What's that?"

"It is Caleb's flagship wine," Liz replied without looking away from Josh. "Are you saying she reviewed Fusion Rock and gave it a negative review?"

Katie chuckled, followed by smiles and head nodding from Josh and Boston. Soon, it progressed to a roaring laugh, and the tension seemed to dissipate.

"It wasn't just a negative review," Josh said. "I'd say she skewered it. I think she rated it a seventy-two."

"That doesn't sound good," I said. "What does a seventy-two mean? Is that like a C-minus?"

Ambrose shook his head from side to side. "It means, well...it means she said it's shit." There was a long pause. "Technically, a seventy-two is drinkable, but unacceptable. It's about as low as you give anything. If something is under seventy, you don't even rate it. When I think back, I can remember a half-dozen wines I've rated in the seventies, but, well, I usually just don't bother writing a review if one comes in that low."

Katie nodded and touched my hand lightly. "If I use the *Wine Spectator* scale, my average rating is probably around eighty-five. That's probably three or four points lower than the average critic." She tossed her head back. "To publish a seventy-two is unusual."

"Definitely," Josh said. "I average closer to eighty-eight."

"Is it lower because it's a Midwestern wine rather than a Californian or European one?" I asked. Everyone looked at me like I was stupid. "I mean, I see ratings on wines at Liz's work, but they're usually French ones or stuff like Merlot and Cabernet Sauvignon. There are not as many grades for Wisconsin wines. If there are, I don't notice them."

"You don't grade something a seventy-two because of the grape variety," Josh said. "I admit to rating Vitis vinifera wines slightly higher than Vitis labrusca, or hybrids, but..."

I put my hand in the air in a stopping motion. "English, please. I hear enough wine talk from my wife. Remember, I'm just a humble locksmith who never took Latin."

"Liz," Ambrose said, "I'm surprised you don't have him trained yet." A few people laughed, and he paused until it subsided. "Josh is saying that wines made from the species of grapes used in traditional wine making may get slightly higher ratings. One could argue it is because they make better wine, or one could argue it's because those grapes are, well, better understood."

"Or critics are used to those wines," Katie added.

"Sure." Ambrose nodded and his gaze locked on Katie's before returning to me. "But the average rating for a wine made with hybrid grapes—which are derived from varieties native to the Old World combined with those native to the New World—is maybe a point lower than those based on Old World grapes. Those made wholly from New World grapes are maybe another point lower. Fusion Rock is a mix of Foch and frontenac, I think, which are both hybrids."

Liz pushed my shoulder. "Hun, a rating of seventy-two sucks, okay?"

"Okay. Got it. Where was this going again?"

"Carpenter's review of Fusion Rock," Ambrose said. "That's from Fierce Heart Winery, which is owned by Caleb and Jenn Iacomini. *They were on the boat.*"

I wanted to say something about the grade making the Iacominis suspects, but Ambrose's delivery already made that point. "Did you guys sample that wine yesterday or this morning? The one Carpenter gave a seventy-two?"

Liz shook her head. After a moment, everyone looked at Boston.

"Fusion Rock is on the slate for this afternoon," she said. "It doesn't seem to matter now, but Carpenter's blind rating of it was something I was looking forward to."

The critics nodded their heads and Josh muttered, "Poor Carp," as he stared at the table.

Ambrose put a hand on Josh's shoulder. "Did you see my text? It's about this afternoon. We're going ahead and doing a double session."

"No, afraid not. I gave the cops permission to look at my phone." He pulled it out of his pocket. "They gave it back, but it looks like they turned it off." He held the sides of the phone until it sprang to life. "What's the plan?"

"Four o'clock," Boston said, looking at her phone. "Oh, shoot."

"What?"

"Got a text from Abby. She isn't coming this afternoon." Her lips pushed out as if pouting. "She talked to her parents, and they're worried about her safety."

"How about Renee?" I asked.

"She had better be here. It's a double session and there's decanting, marking, organizing, and cleaning. Shoot." Boston's lips pushed forward. Then she turned toward Josh. "Do you think Amanda would be free this afternoon? Would she be willing to help? She's done it before. It's mostly reds, so there will be decanting. If not, and if Renee doesn't show, we're screwed."

I thought it an odd request, since we just heard about how Amanda and Josh were separating. But it was better than them asking *me* to help.

"I'll call and ask. She should be off at three-thirty, so maybe she could come over. During summer session, she only works Monday and Wednesday afternoons, so she might be free to come in tomorrow if you would need her then as well."

"Great," Boston replied. "I hate being short-staffed for a double session."

"Either way," Ambrose said, "it's nearly two. Why don't we all catch up on our texts and emails and get some rest? The session starts at four sharp. Josh, ask Amanda to contact Boston if she's willing to come in."

My body felt drained, so a break was appealing. There were murmurs of agreement as people got to their feet. After taking Liz's arm, I led her through the hall, up the stairs and into the bathroom. Then we trudged to our room.

Liz fell on the bed and rolled onto her side. "For once, I'm glad to be married to a security guy."

"What do you mean, for once?"

"What if Abby's parents are right? Maybe we are in danger. Maybe the killer has someone else on his or her list."

"Who would want to kill us?"

"Wouldn't you have said the same thing about Carpenter?"

"No, I wouldn't. She was a divorced woman having an affair with a married man and had dated another of our group. And we just found out that she skewered a vintner's best wine. Plus, she has a YouTube channel or whatever. Who can say what weirdos have been watching her drinking wine in a bikini? Plenty of people had a motive to kill her, including some in our group."

"Shush. Just put that funny thing on the door so no one can break in. I want to take an hour's nap without fear of being murdered."

Chapter 19

With the lights off and the window shade down, I aimed my phone's camera throughout the room, looking for infrared light on its screen. After sweeping the closet, I turned off the camera and repeated the process with the phone's flashlight. Before finishing, I patted the edge of the mirror's frame, stopping at the area where I had felt the stickiness of tape. There was still no device.

"Everything's clear," I said as I took my phone off airplane mode. I checked the closet, verified that the windows were locked, and set up the door stopper. No one would get inside without our knowledge.

I crawled in next to Liz. It was warm in the room, but I left the windows closed. She shoved the bedspread and the thin blanket off the bottom of the bed, leaving only the cotton sheet covering us. Her breathing was low and repetitive. As I pulled her tight, I realized I had heard nothing outside the room. My assumption was that Ambrose hadn't come upstairs. Perhaps, since he had publicly admitted to the relationship with Boston, he wasn't going to even pretend he was sleeping in his own room. I tried to think about something relaxing, but my thoughts drifted to the lock on the shed and the knife the police had found at the bottom of Lake Monona.

If someone brought the knife onboard the *Eloquence*, there were few candidates. It would have been easy for Josh to stow the weapon aboard. It was his boat, and while I helped him pull lifejackets from one compartment, he was the only one who accessed the compartments toward the boat's stern. I also thought of Caleb Iacomini's Hawaiian shirt and the cooler he used to carry liquor bottles. I had assumed he wore the shirt under his life vest to cover his not so svelte physique. Yet it could have allowed him to hide an eight-inch knife, or he could have slipped it inside the cooler.

Ambrose did not wear a shirt, but his boxer-style shorts were long, nearly touching his knees. Conversely, Katie, Abby, Boston, and Renee wore bikinis when they boarded. I had checked them out much more closely than I would admit to my wife. I was sure none of them had an eight-inch knife. Jenn Iacomini was in a one-piece, but I doubted she could have hidden the weapon.

What about Missy's T-shirt? She either said or implied that she wore it to avoid comparing her body with those of the other women. That could have been true. Or might she have worn it to conceal a knife taped to her back or her side? If so, what was her motive?

Years in the security business didn't make me an expert on the criminal mind, but it gave me familiarity with law enforcement, crimes, and criminals. As I went through our group, none of them struck me as a criminal, let alone as a murderer. But my only experience with murderers involved gun-toting teenagers, a drunk with a shotgun, and the thug who had hit and killed Ben Petersik. Perhaps a different type of person committed premeditated murder because of lust, revenge, money, or jealousy.

When Liz's alarm went off, I was on the edge of sleep. She slapped her phone, yawned, and sat up, pulling the sheet off my chest. I twisted over and saw her phone, which read 3:40 PM. Sliding my feet onto the oriental rug, I crouched next to the door stopper. After a few moments, it was off and Liz shot past, heading for the bathroom.

At five minutes before four, I led her down the staircase. Katie was closing the door to her second-story room. She rushed toward us, grabbing Liz's hand and telling her about people talking outside who had kept her awake. Her room faced the front of the house, so if her window was open, she would have heard passing cars and pedestrians.

Boston, Renee, and Amanda were in the event room, arranging wine glasses. It seemed that being legally separated didn't stop Amanda from spending time around her husband.

Ambrose stood in the kitchen holding a plain bagel. He told us there were two bagels and three donuts left. Liz and Katie each took a bagel. I took the final powdered donut as Josh entered the room. He grabbed a cake donut and carried it to his table while Katie and Liz meandered into the event room. Finishing my snack, I remained in the kitchen for a few moments, hoping to nab the last of the food. That's when Missy came around the corner.

Her steps were short, as if her feet were tied together, and she wore pajama pants, fuzzy brown slippers, and a white Green Bay Packers T-shirt. Her hair was unkempt, and she wore no makeup.

"Yo, Cy," she said in her usual deadpan manner.

"We saved you a donut." There was some truth to my statement since I would have saved it...if I hadn't forgotten about her.

With a smile, she set the food on a napkin.

Boston charged into the kitchen. "Missy! Glad to see you. I saved you a bagel."

"Already snagged this. Don't think I can eat much more. But I could do with some water."

"There's some at the table, of course, but let me. Just a second." Rushing to a tray, she pulled off a carafe and a small glass. She filled the glass and handed it to Missy.

"My mouth is really, you know, dry." Lifting the water to her lips, she jerked her head backward and swallowed. "It's like I had a big night on the town or something. I know I look like a disaster."

Ambrose joined us. After getting Missy's assurance that she was up for a tasting session, we strolled into the event room. My stomach thought of the hidden bagel, but I didn't have the guts to ask about it, so I sulked over to Liz's table just as Katie was leaving.

Eight glasses of red wine were in front of us, along with water and the ever-present spit cup. Red wine has more variability in coloring, so my mind was soon in color-grading mode. Ambrose marched to the lectern. I ignored his comments until he mentioned something about Missy. Everyone clapped, so I joined in. Then he asked for a moment of silence in memory of Carpenter. We bowed our heads. Once done, Ambrose returned to his table and Renee approached ours. She made a few comments about the wines, saying all were blends containing Maréchal Foch.

That didn't tell me anything.

"We're glad you made it," Liz said.

Renee smiled. "Abby's parents are a little protective. She feels stupid not showing up, but they pay her bills, so she needs to keep them happy, you know?"

I nodded. "My wife and I are paying a hunk of the bills for our girls, so we know how it feels. All three are in college, though only one is here in Madison."

"Two of them work too," Liz said.

"Their work, our contribution, grants, and loans. That's what we hope gets them through college."

She nodded before getting back to business. "Fortunately, Amanda agreed to help. As for the sessions, we're going forty minutes instead of the usual sixty. I'll be requesting your scores at four thirty-five. I'll check in about halfway through."

She smiled before continuing to Josh's table. Amanda meandered from Katie's table to Missy's, so I assumed she and Renee were handling two tasters while Boston handled Ambrose and other activities. Liz lifted the second glass high in the air, so I got to work.

"I'm kind of at a cross between pale ruby and pale garnet on a few of these." I tapped the glasses, and she nodded as if she had the same view. After writing on my notepad, I provided color grades: three of the entries were pale ruby, two were medium ruby, and three were pale garnet.

Liz and I agreed on six of the eight. The issue was whether we were going with ruby or garnet on two entries. She finally told me she was done and had to move on. That meant she was going with her own grades. I assumed she was correct, since the afternoon light was good.

For the moment, my job as a wine color grader—if I wanted to call it a job—was done. Liz spit into her cup and I shifted to spaced-out mode until the doorbell interrupted us. The previous day, we had talked so much about the press, but the subject hadn't come up today.

It turned out to be the same reporter. I had her wait outside. After verifying that Ambrose wanted to provide a statement, I led him to the porch, closed the door, and waited in the foyer. When he came back inside, he didn't look triumphant as he had after his earlier encounter with the press.

"What's wrong?" I asked.

"They asked me about something Carpenter's ex-husband, Buzz, told the press."

"Her ex-husband's name is Buzz?"

"I don't know if that's his real name, but that's what she calls him. He lives in Chicago. He told the press that he knows who killed her."

"Who?" I asked.

"He says it was me."

Chapter 20

A s wine experts spit into cups, I called Knutsen from our room and told him about Ambrose's encounter with the press. While the detective had not heard from Carpenter's ex-husband, he thought it likely the Dane County Sheriff's Office had contacted and interviewed him. Knutsen put me on hold. Eventually, he told me they were calling Detective Bailey to give her a heads-up about the media interview.

When I came downstairs, Boston had tallied scores for the red blends. Ratings were on the board, but I didn't pay attention. As I got situated, Renee pulled out the bottles one by one. Each reveal resulted in a response from the group, but even I reacted when entry seventy-four, the fourth in this flight, was revealed as Fusion Rock from Fierce Heart Winery. It earned a rating of eighty-seven.

Fusion Rock was the wine Carpenter had given a seventy-two on her vlog. Katie's initial grade of eighty-four was the lowest, followed by an eighty-six from Liz, an eighty-eight from Missy, and nineties from Josh and Ambrose. I didn't know what Carpenter's grade would have been had she been involved in the blind tasting, but I was sure it would have been higher than seventy-two.

The second session was subdued. I kept an eye on Missy and thought she appeared stronger as the tasting progressed. Amanda checked in on her a few times, and I heard Missy's guttural laugh more than once. Perhaps the activity got her mind off the stress of the previous day.

With the day's last session complete, Ambrose walked to the lectern with his hands in the air, as if he wanted the talking to subside. Liz nudged me as he began speaking. "I want to thank you for your professionalism." His deep voice oozed charm, and he nodded as if encouraging the group to be positive. "This has been an incredibly difficult and, um, stressful day. You, however, pushed through and I appreciate that. It's been strenuous for me as well. Also, I appreciate Amanda joining us on short notice. She's a lifesaver."

The speech felt overboard, but everyone clapped. For some reason, I joined in.

"There are two days left." He cleared his throat as if he were about to sing. "We will finish our event. However, after talking with a few of you, I, well, canceled tonight's planned ghost tour."

I nudged Liz's shoulder. "Madison has a ghost tour?"

Her eyes widened. "Shush."

"Boston and I still plan to go to a restaurant for dinner in about..." he checked his watch, "twenty-minutes. It's just a casual tavern. You're all invited, but I'll understand if you prefer staying in or doing something on your own."

Josh raised his hand. "Afraid Amanda and I will not make it tonight. We decided to spend the night at home, just to get away from the stress. We'll be back in the morning. Amanda is off tomorrow, so she'll help again."

"Great," Boston said. "We appreciate it."

"Heading home for the night is understandable," Ambrose said. He looked toward us, and his eyebrows rose. "How about the Bartholomews? Are you joining us for dinner?"

Liz looked at me before responding. "Count us in."

Renee said she would join, as did Katie.

That just left Missy. "Don't know how much I'll eat, but I'll go." She chuckled. It sounded like a bad Santa Claus impression. "Besides, I'm not staying here by myself."

"Great then," Ambrose said. "We'll meet out front in about twenty minutes."

Everyone agreed, and Renee cleared glasses from Josh's and our tables. Liz carried a tray into the kitchen; so, feeling the need to be useful, I arranged glasses on the counter as Amanda wiped down the windows. Once the tray was cleaned and stacked, Liz took a soap-drenched washcloth to the circular tables in the event room. Minutes later, Boston told me that, though she appreciated my help, I was in the way. She ushered me out of the kitchen. It seemed I was less useful than my blind wife.

Pulling out my phone, I sat on the porch steps and checked the weather forecast. Soon, Josh came out carrying a duffle bag.

He sat next to me. "Once Amanda finishes, we're heading out. Boston won't make her deal with most of the cleanup."

"It was good of her to help. I take it she's worried about you." I put my phone away. "Or is she nervous about being left home alone when there's a killer on the loose?"

"Nah." Josh laughed. "Amanda spent six years on active duty in the Marines and still serves in the reserves. Nothing scares her. She probably thinks I need support, as crazy as that sounds, considering what Carpenter was to me."

"That does sound crazy. Especially since she seems to know the full...extent of your and Carpenter's relationship."

His gaze followed cars as they passed. "We may have drifted apart, but we're still friends. I think we've always been better friends than partners. Maybe that's why she's not all that upset. I mean, she has known about me and Carpenter for a while. She still wants to work through it, even though I've filed for separation. The most important thing to her is our friendship. That's why she's been so patient with me. More patient than anyone should expect."

"That's big of her." The comment sounded stupid, so I changed the subject. "You live in town, right?"

He nodded. "Southwest side. It's maybe five miles from here, not too far from where Westgate Mall used to be. Do you know the area?"

"Sure. I know it well. We're not that far from you, though we're further south, just outside the city limits."

The door behind us pushed open, and Amanda greeted us with a smile. She had changed from her work outfit and wore a baseball cap, long shorts, and a sweatshirt with its arms cut off. Her medium-length hair was in a ponytail, which poked through the back of the hat. She looked like what I expected a Marine reservist to look like. They started down the stairs before Josh said something to her and ran back inside the house.

Amanda leaned against one of the porch pillars, saying he had forgotten something. A wisp of black hair fluttered in front of her eyes. "Cy. Someone said you used to own part of MB Lock & Security."

"Yeah. Spent thirty years with them."

"I've seen MB commercials for years on TV and I've heard them on the radio. Though I don't know if I've seen any commercials with you in them. How did you get that gig?"

It felt like she was interviewing me, as if she thought I was a suspect. There was no harm in responding, so I went with it. "I like locks. Always have. As a kid, I wanted to be like Newkirk in *Hogan's Heroes*, though he was usually cracking safes rather than picking them. During high school, I got a certificate in locksmithing and once I graduated, a two-year degree in it. Whether it be taking locks apart, cracking them, picking them, or putting them back together, it was always my thing."

"Funny, I didn't think locksmiths picked locks that much. I thought they mostly installed locks and made keys. Shows what I know."

"Yeah, the parts I like are only a small part of being a locksmith, but they are the parts that drew me in, and they are the parts I love."

It appeared she was about to ask a follow-up question when the door opened and Josh came out. They waved goodbye and clambered toward the sidewalk. Before they crossed the road, the B&B's door opened again. This time it was Missy. She had her hair in a tight ponytail, which made it look less greasy, but the scent of lake water remained. Jeans and blue tennis shoes replaced pajamas and slippers.

"What's up?" she said. It was her way of saying, "Hello."

"Not much."

"Where's your wife? I've never seen you without her."

People were increasingly seeing me as Liz's appendage. "She's cleaning up with Boston and Renee. The other server...Abby...she dropped out and, while Amanda helped with the session, I don't think they expect her to do cleanup."

"Can't blame Abby. If this wasn't such a big deal for me, I'd drop out as well. I mean, I already look like an idiot, going to the hospital and everything." Her tone was emotionless. "Did you hear I passed out near the dock? When I woke in the hospital, sand was in my ear. I don't know if I rolled down the beach toward the water or if they turned me onto my side. Knowing my luck, it was whatever was more embarrassing."

"Don't worry about it. No one gives a rip."

"And I threw up twice."

"It's over. It's not a big deal."

She laughed. "It is a big deal. It sucks, you know, for a super taster and a super smeller to throw up."

"Yes, I've heard. Remember, I'm married to one."

She nodded. "Changing the subject, did you see the video of Ambrose? The one from today?"

"Video? No."

"The TV lady ambushes him. It happens right here." She patted the wooden porch. "The video's posted on the TV station's website. Just a second."

She pulled out her phone and, in a moment, a two-minute video began. The sound was tinny but clear. It started with the blonde woman reporter standing in front of The Larson Place. It flipped to a shot of a dark-haired, dark-featured man on a porch that didn't look all that different from the one Missy and I were on. Except this guy had biceps as big as my thighs.

"That's Carpenter's ex," Missy said.

"The love of my life is gone," the man said with a sniffle. "We may have been divorced, but I still loved her and she still loved me. I just saw her on Monday morning. She was as beautiful as ever." Shaking his head, he took in a few measured breaths as if he was about to do a set of squats. "It makes me so, so pissed."

His right hand lifted and pointed directly at the camera. "I'll tell you this much. Whatever happened to her, I know whose fault it is."

"Who is that?" an off-camera voice asked. "Whose fault is it?"

"Ambrose Houser!" The man's eyebrows shot upward and his thick mustache shook. A vein on his neck seemed to pulse and his face reddened. "The slimeball stole her from me and tossed her aside when he'd gotten what he wanted. She was a threat to him, so he's killed her, or he's put her into such despair that she..." He wiped his eyes. "That's the complete story. If he killed her, I expect the cops will throw the jerk behind bars. If she killed herself, I'll sue his ass in court, since he would have been the one to drive her to it."

The clip of the ex-husband ended, and the video flipped to the reporter in front of The Larson Place B&B. I was surprised to see myself open the door and announce that I would get Ambrose Houser for a statement. It made me look like Ambrose's assistant instead of Liz's. Then he came outside, holding a notepad to his chest.

"Do you have a response to being blamed for Carpenter Dalbesio's death?" She stuck the microphone in front of his face.

"Blamed? Me? What are you talking about?"

The microphone disappeared for a moment. "Ms. Dalbesio's ex-husband, Leonardo, claims you broke up their marriage, and he claims you are responsible for her death."

Ambrose looked crestfallen. "Me?" he muttered. Then his eyes lit up and he pulled the microphone to his lips. "I had no reason to do anything to Carpenter. We were friends. And she did nothing to herself. She was happy. She and I were past any disagreements."

"Why did Mr. Dalbesio accuse you?"

"I can only think of one reason." Ambrose looked directly into the camera. "Guilt."

The reporter summed up the story and the confrontation in about twenty seconds. Missy turned off the video. "What do you think? The guy looks dicey. Carpenter's ex, I mean. Ambrose pretty much, like, accused him of killing her."

"Yeah," I said. "But the ex wasn't on the boat."

And, as far as I knew, he wasn't in Lake Monona when someone slit Carpenter's throat.

Chapter 21

A mbrose led the seven of us to the restaurant, holding his phone and telling us when to turn. Liz was talking with Katie, so I walked alongside Ambrose. Once he realized I knew the area, he slid his phone into a pocket and let me navigate the rest of the way.

Like the place where we ate the first night, the restaurant was across from the Wisconsin State Capitol. This time, we were on the north rather than the east side. Though we didn't have reservations, the establishment had ample outdoor space. The tables were perpendicular to the street and the restaurant's façade. Each table sat at least a dozen people, so we took an open one. Grabbing the chair closest to the street, I leaned my arm against the metal barrier that defined the dining area.

The menu included a dozen wines by the glass, but only one was from a Midwestern winery. Katie ordered an inexpensive brut Cava from Catalonia, which she said sounded appealing. I perused the draft beer listing, settling on a German pilsner since it was two dollars less than every other tap. Liz bought a Scotch that cost four times more than my beer. I was too stunned by her order to notice what everyone else was drinking.

Black umbrellas hung overhead, protecting us from the afternoon sun and fluttering in the wind. After bringing our drinks, the waiter gazed up at the sky, appearing to note that the building was now shading the table. Lowering the umbrella, he tugged a handle, pulling it tight to the metal structure. Then he wrapped the handle around the canopy, pulling so it held itself closed with Velcro.

Leaning between me and Liz, he did the same process on the second umbrella. But this time, he didn't pull the handle tight enough, so he undid the Velcro, and pulled it tighter. I muttered thanks as he stepped away.

"That's what it sounded like," Liz said, leaning into my shoulder while holding her expensive Scotch in one hand.

"Like what sounded like?"

Her cheek touched mine. "Remember when we were on the boat? Maybe five minutes before everyone got back from swimming I heard a weird noise. I couldn't place it, which is so odd for me. Regardless, that's what it sounded like."

I struggled to remember what she was referring to. "It sounded like the wind blowing through the umbrella?"

"No." She pushed against me, and her hand lifted higher. "Remember, I said it was a kind of slurping or a snake-like sound?"

I was eying the Scotch. "Careful with your drink. That's too expensive to spill."

She let out a huff. "It was like the sound of the Velcro being pulled off."

My mind returned to the boat excursion, and I remembered her mentioning a sound. It wasn't something I had heard, but she always had better hearing than I did. The difference had become more noticeable since her eyesight had faltered. "You think someone pulled on something? Maybe some lifejackets had Velcro. Perhaps someone adjusted their strap?"

She shook her head, looking unsatisfied. "I remember thinking it was something on or under the boat. The boat moved a touch after I heard it. I'm not saying it was Velcro, just something that sounded like it."

Leaning back, I took a sip of my beer. "How about tape? Could it have been someone pulling tape off something? Like duct tape, maybe?"

She looked at me and smiled. It was a natural smile, so the cheek facing me barely rose. "That seems right." Her eyes closed. "It sounds right."

"Did you mention the sound to the cops when they interviewed you?"

"No." Her eyes opened. "It had slipped my mind, though I'm not sure I would have mentioned it anyway. Did you?"

"Definitely not. I had forgotten about it."

Katie, who was on Liz's other side, reached across and touched my shoulder. I shuddered. Liz and I turned toward her and Missy leaned in from across the table.

"Cy, we got a question for you," Katie said. A gleam was in her eye. "How did you and Liz meet? More importantly, how did you woo her?"

Missy laughed. "Let me guess." The three of us looked at her, so she continued. "Liz locked herself out of her car. She called for a locksmith, and you show up and you, like, get her into her car and don't charge her. Instead, you give her your card and you get her number."

"That's not too far off," Liz said, and the three women laughed. "I had just started my first professional job out of college. There I was, all of twenty-two on maybe my sixth day of work, and it was the first day I opened by myself. This was the Meadowridge Branch of the Madison Public Library System. I was running late, got to the entrance, and realized I had forgotten the keys to the front door."

Leaning in, I decided to give them my version of the story. "I'm writing up a report in the van after getting the owner into the pharmacy next door. Then I see this beautiful woman with more hair than Dolly Parton hopping up and down like she just lost a bet or something. It got me curious, so I go check on her."

Liz put her hand up. "Let me finish." She stared me down before continuing. "I'm sitting there calling myself an idiot. He comes up and says, 'Locked out, Miss?' I was mortified. Embarrassed. I admitted it but told him I was going to look in the car. I was hoping the keys were on the passenger seat or something. Of course, I knew they weren't, but I had to check. When I come back, he's holding the front door open." She chuckled. "I just looked at him, and he was so young and cute and cocky. Without thinking, I gave him a kiss on the cheek. I'd never done that to anyone, ever. But before I pulled away, he had his arms around me and somehow our lips met."

"How romantic," Katie said.

"You're lucky she didn't slap you," Missy said, looking at me. It was quiet for a moment, then everyone laughed.

"I passed her my business card and wrote my personal number on it. She gave me her number too, so I called her that night and we had our first date."

"I had to call my dad and get him to bring the keys from my house so I could lock up," Liz added.

"Sounds like things moved fast," Katie said.

"Not really." I shook my head. "Her parents didn't want their college-educated daughter dating a lowly locksmith. They thought she was slumming. Her mom came from a poor family in Greece and was very class conscious. She thought it ridiculous that Liz even gave me a second look. Her dad just thought I was a slug, since I didn't have a university degree."

Stories of our courtship continued, and though I enjoyed hearing the joy in Liz's voice, it was more fun when I was still a small businessperson. Now, it was as if people asked because they wondered how I got her to date, let alone to marry me.

The food came out after a few minutes, ending the discussion. We ate, and I sucked down a second beer. After paying, Renee headed home on her own and the rest of us started back to the B&B. Ambrose asked Liz and me to take the lead, though it seemed silly since there were only three turns on the ten-minute trek.

"Why did you ask about whether I told the cops about the sound we heard on the boat?" Liz asked as we walked. I hadn't heard it, but didn't bother to correct her. "Do you think it's important?"

"Might be." Pulling her closer, I glanced back at the rest of the group. "I've been thinking about who might have been able to sneak an eight-inch knife into the water. Josh could have certainly hidden it on himself, as could have Caleb, Ambrose, and even Missy. None of the others would have been able to hide anything that big and awkward. I mean, their swimsuits were pretty revealing."

"Even I noticed that," she said.

"Yep. But what if the killer had hidden the knife on the boat's hull?"

Liz's eyes widened, and she looked back at the group. "You're saying someone taped the knife to the boat?"

"It's an idea. Someone pulling the tape off one of the tri-toons would explain the sound. And it could explain how the killer got the knife into the water."

She nodded. "Yes. Yes, it could."

Chapter 22

After passing the Dane County Courthouse, The Larson Place came into view. A pair of uniformed law enforcement officers stood near the porch. We slowed, and there was muttering and whispering from our group. Once in front of the building, I realized they were sheriff's deputies and not City of Madison police.

The deputies met us on the walkway that connected the sidewalk to the porch. The older one appeared to be in his late twenties and had a pimple at the tip of his nose. He introduced himself and said they were looking for Ambrose Houser and Boston Cruz. The pair raised their hands and stepped forward. The deputy asked them to accompany them back to the station.

"Another interview?" Boston said. "You're kidding." Her head twisted, and she turned in a circle. I assumed she was looking for a police car. "How do we get there?"

The deputies exchanged glances. "We came on foot, Ma'am." The older deputy pointed at the Dane County Courthouse behind us. "Headquarters is next to the courthouse. It's quicker on foot, less than a five-minute walk."

Boston glanced at the building and then at the deputies. "Okay." She looked contrite.

The four of us who remained watched as the leader of the event and his partner were taken away.

"The cops don't really think they did it, do they?" Missy asked once they turned the corner. Her voice was even flatter than usual.

"You two were in the water with them," I said, nodding at her and Katie. "Did either of them ever get close to Carpenter?"

Katie leaned in, her brow furrowed. "I doubt it. Ambrose and Boston were always together, but they were also with Renee and Abby."

"Except when they raced around the boat," I said. "They had to have left Ambrose and Boston by themselves."

"Oh, you're right." Katie pointed at Missy. "They raced against us."

Missy nodded. "There might have been time. But just barely. Those two from Fierce Heart Winery were closer to Carpenter most of the time. They and Josh, of course, would have had the best opportunity. If Ambrose and Boston did it, they had to be in cahoots. Same with the vintners."

"Cahoots, huh?" I shook my head. "How about Renee and Abby? Were they near Carpenter during the race?"

"No way either had a knife," Missy said. "A knife wouldn't fit inside a bikini." She pointed at Katie. "Same goes for her."

Katie tilted her head back. "If someone had given one of them the knife when they were in the water, they could have, like, come up behind her when they did the race. It doesn't seem likely, but it's possible." She tilted backward, but her long neck stretched forward. "I can't believe we're talking about this. I can't believe that someone in our group is a murderer. None of us are that way, you know?"

The women muttered agreement. Then we started toward the steps.

"So, who won the race?" Liz asked. "The one between you two and the servers."

"They killed us." Missy stopped at the bottom of the steps, lifting a hand to her lips. "Oops. Bad choice of words."

We exchanged glances. "No problem," I said. "Figure of speech. It would have been hard for them to do something to Carpenter while still winning the race, wouldn't it?"

Everyone nodded, and Katie hopped up the steps and unlocked the front door. "What are you all doing tonight? It's only seven-fifteen."

"Cy and I are going for a walk," Liz said. That was news to me.

Missy started up the stairs. "I'm locking my door and reading until I fall asleep, which won't take long. I've been perusing Ambrose's book on New England wines, but I need a break from all this." She motioned toward the building. "I'm going to pull out my Kindle and read a trashy romance."

Katie chuckled. "Sounds like a plan."

"I haven't even seen it before," I said. "Ambrose's book, I mean."

"Oh, get real." Liz tapped the top of my head. "It's been out for the last few weeks. You've seen it many times. You just haven't paid attention."

She was probably right, but I tried to look innocent.

Missy unzipped her fanny pack and pulled out a paperback. The cover showed an outline of New England, with two bottles of wine in the foreground. It looked familiar, so Liz was undoubtedly right. "You can check it out if you like," she said. "Just give it back before we head home."

Taking the book, I flipped through pages of text and color photos. Turning it over, I chuckled at Ambrose's headshot. "He nailed the glossy," I said. "It's like he's trying to be the wine hunk or something. Too bad there isn't a picture of Carpenter."

"She's not the author." Katie took the book from my hand and found a page toward the back. "Here we are," she said, handing the open book to me. There was a group shot of Ambrose, Carpenter, Josh, and Katie. It was a color photo of an attractive group, but it was Carpenter who jumped out.

Missy reached for the book, turned the page, and handed it back to me. "Local authors are just listed on the next page." I reviewed the list of tasters by state. "It's just as well that my photo won't be alongside theirs. I'd be the homely one."

Missy was far from homely, but I understood her point.

"Don't be silly," Katie said. "Besides, I'm not sure anyone will want their picture in the new book. My guess is they'll have separate photos so they can include Carpenter. Josh, Ambrose, and my photos will look like a suspect line in her murder investigation." Her breathing increased, and she leaned forward.

Liz and I both stepped toward her. "Are you okay?" Liz asked.

She dropped to a knee. "Sorry." She looked up at us, her chest heaving. "I'm sitting here thinking and talking about the impact Carpenter's death will have on my career." Leaning forward, it looked as if she was going to say a prayer. "It's so self-centered to be thinking about myself. It's awful of me to be thinking about whether someone's death will be good or bad for my career."

Liz and I exchanged looks.

"At least you, like, admit it," Missy said. "I've thought about it too." She stepped closer. For a moment, I thought she was going to put a hand on Katie's shoulder. "I had the same thoughts. Might this end up on some true crime documentary? If so, would it help my name recognition, or would people look at me as a suspect?" She shook her head and batted her eyes. "Someone died and I'm thinking about myself. How awful. So, I'm just like you, though I didn't have the guts to say it out loud. Until you did."

Liz pulled Katie up and they hugged. Then I backed away and Missy patted both of their shoulders. Soon, they pulled her in, and I waited while the three hugged. It was true they were being self-centered, but that was natural. The discussion made me think about how an unsolved murder was making me feel guilty. I wanted the murder solved as much to assuage my feelings of guilt as to help anyone. In a way, I was as self-centered as them, if not more.

"I'm not usually a hugger," Missy said as she pulled away.

Liz took the book from me and gave it to Missy. "You might as well keep it," she said. "Cy won't do anything but look at the pictures."

Missy slid the book into her fanny pack. She went up the steps and unlocked the door. With a wave, she stepped inside.

Katie looked back at us as she grabbed the open door. "You two have a romantic walk. I'll do the same as Missy and get a good night's sleep. Let me know if the cops arrest anyone." She disappeared inside and the door closed.

Chapter 23

I wanted to go inside so I could visit the bathroom, but Liz started for the sidewalk, wiping her eyes. I followed, thinking about how we could help solve Carpenter's murder. For the first time, I was not wholly focused on my guilt. It was about more than her being killed when I was captaining the *Eloquence*. It was about Carpenter and Liz, Missy, Katie, and everyone who was on the boat or who knew her.

Though I had been dreading this event and the prospect of spending several days with wine snobs, I realized I liked them. Maybe not quite all of them, but most. Perhaps I would have felt differently if I were still performing for Carpenter's followers, but this crime had to be solved. If not, it would follow all of us.

We walked silently for a few minutes before I remembered that Liz had suggested the walk. "Is there a reason we're out here? Do you want to talk about the murder?"

"Yes." She wiped away the last of her tears. "You should call Bailey. Tell her about the tape sound. Maybe it's important."

"Sure. Suppose it could be." I glanced at the courthouse across the street on our left. "I wonder if Boston and Ambrose are being questioned. Knutsen and the MPD interviewed them earlier. Bailey is probably following up on stuff they learned from the ex-husband. Either that or they found fingerprints on the knife."

"Fingerprints?" Liz stopped walking. "Can they lift fingerprints from something that's been in the water?"

"No idea." I pulled out my phone. A quick search brought a list of links. I clicked on the first. "Says here, they can recover prints off something that's been submerged for days." I returned the phone to my pocket, took Liz's hand, and we continued our walk. "Though that's probably when someone touches it out of the water and throws it in. Don't know if it would be as likely if the knife was underwater when the person touched it."

"But it's possible? Let's hope they've made a breakthrough."

"Yeah. Sounds like it's possible, but we can't wait and hope." Letting go of her hand, I pulled out my phone again. "I'm calling Knutsen. We'll see if he's still in. Otherwise, I'll leave a message and he'll get back to us tomorrow."

"Shouldn't you call Detective Bailey since she's in charge?"

"Nah. I've known Knutsen for years. He'll be upfront with me. At least as much as he can be."

He answered after three rings and told me he was walking to his car, going home for the night. After explaining that we remembered something about the boat excursion, he suggested we meet outside the Monona Terrace Convention Center. It was only a block from where we were and near Knutsen's office. As we got closer, I spotted him crossing the road heading for one of two long benches.

He sat, but as we approached, he rose to his feet. Though I could see stubble on the side of his head, the sunlight still glinted off it. "Liz, Cy." We shook hands, and he and I sat while Liz stood in front of us. "What's up?"

Deferring to Liz, I waited for her to speak as a pair of bicycles whisked past, carrying teenagers with peach-fuzz mustaches.

"I remembered something about the boat outing. It was dark when we were on the lake, so I mostly had my eyes closed. Sometimes, it's better to see nothing than to see blurry lights and movements in front of me."

He nodded. "Understandable."

"When I do so, I focus on sounds and smells. A few minutes before Josh called for everyone to come in from the swim, I felt a bump underneath or on the side of the boat. The bump caused the boat to lurch ever so slightly, and I heard a sound."

"What kind of sound?"

"An un-sticking, like someone was pulling Velcro or peeling off a piece of duct tape."

"Duct tape?" He reached into his coat pocket, then patted his pants. He appeared to give up on finding whatever he was searching for. "Are you sure?"

"I'm sure I heard something." Unzipping her purse, she pulled out a container of orange Tic Tacs. After tossing a few into her mouth, she offered some to Knutsen. He smiled, so she shook four into his outstretched hand. "Anyway, I commented to Cy about the sound, but it didn't seem important, and it slipped my mind until tonight when our server at dinner pulled Velcro off an umbrella. We talked about it, and Cy had been wondering how someone could have gotten such a large knife onto the boat and into the water without being seen. He suggested that maybe someone taped it to the boat with duct tape or something similar."

The detective's gaze jumped between me and Liz. "Do you think duct tape would hold a big knife like that in place underwater?"

"Remember, this is a tri-toon," I said, acting as if I was an expert, though I hadn't even known what a tri-toon was prior to Tuesday evening's excursion. "There are three toons. A portion of the middle toon wouldn't be easy to see, even the part above the waterline. All someone would need to do would be to swim up to the toon and pull off the tape while holding the knife's handle. They'd then be in the water with a knife. Once they used the knife, they'd drop it, since they couldn't bring it back onto the boat."

Knutsen stared straight ahead, nodding his head slowly. "It's an interesting idea, and one we could test pretty easily." He turned, looking me in the eye. "If it was above the waterline, the stickiness of the tape—whatever that's called—"

"Adhesive," Liz said.

"Yeah, the adhesive could still be on the pontoon thing, wouldn't you think?"

I didn't know but nodded affirmatively.

"Unfortunately," he said, "we'll need to wait until tomorrow to check. The boat is at a club with a secure entryway. The sheriff's office has it cordoned off, but no deputies or security guards are monitoring it. I don't want to call Bailey this late. She's probably home by now."

"Can't you go there on your own?"

He looked at his watch. "I could, but the club is closed, and a security code is required to get onto the dock. Bailey didn't share it with me. Not because it's a secret or anything, but because we didn't see me needing it."

"I could get you in," I said.

Knutsen chuckled and got to his feet. "Cy, we're not breaking in. The last thing I need is to piss off the sheriff's office or the yacht club."

"I know Josh's access code."

"You know his code? How'd you manage that?"

"Josh entered it when we arrived that night. And I'm...observant."

He shook his head and licked his lips. "Okay. Guess it won't do any harm." He laughed, then looked at Liz. "I'll have to make sure I don't log into my computer with him around."

She nodded. "I often worry about what he'd have done with his life if he wasn't a locksmith."

Knutsen glanced at his phone, then slid it into his pocket. "Let me call my wife first, so she knows I'm going to be late. When we get to the dock, I'll send Bailey an email to cover my ass. Preferably, I'll tell her I'm doing something before I actually do it." We got to our feet and he patted my shoulder. "Okay. Let's go look and see if we come up with anything interesting on the boat."

"Are you okay with us coming along?" I asked.

He laughed. "If the boat is still in the water, someone's got to jump in and get wet. That someone won't be me."

I shook my head, knowing my role.

Chapter 24

The structure where Knutsen had parked was only a block from where Liz and I had met with him. It was also across from a hotel. Rather than walking with him to his car, I ran inside the hotel and visited the restroom. Once done, I rushed out, finding Liz leaning against the brick half-wall that lined the property. A queue of cars waited to exit the lot, turning right onto the one-way road.

After a few minutes, a silver Toyota pulled out, changed lanes, and stopped in front of us. Opening the back driver's side door, I ushered Liz inside. A horn blared as she slid across the seat. Crouching down, I pulled in beside her. It was a compact car, and the driver's seat was pushed back. It was tempting to comment on the tight accommodations, but I kept my mouth shut.

"I feel like I just picked up two suspects," Knutsen said, looking at me in his rear-view mirror.

"Cy didn't want to bring me around to the traffic-side," Liz said, "and he didn't want to leave me in back all alone." She shook her head. "He's protective of his blind wife, you know?"

"You don't seem blind to me," he said as the Toyota merged into traffic. "Hope that doesn't sound condescending or anything."

"She can see things directly in front of her when there's enough light," I said. "It's not really a problem in the daytime." There was silence as the sedan meandered through the streets and finally turned onto John Nolan Drive. To our left, I saw Lake Monona and envisioned the tri-toon *Eloquence* anchored on the lake. "Did you hear that the sheriff's office brought Ambrose and Boston in?"

"Yes, I heard," Knutsen replied, looking at me in the rear-view mirror. "The victim's ex-husband doesn't think too highly of Ambrose Houser. That's not surprising, since it sounds like he stole his wife."

"And then unceremoniously dumped her," Liz said.

"Where did you hear that?"

"Someone said it." I answered and turned to Liz. "Katie, I think. Though I think Liz added the *unceremonious* part."

She nodded. "Yes, it was Katie."

"Ambrose told us a different story. He claims it was Carpenter who ended their relationship. Not the other way around."

Liz and I looked at each other. "Really?" I said. "That's not the impression we had."

"Maybe he's trying to appear to be the nice guy. We'll figure it out." Knutsen's gaze shifted between the road and the mirror. "I don't know what his motive would be. You could say jealousy, but my impression is that he couldn't have killed her without that Cruz woman seeing something. If that's the case, Bailey should be able to get her to turn on him. You hearing any rumors?"

"Now we're sources?" I said with a chuckle.

"Hey, you called me."

"We're probably hearing less than you." I looked at Liz before continuing. "I'm sure you already know this, but Carpenter was pressuring Josh to divorce, even though he filed for separation."

Knutsen lifted his eyebrows. "I hadn't heard that, but I haven't read his interview transcript yet. The plan is to give it a quick review before going to bed."

"How about Josh's wife?" I asked. "Did someone interview her? If so, did you read her transcript?"

"Yes, and yes. I actually listened in on her interview, but I can't talk about witness statements."

"Interesting though." I glanced at Liz. "You listened to hers, but not Josh's. Do you see her higher on the suspect list?"

He shook his head while keeping his eyes on the road. "The murdered woman was having an affair with a married man. It's natural for us to be interested in the man's spouse."

"Naturally," I said.

"Any other rumors?"

"The women at the B&B are paranoid that Carpenter might have been killed by mistake," Liz said. "They're concerned that one of them was the intended target."

Knutsen chuckled. "Worrying is understandable." Turning his head to one side, he glanced over his shoulder at Liz. "Sorry if it sounds like I'm dismissing their concerns. Both the victim and Katie Coolidge were wearing white bikinis, so I get that someone might confuse the two in the water. But there were only ten people, plus you, on the lake. I can't see someone from the boat not being able to tell them apart."

"What are the theories?" I asked. "I realize you can't tell us everything, but most of it is common sense."

A motorcycle abruptly pulled in front of the car, and Knutsen placed a hand on the horn, but held off on honking. "We have been assuming the killer was on the boat, but we're not ignoring the possibility that someone else with a motive swam out to the boat. That could include Amanda Peterson, the victim's ex-husband, or someone we don't yet know about."

Liz's brow scrunched down. "Could a person swim that far with no one noticing?"

Knutsen nodded. "It's possible. If the person had scuba or fins and snorkeling gear, it would be very doable. In case you're wondering, both Amanda Peterson and Leonardo Dalbesio are at least competent swimmers. The bigger issue, however, would be how the person would know precisely where the boat was on the lake. Lake Monona covers over three thousand acres, and multiple boats were on the lake after sunset. Josh Peterson claims he didn't tell anyone where exactly they were going on the lake. Says he didn't really know until he got out there."

"How about Carpenter's phone?" I asked. "Liz and I allow each other to find where our phones are. We started doing that when her sight deteriorated. Maybe Carpenter's phone allowed someone to track her location."

"The techs checked her device, and it didn't have any tracking. Neither did Josh's. They'll run the same check on the phones of the two they brought in tonight. Bailey might ask you two for access as well. I know they already asked for location access from the telecom providers, but they didn't search the devices themselves other than checking for photos of the outing."

"Why would we share our location with someone else?" Liz loosened the seat belt strap and leaned forward. "My husband would never allow that. He's a safety tyrant, you know?"

"The idea would be that someone hacks your phone or steals your access code," Knutsen said. "They could then download an app which would share its location with someone else. Maybe a hacker accessed your phone or someone else's who was on the boat to track where the boat, and therefore, where Carpenter was."

"Okay." She pulled out her phone and handed it to me. "Check mine."

Liz and I shared our phone locations, but multiple apps and hacks would accomplish the same thing. Instead of telling her that, I checked for what I knew. The only access her phone granted was to mine and to one of our daughters.

"Good," she said after I told her. "I'd hate to think I had something to do with Carpenter's death."

"Other theories?" I asked Knutsen. "Any chance someone hired a professional to kill her?"

"A hired killer is always a possibility, but it doesn't feel right. Professional killers typically shoot people rather than swimming to the middle of a lake to cut someone's throat." The car passed a hotel before merging onto the highway.

"By the way," I said, "did you find a match for the knife set in the shed?"

"Nope. There was a set, but it differed from the murder weapon."

There was a brief silence before Liz leaned forward. "What if you find adhesive on the boat?" she asked. "What does that prove?"

"You want me to take this?" Knutsen asked while looking at me. "Or do you want it?"

Flattered that a detective in the City of Madison Police Department's Investigative Services Unit thought I knew the answer, I took a shot. "It would mean that someone who was on the boat killed her. If you were going to swim to the boat, you'd just bring the knife with you."

"Exactly," Knutsen said. "Why tape a knife to a pontoon? You do it because you're on the boat and can't take a weapon aboard and into the lake without it being seen."

We exited the highway and turned onto a side road. The road snaked along the lake, providing a view of lakefront homes, some nearly a hundred years old, others newer and larger. There were occasional sightings of docks which seemed to sit behind every home.

When we arrived at the yacht club, the parking lot was almost empty and the gate leading to the docks was closed. We hopped out, and I nodded toward a covered boat sitting atop a trailer, which was surrounded by police tape. Knutsen went to the front door, but it was locked. He asked me to hold off on opening the gate until after he sent his email.

"Okay, Cy," he said. "Do your magic."

Entering a code into a keypad wasn't magic, but the gates pulled apart just as if I had said, "Open sesame."

A large black truck, which was sitting at the boat launch attached to a boat-filled trailer, suddenly roared to life and pulled forward. We waited a moment, and Knutsen mumbled something. The pickup stopped, and he walked to the driver-side door.

After a conversation, he joined us in front of the boat. "Just wanted to make sure they knew I was the police. Fortunately, he didn't comment on me being MPD."

"We're in the City of Monona, right?" Liz said, referring to the suburb that sat along the lake's eastern shore.

Knutsen nodded as he slipped under the tape. "Technically, I'm operating under the direction of the Dane County Sheriff, who is working with the City of Monona Police." He pointed at the *Eloquence*. "There are three pontoons on this, like you said. You won't get wet after all, but I need you to help me find where the tape might have been. Touch nothing. I don't want to mess with potential fingerprints." He pulled off his jacket and laid it on the asphalt.

Liz was holding onto the police tape with one hand, so I let go of her, ducked underneath, and dropped to my knees. There was no creeper to lie on, so Knutsen and I crawled on the blacktop beneath the trailer, entering from the front. Using my phone as a flashlight, I examined one silver aluminum toon while Knutsen started on another. I knew what I was looking for but was doubtful I'd find it without using my hands.

Knutsen apparently came to the same conclusion and agreed we could use sheets of paper which he found in his trunk. I patted a sheet against the toon, pulled it away, then moved it to the next spot. The idea, he said, was to touch the aluminum without impacting tape residue or fingerprints. I didn't know if that would do any good, but I went with it, deciding to go up one side and down the other. While I searched, Knutsen paused and spoke to a few boaters who were coming in for the night, curious about what we were doing.

As I approached the last four feet of the middle toon, my shoulders ached. Patting the paper against the toon for what seemed like the three-hundredth time, it suddenly stuck to the aluminum. As I lifted myself onto one elbow, the paper drifted to the blacktop. I aimed my flashlight at the spot.

Something was there. Adhesive residue.

Chapter 25

Within seconds, Knutsen was next to me on the blacktop, highlighting one advantage of youth. I kept the flashlight beam on the spot. While the light glinted off the silver aluminum, there was an area where it reflected differently. The detective nodded, then had me wait as he got something to mark the location. As I slid from underneath the boat, he laid a dirty baseball-size boulder beneath the location. Then he called Detective Bailey. Following a brief discussion, he pulled me closer, saying he would not tell her he had brought us to the dock.

Cooperation between police departments was important, but there was an inherent defensiveness, so I understood his concern. Yet there was still the matter of getting us back to the B&B. While I enjoyed walks with my wife, I wasn't up for a nearly two-hour death march. After making a few phone calls, he contacted a taxi company and gave me twenty dollars.

"That won't cover it," Liz said. "A cab ride is a flat three dollars, plus three fifty per mile. We're probably looking at five miles, so that comes to twenty dollars and fifty cents. Add in tip and we're talking twenty-five dollars."

Knutsen looked at me as if expecting me to disagree with my wife.

I knew better. "Liz knows these things."

He let out a puff before pulling out his wallet. "All I got is a ten."

"We'll take it." I snatched the bill from his hand. "Remember, we have three daughters in college. Easy come; easy go."

He seemed transfixed as he watched the money go into my wallet.

"What will go on here?" I asked. "Is Bailey coming herself?"

"Oh, no." He licked his lips, then motioned toward the boat. "She's sending someone to look at it."

"A forensic examiner?"

"No, just a deputy who she says can handle it. The boat is in their custody, so I don't want to confuse things by processing evidence myself. I'll let him check for prints and verify we found tape adhesive. If so, they'll figure out what type of adhesive and determine how long ago it was applied."

Before asking another question, I spotted two men approaching from the dock. We backed closer to the *Eloquence* and Knutsen stuck a hand into his pocket as if he was going to pull out his identification. But the men just said, "Evening," and continued past, exiting through the gate.

"At least this should simplify things for you and Bailey," I said after the men had left. "Now you've got only nine suspects."

Liz let out a chuckle. "Nine suspects?"

He shook his head. "It doesn't help that much. This additional evidence may eliminate a professional killer. That's good, but the chance of a hired killer was already remote. It will allow Bailey to pause efforts to identify any mysterious payments made by one of Carpenter's acquaintances or enemies. We can also ease efforts to identify all the boats that were in the water that evening, and we'll stop reviewing shoreline videos."

"Shoreline videos?" I asked. "What do you mean?"

"If it was the ex-husband, Josh's wife, or someone else who wasn't on the boat, they'd have to come into the water either via boat or from shore. Private homes with docks make up most of the shoreline. A good percentage of those homes have some sort of security cameras on their docks. MPD, along with the City of Monona Police, were working with homeowners to view them for that evening. We've already accessed city and county cameras. Turville Point and Olbrich Park are probably the only areas where a person could enter the lake without the risk of being seen or recorded."

"Olbrich Park?" I glanced at Liz. "That's way on the other side of the lake."

"Yes, but we were trying to cover every base. We're halfway through the process of obtaining security videos, but assuming the adhesive tests come through as we expect, we'll scuttle that search. We'll also stop background checks on folks who were in the other boats that were on the lake."

"Does that include the dick in the motorboat who was getting close to us?" I asked. "I'm sure people told you about that boat."

The detective nodded. "Yes, we know whose boat it was. Three men were on board, all in their early twenties. There's no connection between them and Ms. Dalbesio."

"At least this eliminates Amanda and the ex-husband," Liz said, a hint of hopefulness in her voice.

"Yes, though we already counted out Amanda Peterson and Leonardo Dalbesio."

"Really?" I was surprised.

"Yes. Amanda's neighbor saw her milling about in the house that evening just after sunset. Supporting that is the fact that Amanda's car was home all night. Josh's was parked downtown since he arrived from the airport on Tuesday morning. Her car has one of those apps that track where the vehicle is. On Tuesday, it was downtown for dinner. Afterward, she drove home. It was in the garage when everything went down, and she was in the house the whole time. We know that because we got her phone activity from her cell phone provider. Both she and Josh gave us permission and gave us access to their phones."

"Her phone was in the house. Couldn't she have left it at home? Or are you relying on the neighbor's statement?"

"Amanda's phone shows there was movement within the house a few times throughout the evening, just as she claims. She couldn't have left it and went out in another car or something. The neighbor's testimony supports this. As for Leonardo Dalbesio, or Buzz, as he's called, he came to Madison on Sunday but left for Chicago on Monday morning. His phone shows he was at his apartment all of Tuesday. His girlfriend confirms it. Unless she's lying and he drove back to Madison without his phone, he's got an alibi."

"Looks like we're not making things easier for you, after all."

"Definitely not. We thought we could exclude those who were on the boat who couldn't have gotten on and then into the water with a concealed eight-inch knife. Now, everyone who went swimming is a suspect. In a way, the tape expands the number of suspects, though a few have no motive. The two college students come to mind."

"How about the Iacominis?" Liz said.

Knutsen smiled. "I've already said too much. Plus, I've given you five dollars for your daughters' education."

I patted Liz's shoulder. "Give the poor man another Tic Tac."

Only half a dozen remained, which may have been why she handed the plastic container to him. He shook a few directly into his mouth. For a moment, I thought Liz was going to tell him about Carpenter's review of the Iacomini's flagship wine, but she looked at me and seemed to decide against it. The conversation instead turned to the boat itself. We told Knutsen about helping Josh to launch it. I mentioned I was surprised that the deputies had left the boat unguarded.

He shrugged his shoulders. "I'm sure Bailey will be second-guessed on that, but the crime occurred in the water. She probably didn't see the boat as key since they already combed through it; I know I didn't."

We nodded our agreement as a taxi pulled up to a nearby curb. Knutsen and I shook hands, and Liz gave him a wave as we left through the gate.

The ride back was quiet until we drove past Olin Park alongside the lake. It was after sunset but well before twilight, so at least a dozen boats were in sight. I was unsure of what Liz could see, so I pointed them out, telling her whether they were sailing vessels or motorboats.

When we were a few blocks from the Larson Place, Liz told the driver to let us out. For a moment, I was confused, but I realized it made sense, as we had claimed to be going for a walk. We didn't want to tell the murder suspects sharing our B&B that we had cut our walk short to meet with the police.

As we walked on the sidewalk, Liz's phone buzzed. It was a text from Ambrose saying he and Boston had just gotten back to the B&B after being "grilled separately" by sheriff's detectives. The note said the third day's tastings would continue as scheduled.

"Are you okay with staying tonight?" I asked as we approached The Larson Place.

"Yes. Assuming you're sure the room is secure. There is no weak link that would allow someone to get inside our room?"

I considered the question for a moment before responding. There was always a concern that the building owners might give Ambrose the ability to access our room. But it would be foolish of him to do so. If something happened, the police could identify who entered any room and when. Even if someone got the access code or picked our lock, the door jamb would prevent them from entering.

"The windows are the weak link," I said. "Though I'm not concerned. I feel we should be here, and I still don't think anyone would come after us."

"Agreed. Anything you can do about the windows to make them safer?"

We were on the third floor, which normally would prevent anyone without unique skills from accessing the windows. But they faced the back of the house and the portion of the roof that covered the event room was just outside. There was a ladder in the shed and if someone got onto the second-floor roof, they could get to the windows. Even if we locked both, a person could enter if they had the right tools.

"I have security bars in the car's trunk." Few husbands could make that claim, but Liz didn't seem impressed. "Let's pick two up before we go back."

"What will those do?"

"A bar goes across the inside of a window. If someone would, say, cut a hole through the glass and reach through, they still wouldn't be able to open it. They could, of course, take off the security bar, but that would be an extra step, and it's easier said than done."

"So it's not perfect."

"Not perfect, but it addresses the weakness. Also, I'll check out back and make sure the cop that went through the shed got it locked back up. That way, no one can get to the ladder without picking or cutting off the lock. If they can't access the ladder, then they can't get onto the roof unless they bring their own or have some boss skills or tools."

She nodded her approval, so we swung by the parking lot and picked up the security bars. By the time we got to the B&B, stars were visible in the sky. I held Liz's hand as we walked into the backyard. Pulling out my phone, I checked the lock. It was as pristine as ever. Then I peered into the shed through the window to make sure the ladder was still inside.

Once done, I led her into the house. A light was on in the kitchen, but we saw no one, so we left it on and went up to the third floor.

She was worried, but I was determined to have a restful sleep.

Chapter 26

L iz tossed and turned all night, and I opened my eyes at even the slightest sound. It seemed that the only time I was in a deep sleep was when the alarm went off. Liz shook me as it buzzed. Normally, I would have just gone back to sleep, but I had to undo the door jammer, and I needed to get ready while she showered.

When we went downstairs at eight forty-five, I heard laughter from the first floor. It felt as if nothing was amiss. Entering the kitchen, we found Josh, Katie, and Ambrose at the table. Boston and Amanda were milling about in the event room while Renee was toasting bagels and bread. There was even a plate of rolls in the middle of the table.

Everyone said hellos and good mornings. Cumulous clouds showed through the event room's windows, and I watched Amanda rush about, carrying a half-full wine decanter and a bottle enclosed in a cloth cover. Covering bottles was key to the blind tasting.

Ambrose discussed his interview with Detective Bailey. "The police are sure I'm guilty," he said. "This time, however, I had a lawyer join me. Josh had given me his number. Though he's a divorce lawyer, he put me in touch with, well, one who does criminal defense." He nodded his head. "The man's name is Parson Little."

"Sounds like someone from a Jane Austen book," Missy said as she sauntered into the kitchen. She wore black leggings and looked as if she'd showered. Taking the remaining stool, she slid in between Josh and Katie. "You guys got anything to eat? I'm starving."

Katie patted her shoulder. "That's probably a good sign since you didn't eat much yesterday."

"What about Boston?" I asked Ambrose. "Did she have a lawyer with her?"

"Yep. Same firm as Parson Little. A woman. I didn't catch her name, but I think she's Parson's assistant or understudy or, well, whatever they call a junior lawyer."

Renee slid plates and butter knives in front of Liz, Missy, and me. The three of us grabbed bagels. While Liz buttered hers, I looked around and decided this was a good time to check on the shed. Saying I would be back in a moment, I slipped away, bagel in hand.

In the daylight, the paranoia we had fallen into the previous night seemed overblown. There was no reason to believe that the killer was after anyone other than Carpenter. Even if they were, they couldn't have been after us. Yet I wanted to look at the shed one more time to make sure no one had tried to access the ladder. We had one more night in the B&B and I preferred doing it without being paranoid.

It was warm and muggy, but a haze hid the morning sun. A clump of low-lying clouds raced toward the house, and I noted a pungent scent that I associated with a coming storm. Looking to the southwest, the sky looked even darker. I pulled out my phone and reviewed the day's forecast, which called for morning storms and a clear evening.

The backyard was as I remembered, and the Master Lock still guarded the shed. I lifted the lock with two fingers and aimed my phone's flashlight at the keyhole. There were no scratches. Certainly none near the keyhole, which might have implied that someone other than me had picked it.

With my hand cupped against the window, I directed the phone's flashlight inside the shed. The unlucky police officer who had searched the area for a knife set had moved the boxes, but the ladder, the canoe, and the bicycle were in the same spots.

Before returning to the house, I looked around the backyard. The owners didn't manicure the area as they did in the front. Instead of a healthy lawn, a mix of prairie grass and weeds surrounded the shed. On one side of the structure, the grass was pushed down in two parallel lines. I shrugged my shoulders, wondering what would leave the impression. Turning away, I realized it could be the partial outline of a ladder.

I stared at the house. Through the window, I saw Renee's back and another person in one corner who I thought was Missy. My gaze rose to the roofline, which stood perhaps twenty or twenty-two feet. Walking toward the house, I crouched down and searched for a spot where a ladder's feet would have sat if someone had leaned one against the roof gutters.

There were a couple of possibilities, but when I looked up, I spotted a filled table through the window. I realized it was time for the next session, so I rushed around the building, slowing as I entered through the front door.

"Since Cy is back, we'll start," Ambrose said. He abandoned the lectern and strolled to his table.

Humbled, I slouched down next to my wife.

"About time," Liz said. "Were you visiting your girlfriend, the lock, again?"

I ignored her comment and examined the line of wine-filled glasses at our table. "I was thinking about the weak link in our security that we had talked about. The window." I put my lips to her ear. "It appears someone had that ladder out recently."

"Last night?" she mouthed.

"Don't know." I spotted Renee approaching, so I pulled back and waited. She gave us a rundown of the first flight and handed me a glass of water.

"How do you see these?" Liz asked, motioning toward the wines on our table.

The first one appeared to be medium gold, but as I lifted it, I realized it was lighter than I initially thought. With the glass between my eyes and the window, I announced it was pale gold, then set it down. She agreed without discussion. As she asked about the second entry, lightning struck.

"Whoa!" Missy said. Thunder followed seconds later, and she looked nervously about.

"The second one?" Liz repeated. "Deep gold?"

That sounded too dark. Picking up the glass, I swirled the wine, then held it between myself and the window. My thought was that it was medium or perhaps pale gold. It definitely wasn't deep gold. Another bolt of lightning lit the area, and I realized how dark the room was. That explained why Liz was struggling with the grading.

For a few minutes, I had to forget about the ladder and the shed and to focus on the wine. There were five critics, and I assumed Ambrose would consider everyone's visual grading when summarizing each wine. Liz wanted perfection. She wanted every aspect of her review notes to be accurate, not just the ratings. This was the only time she actually needed me, so I took the responsibility seriously. If I didn't, I'd feel even more unnecessary.

After some discussion, she went with my color grades, only questioning the fourth entry. Raindrops pelted the window as she sipped and spit. The storm was loud, but she ignored it, closing her eyes for long periods, which I took as a sign she was concentrating. After thirty minutes, Renee collected Liz's ratings, and we waited as Boston detailed them on her whiteboard.

"For the first time," Boston said, "Katie loses her title as the Russian judge."

Katie's mouth dropped open, and everyone but me laughed.

"What's a Russian judge?" I asked my wife.

"The judge with the lowest ratings," she whispered.

"Who beat me?" Katie asked. "Was it Liz?"

"You got it." Boston looked at Liz and then back at Katie. "You were identical on six of eight. While you were one point lower on one, Liz was two points lower than you on the other."

Katie threw a fist through the air in mock defiance, as if she was upset about losing the title. Then she clapped and looked toward Liz. After a brief discussion, Boston started on the flight's first entry. Ten minutes later, they agreed upon a rating for each, and Ambrose announced that the next session would begin at ten thirty.

"What was this about a ladder?" Liz asked as people filtered out of the event room. "Is it a concern?"

I glanced to one side and spotted Katie approaching. "Could be. Could even be worth talking to Knutsen again."

Chapter 27

In the next session, Katie took back her title as the Russian judge, coming in two points lower than Liz, who had given the next lowest ratings. Ambrose announced they would go to lunch at a place on King Street. Liz and I wouldn't join them, as I had already called Knutsen and he agreed to meet us outside the Wisconsin State Capitol Building at twelve-thirty. The detective said he planned to grab a burrito from one of the food carts that lined the Capitol Square. He would be on one of the raised curbs that encircled sections of the Capitol Lawn.

There was no way Liz would eat Mexican food while doing a wine tasting, so we picked up bagels at a New York-style deli. Hers was plain, but both of mine had sesame seeds. Eating as we walked, we finished before spotting Knutsen sitting on a curb, a row of bushes at his back. He was wearing a sport coat, but his tie was loose, and his pant legs lifted high, revealing brown socks that didn't match his blue pants and black shoes. The sun was pushing through the thinning clouds and its light glistened off his cleanly shaven head.

"Got some news for you two," he said. Him having news was a surprise, since I was the one who asked for the meeting. This time, Liz sat beside him while I remained standing. "The Dane

County Sheriff's Office analyzed that spot on Josh's pontoon boat. It's from duct tape, just as you suggested. The residue is consistent with a single six-inch piece put on the boat from a two-inch-wide roll." He shrugged his shoulders. "But there is a problem with the idea that it was used to hold the knife."

"Too short?" I remembered the weapon was eight inches long, so I expected the piece of tape to be at least nine or ten inches. "Could it have been set perpendicular to the tape? That wouldn't hide the knife, but it could hold it in place."

"We thought of that," Knutsen said. "Problem is that the residue is consistent up both ridges for the entire length of the tape. The only break in the residue was in a circular pattern near the middle of the tape's length. It's like the tape was used to secure a half-dollar coin."

"You're saying it couldn't have held a knife?"

Knutsen pulled out sunglasses and held them in front of his knees. "I wouldn't go that far. In theory, the person could have put the tape on, then taken it partially off and then put the knife in perpendicular, as you said."

"But then, how did that circular pattern get there?" Liz asked.

"That would be the question," he said, gesturing at Liz. "They also looked at the rest of the pontoon, searching for more tape and for prints. Nothing came up. Not even Josh or Amanda's prints. Maybe that's not surprising since there's no reason for a boater to be touching that middle pontoon. Also, there was no adhesive on the knife."

There was a long silence. "What does this mean for your investigation?" she asked.

"It brings us back to where we were yesterday morning. We can't limit our suspects to only people who were on the boat that night, but of those on the boat, our focus is on those who could have brought an eight-inch knife into the water. As you know, that would be Josh Peterson, Ambrose Houser, Caleb Iacomini, and Missy Brown."

"Then what was stuck onto the toon?" I asked. "Do boaters routinely tape something to the hull or to a pontoon?"

"No." Knutsen shook his head. "Bailey talked with the folks in their Marine Enforcement Unit. The only suggestion they had was that a boater might try to hide illegal drugs by taping them to a hull. I got the impression that they were reaching for any idea that might explain the tape."

I thought about the tri-toon boat and struggled to imagine any reason to tape something to the inner toon. "Could the killer have done it just to throw you off? Maybe taped it there to make you think there had been a knife there, which would make you think the killer was in the water?" As soon as the words came out, I knew they sounded stupid.

"You're suggesting someone put tape on the boat to confuse us? That makes no sense. What are the odds that one of you heard it and we found it?" He placed the sunglasses on his nose. "It's only because of Liz's sense of hearing and your persistence that we found the adhesive."

I stared at the sidewalk in front of me, watching an ant disappear into a crack.

"Don't you have something for me?" Knutsen said, breaking the silence. "Isn't that why you wanted to talk?"

"Oh, yeah." I sat next to the detective and my mind raced as I remembered my trip to the Larson Place's backyard. "This morning, I was nosing around the shed at the B&B. Do you remember there was a ladder in there?" Once he nodded, I continued. "I am pretty sure someone used it recently. An outline was visible from when it lay in the grass along the side of the shed. And then, about six feet from the house's roofline, I noted two separate indentations. It appeared that the ladder had been used to get someone onto the roof."

"The roof of the Larson Place? Isn't that three stories?"

"In front it is. In back, it's only two."

"What are you thinking? Why would a person go on the roof?"

Liz leaned forward. "All of us at the house are worried. Worried the killer might not be done."

Sunglasses hid Knutsen's eyes, but they were likely wide open. "You're suggesting a person went onto the roof to get at someone else in your group? I haven't heard about a break-in or any problems at the B&B."

"Nothing that we know of," she replied. "But Cy put security bars on our windows. Maybe someone climbed up there but couldn't break in because of that."

I reached behind Knutsen and tapped Liz's shoulder. "Or perhaps they were going to Ambrose's room, but found he wasn't inside."

"Yes," she said. "Maybe the killer is after him, but it didn't work since he was not in his room."

Knutsen turned back to me. I sensed him wanting to tell us to stop wasting his time. Instead, he got to his feet. "Well," he said with a sigh. "That's not nearly enough information to convince me that the killer is after someone else. The ladder is obviously there for a reason. The owner or a maintenance man may have used it a few days ago or even a week ago. We can check on that the next time we speak with the owners. Until then, I will direct a drive-by or two for tonight. That's a favor.

They can pull in and just check the shed and the building's perimeter. Otherwise, I need to go."

"Okay, I get it," I said. "We're being paranoid. But getting back to the boat, Liz still heard something, and we found tape residue on the toon."

The detective adjusted his glasses and shook his head. "Don't know what to say, other than that it probably wasn't used to secure a knife. We'll ask Josh if he knows about it. Possibly it's something he taped on weeks or months ago."

A thought came to my mind. "How about a tracking device? Could the tape have been used to attach a tracking device to the boat?"

Knutsen smiled. "Bailey and I talked about that as a possibility. But why bother with tape? Nowadays, there are tons of good GPS trackers on the market that are magnetic and waterproof. Why bother taping it to the boat? It makes no sense."

"Toons are aluminum," I said.

He shrugged his shoulders. "So what?"

Liz stood. "Aluminum is paramagnetic."

He plucked off his glasses. "What does that mean?"

"Aluminum is not magnetic," she said. "In order to affix a device to it, you'd need tape, rope or something."

Knutsen looked to each side, then fixed his gaze on me. "Are you sure?" We both nodded. "I guess that rings a bell, but Bailey and I talked about it with two other detectives. None of us..."

"I'm a locksmith," I said. "It's common knowledge that aluminum isn't magnetic, though maybe people rarely think about it. For me, it's different. Metals are core to locksmithing."

Chapter 28

Knutsen stayed for a few minutes, talking about the possibility of the tape having been used to secure a tracking device. He didn't seem convinced, but it raised the chance that the murderer might not have been aboard the *Eloquence*.

I lifted a finger theatrically into the air. "The adhesive shows that *someone* taped *something* to the toon."

Knutsen laughed. "It was possibly a good luck charm or something."

"Or a Saint Brendan the Navigator medal," Liz said.

I didn't want to ask, but I had to. "Who is Saint Brendan the Navigator?"

"The patron saint of boaters."

I should have known.

"That's as good a guess as any," Knutsen said. He turned away, waving us to join him as he started back to the City-County Building. "I'll mention the tracking device idea to Bailey. It would be her call and her divers that would search for it at the bottom of the lake. When I talked to her this morning, she said her focus was on finishing the search for shoreline video of anyone entering the water. Thus far, we have nothing, which implies it was one of your friends on the boat."

Liz and I caught up with him as he paused at the intersection. "If it was a person who was on the boat, is the investigation screwed? None of them is going to suddenly remember seeing a knife or seeing someone coming up behind Carpenter. Do you just bring people in and hope the killer messes up?"

"Unfortunately, that's about all we can do." The light turned, and we crossed in front of a pair of Madison Metro buses. "Every person on the outing, including you two, says they saw nothing. Though we have multiple people in that group who had a motive for wanting Ms. Dalbesio dead, none of those motives are strong, and no one from the group has a history of violence."

"How about Amanda?" Liz asked. "Doesn't she have a classic motive if she thinks Carpenter stole her husband?"

The detective stopped walking and waited until a group of suit-clad men passed by. "The interviews with Amanda and Josh made it clear that their marriage is at its end. As you know, Josh filed for a legal separation."

Liz stamped her foot as if she were trying to make a point. "Maybe that's what Josh wants, but maybe Amanda doesn't want a separation or a divorce. She seems nice, but maybe she took out her rival for his affection."

Knutsen leaned closer to her. "I doubt that. She admits to things that make it clear that they have both moved on."

Liz snapped her fingers, smiled, and looked at me. It was her natural smile. "Amanda is also having an affair."

"What makes you say that?" I asked.

"I told you she's been in the liquor store, but she had also been at the restaurant." Her eyes closed. "I'd seen her a few times, but never with Josh. There was someone else. A guy.

Tall, dark-featured, and handsome." Her eyes opened, and she looked at Knutsen. "I didn't get a good look at him, but it wasn't Josh. I'm right, aren't I?"

Knutsen looked about nervously. "Let me just say that your suggestion is consistent with what we have learned from Amanda's statement and from our investigation."

"So she *was* having an affair!" Liz announced.

"Jesus, keep it down." Knutsen backed off the sidewalk and leaned against a mail slot outside a bank. "Let's just say that we're convinced that Amanda is no more invested in the marriage than Josh."

"Then why are they still together?" I asked. "Why stay married to someone you don't love?"

"It could be she still loves him," he replied. "My impression is they both care for each other, but not as lovers. Now they are just friends. There's no longer any..."

"Spice?" Liz suggested.

He nodded his agreement and put up his hands as if surrendering. "You can see where this leaves us. The state of their marriage doesn't clear Amanda or Josh as suspects. Maybe Amanda still was jealous. She possibly felt spurned and was angry at Ms. Dalbesio. But murder?"

"It doesn't seem right." Liz said. "Would she be so angry at the woman he was sleeping with that she'd cut her throat when she's sleeping with someone herself?"

We all nodded for a few moments. "Do you know about Carpenter trashing one of the Iacomini's wines?" I asked.

The detective nodded. "It's a motive, but not a very good one. Wineries get crappy reviews all the time, but that doesn't lead winery owners to take out the offending critics." He looked back at Liz. "If so, you'd better go into a different line of business."

"How about Ambrose?" I asked. "He used to date Carpenter, right?"

"Yes. Mr. Houser has had relationships with at least a dozen women since getting divorced a few years ago, including three who were on the boat outing: Carpenter Dalbesio, Boston Cruz, and Katie Coolidge. That doesn't mean he would want her dead."

"Katie?" Liz said in a disappointed voice. She turned toward me. "I hadn't known or expected that."

Neither had I. "Are you looking into whether Carpenter might have been blackmailing Ambrose, Josh, or someone else?"

He paused on the sidewalk, looking in both directions before continuing. "Cy, we're considering everything, but remember, the Dane County Sheriff's Office is running things. Bailey and I talk strategy, but I doubt she tells me everything she's doing. Also, keep in mind that I'm only giving you information because you're sharing with me and because I know you have discretion. None of these discussions leave you two, right?"

Liz and I nodded.

"Bailey and I hope to find a more substantive motive. We saw possibilities with the ex-husband and Amanda, but after digging in, neither motive feels strong. Besides, both have alibis. That's not to say we've given up on them as suspects. We continue to look for financial transactions that might imply that someone hired a professional to kill Ms. Dalbesio. But it's probably a dead end since, as I told you, hired killers don't typically swim out on a lake and cut someone's throat." A police cruiser drove past, and Knutsen waved.

"How about money?" I asked. "If Josh and Amanda got divorced, would that cost her money? Do she and Josh have a prenup?"

"There's no prenup." The detective pushed his sunglasses back to the bridge of his nose. "Their principal asset is their home, which, net of the mortgage, is valued at about two hundred and fifty thousand dollars, though they both have about fifty thousand in IRA accounts and Josh has a trust fund worth about two hundred thousand. They have a boat, but there's a loan on it. The two each make about fifty thousand dollars a year. Hers comes from being in the reserves and working for the school district. His money comes from his work as a wine consultant and from the trust fund. I understand that his family is well-off, but he seems to be just getting by."

"Okay. Money doesn't sound like a motive for Amanda." I shook my head and tried to think of a reason someone would slit Carpenter's throat. "There's got to be something else. Something we aren't aware of."

Knutsen nodded. "There's a secret. One that explains why the killer would choose such a bloody and personal way to kill."

The three of us stood in front of the City-County Building, nodding our heads. We shook hands, and the detective climbed the steps. Liz grabbed my hand, and we started toward The Larson Place.

"We've got one more night." I pulled her tight. "I'll be glad when this is over."

She let go of my hand and stopped. Then she pulled out her phone and turned toward me. "I got a text from Ambrose. He's wondering if I would be available in early September to go to Lincoln, Nebraska, for their next tasting event."

"Nebraska?" It sounded like a nightmare. "You want to go to another one of these? You're pulling my leg."

"No. No, I'm not."

Chapter 29

The idea of another tasting event with the same group of people sounded crazy. If Carpenter's murder was still unsolved, it would make for a stressful trip. Making it worse, we'd have a long drive to Lincoln.

While I hoped she wouldn't be interested, I knew better. It was only one more event, but she likely saw it as an opportunity to be viewed as more than just a local critic. Ambrose's note asked her to meet with him and Boston to discuss the opportunity. His text suggested they talk before or after the afternoon session.

The B&B's common areas were empty, but the others arrived minutes after we went to our room. With Liz's hand in mine, we walked downstairs, finding Josh and Missy at the kitchen table. Amanda was cleaning the event room windows, and Renee came up from the basement carrying two covered bottles of wine. After a few minutes, Ambrose and Boston joined us. Small talk continued, but eventually Liz asked Ambrose if they could talk about his text.

He invited her to join him and Boston in his room. He said I could come along, which was good since I didn't want her alone with two murder suspects, especially one with a hairy chest and a lush baritone voice. Liz may have been ten years older than Ambrose, but I would not put anything past him.

The four of us ascended the stairs, and I wondered if this would be the first time he'd been in his room for days. Except maybe to retrieve the gaudy robe he wore the night before.

As the door closed, Ambrose grabbed a pile of folded clothes from atop the bed and placed them inside a suitcase. A combination lock hung off the luggage. I was familiar with all the TSA-approved locks. With the right tool, I could open this one in three seconds. Staring at the device, my mind saw the keyway and the pins, and I imagined just how the pick would slide in.

The rest of the room looked unused, and a fresh breeze brought in the faint scent of the lake through the open windows. Both of his windows at least had screens.

Ambrose sat on the edge of the bed as Boston pulled a chair from its desk and motioned for Liz to sit before joining him on the bed. I leaned against the desk and waited.

"We know this tasting has been, well, a nightmare," Ambrose said, his gaze hopping between the two of us. "But I assure you, this is nothing like a normal event. The tastings are usually enjoyable trips which allow everyone to visit new and interesting locations and try good wine. This is our fifth session, and we have four more booked over the next several months. The next one is in Lincoln. Like this one, it's one of our smaller events and will take place over four days. It is our only event that includes wines from multiple states. In addition to Nebraska, it covers wineries in Kansas and the Dakotas. We'll end up with a similar number of entries as we've had here in Wisconsin."

"Those are states whose wines I know little about," Liz said.

He patted his hand on the bed. "That illustrates why folks in those areas will benefit from my book. While we normally have two local tasters at our events along with my four regulars, this tasting has three locals. It's a PR thing, you see. Though Nebraska and the Dakotas have very few wineries, our funders want local input. Fortunately, the folks in North and South Dakota worked together with us, allowing us to choose one taster to, um, represent both states."

Liz nodded. "With Carpenter's passing, you will have six tasters for the Nebraska event. There will be you, Josh, Katie, one from Kansas, one from Nebraska, and one from the Dakotas."

"That's where we're sitting. The problem is that Josh is, well, iffy for every event. If he misses this one, it puts Katie and me in the minority. I hate to be in that situation."

"What do you mean by Josh being iffy?" Liz asked.

He looked at Boston and his manner became somber. "His mother is very ill. Cancer."

"It's sad," Boston said. "The doctors estimate she's got six months, but they caution she could go any time. He's the only child and the only family she's got left, so he wants to be there when it gets to the end. Ambrose has, naturally, given him permission to bow out at any moment as necessary."

"Yes, of course," Liz said.

"If he suddenly bows out, why does it matter?" I asked. "Can't you bring in local tasters that you can trust? Liz knows her stuff, and she's a local critic."

Ambrose let out a loud breath, then spoke in a calm, reassuring voice. "Every taster who has taken part in an event for this book and for my previous one has been competent.

Each one has taken the job seriously. However, tasters are often advocates for the wineries in their region."

"The average local critic's grade has been nearly three points higher than the grades given by the national critics," Boston said. "That's based on the nine events I've been involved in. You, Liz, have been an anomaly. Your grades have aligned with the national critics and have been slightly lower than the average given by Ambrose, Josh, Katie, and Carpenter. It implies you are a critic who not only fights the tendency to favor wineries from your home state, but one with a palate that picks up the same things as Ambrose, Katie, and Josh."

Ambrose brushed at his mustache. "Quality, well, matters. My concern is that one mismanaged event could bias our results toward one state or region. In you, I see a person Josh suggested. Someone who has gained Katie's respect, and whose numbers speak for themselves."

"Thank you," Liz muttered. Her lips pushed together and her skin flushed. She wanted to smile. I just knew it. But she held off.

"At this point, I'm only offering you this one event," he said, "but Josh's situation means I might need you for one or more of the remaining events. It could be something to catapult your career to the next level. If you end up in three or more events, I'll list you along with the national critics."

Liz's chest lifted with each breath. Excitement exuded from her. "Sounds great." She turned to me. "Assuming Cy can join me."

"Well, yes, though there is one thing." He paused, and his gaze switched to me and back to Liz. "We have a budget for Lincoln, which was already stressed since we have an extra taster. If Josh and you are both able to attend the event, we will be fully staffed. If we add in Cy's travel, we may be, um, over budget."

In other words, he didn't want to pay for the plus one's travel. While I felt myself shrinking, I would not let my ego stop her from getting this job. "We'll drive," I said. My voice was loud, as if I were afraid no one would hear me. "Liz would have her own room anyway, so adding me doesn't change the lodging cost. I didn't get a per diem for this event, so I'm fine with not having one for the Lincoln trip. My only cost is a few extra bagels. I'm an inexpensive assistant."

Liz patted my knee. "I would love to go. Rather, we would love to go."

"Then it's set!" Ambrose boomed.

My mind went fuzzy as they talked about the timing and the details of the event. For a moment, it felt as if I really was shrinking, and I stared at Ambrose's travel lock and it seemed to grow larger. Focusing on the keyhole, I saw scratches, which was what I expected. Scratches resulted from a lock being opened. It was probably just Ambrose unlocking his own suitcase, but sometimes the TSA opened combination locks using their master key. There were also stories of airline employees rifling through people's checked bags. There was no way to know who had opened his luggage, but it had been opened many times.

Liz said something to me, and I rubbed my eyes as she got to her feet. I realized I was still taller than her five foot-five frame, and everything was normal again.

Chapter 30

Heavy reds comprised the afternoon session. The aroma of spices and berries was apparent from the start. Staying on the right side of the law, I focused on color. The first two were difficult, and I struggled to break them between tawny, garnet, ruby, and purple. But despite residual clouds, the light was good, so Liz ignored my waffling and went with her own color grades. As she sipped, I looked around the room, watching Josh spit into his red cup while Katie, her mouth dangling open, held a glass of wine against the backdrop of the off-white wall. Renee zipped between me and the rear window. Behind her, I saw the shed and the nearly virgin Master Lock that protected its contents.

The lock was never far from my thoughts. As I stared outside, Renee returned and gathered Liz's ratings. My mind felt hazy, so I asked if I could take a trip to the restroom. To my surprise, she allowed me to go, telling me it was okay since Liz had already submitted her ratings.

I washed my face in the first-floor bathroom, drying it with paper towels. When I got back, they were arguing about the score for the flight's third entry. The wine received mid-eighty ratings from Katie, Ambrose, and Liz, but ninety-two from Josh and Missy. It was the biggest disagreement since the first day's sparkling wine argument. Josh and Missy reduced their grades by one and Liz went up one, but that wasn't enough. Boston decided they would never agree, so she calculated an average score, ending the discussion.

When the session finished, Ambrose stood at the lectern and announced their final evening event. It was a trip to the Memorial Union Terrace followed by dinner at a downtown wine bar, which Ambrose claimed had a perfect view of the Wisconsin State Capitol.

The terrace looked out onto Lake Mendota on the opposite side of the Capitol as Lake Monona. It was a wonderful spot but was a twenty or twenty-five-minute walk from the Larson Place. I was relieved to hear that Amanda would shuttle people from the B&B to the location. Once Liz was ready, we headed to the kitchen where we found Missy, Katie, and Renee sharing a bottle of white wine. Liz joined them, but I couldn't get my mind off the shed, so I said I would meet her outside.

Josh was sitting on the steps, waiting for Amanda who was retrieving her SUV from a nearby parking lot. I nodded to him and continued around the building. Despite the morning's rain deluge, the grass behind the house was dry. I walked to the shed and peered through its window. The ladder, canoe, bicycle, and boxes were still inside. Then I fixed my gaze on the lock. Holding it with my left hand, I peered into the keyhole, remaining impressed by the lack of scrapes and marks. It looked so perfect it had to be brand new. Looking inside the shed, I stared at the canoe and thought again about what happened when I was temporary captain of the *Eloquence*.

Putting the lock down gently, I walked toward the driveway and spotted movement inside the house. It occurred to me that the women were watching me. Liz was probably joking about me taking another look at the lock. Hopefully, she didn't tell them about how I talked about locks.

Josh was still on the porch, so I sat beside him. He was wearing black sunglasses and a striped button-up cotton shirt. I thought of him as a redhead, but the sunshine gave his hair more of a strawberry blonde appearance.

"How are you holding up?" I asked.

He was about to reply but halted, shaking his head. "I'm just so empty." The words were barely audible.

"Sorry. I can't imagine." What else could I say?

"You know the worst part?" He waited until I admitted I didn't. "The worst part is that I don't have an official relationship with Carpenter. People don't realize how absolutely devastating this is for me. Except the police, who are worse. They act like the more I admit to loving her, the more likely it is that I killed her. It's surreal."

"That has to be weird."

"Making it worse is that I told them that Carpenter had pushed me away a bit. I had promised her I would divorce Amanda, but I was dragging my feet. She questioned whether I was really going to do it, but I was. I was just being weak, you know?"

I nodded knowingly, because I didn't know what else to do.

He shook his head from side-to-side. "Maybe the most frustrating part of it is Amanda. She acts like Carpenter and I never happened. She knows that's not true, but she can't really console me, which I understand. There's nothing she can do but pretend everything's okay and nothing happened. It almost makes things worse."

With a nod, I patted his shoulder. "What did she think about Carpenter giving you pushback and encouraging a divorce?"

"Amanda didn't even know. Like I told you, Carpenter was just trying to make me do what I already said I would do. Telling Amanda wouldn't have accomplished anything. She already knew where our relationship was going." He blew out a large breath. "Is it okay if we talk about something else? Something to get my mind off reality."

"Sure." It took a moment before I came up with a different topic. "Ambrose asked Liz to take part in the next event. The one in Lincoln, Nebraska, of all places."

"That's good. Your wife knows her stuff. I knew that when I recommended her, but I've been impressed with how she judges and her professionalism. I watch her re-tasting the entry as we talk about it. Her eyes are closed and her lips move and you can see her thoughtfulness. Boston told me her notes are impressive. Ambrose appreciates good review notes."

"She's got awesome taste buds and a crazy sense of smell," I said. "The biggest advantage is her mind. From her time working as a librarian, she's obsessive about creating order and she has a ridiculous memory. She's able to remember and classify every smell and taste and color. It makes her annoying to cook for."

Josh laughed. "It's great that she'll be in Lincoln. I don't know if you've ever been there, but it's a more interesting town than you'd think. Like Madison, it's more than a university town."

"Going to another tasting is a little disconcerting, though," I admitted. "It's one thing to stay one more night when you're worried about there having been a murder. It's another thing to sign up for another three nights. We'll do it though. It's important to her."

"Actually, it will be four nights, just like this event." He flipped up his sunglasses and looked at me, squinting into the evening sun. "You and your wife will only spend three nights here since you live in town. I was visiting my mother, so even though I live in Madison, I didn't show until Tuesday morning when I flew out of Boston. I didn't get in until that morning. Everyone else is staying four nights."

"We have talked so much about Tuesday night, the night of the boat excursion, that I had forgotten that people were here the night before. Guess that means we'll be in Lincoln for four nights since we'll be driving. Ambrose doesn't want to pay for two plane tickets."

"Oh, Ambrose." Josh shook his head. "He's always focused on the bottom line, isn't he?"

"How does he pull it off? I'm obviously clueless about this wine stuff, but I'm not a novice when it comes to business. What sort of sales does he expect from a book on Midwest wines? He's paying Liz four hundred dollars for the event. With six critics, and adding in travel and the B&B, I'd think a single tasting event would cost close to four thousand dollars."

"Believe it or not, Ambrose gets tourism boards and local arts organizations to fund the tastings. They'll use grant funds to pay for lodging, wine tasting fees, per diem, parking, and travel."

"That's a pretty good angle. I thought the publisher funded the events."

"Working with government and tourism organizations is the only *angle* that would allow for a book like this to take place. It's not cheap. I actually found this place for him. He was interested because he could get it at a deep discount since they were still remodeling when he booked. Amanda and I did a final walkthrough a few weeks ago for him. I was relieved, as I had been concerned that things wouldn't be ready."

A black SUV pulled into the driveway, interrupting our conversation. "There's Amanda," he said. We both stood. "Are you heading to the terrace with us?"

"No," I said, though we had planned to go. "Liz and I are meeting our daughter for dinner, so we're gonna skip." It was a lie, but the thought of watching boats on the lake sounded painful, and I had an idea I wanted to pursue.

"Oh. Good for you. Have an enjoyable one." He nodded and walked toward his wife.

I rushed inside and spotted Boston and Ambrose near the front room's fireplace. "Amanda is back," I said. Then I went into the kitchen where the rest of the women were cleaning. I told them about Amanda, and they talked about how many people could fit in her vehicle and whether they would go in the first group or the second. I took Liz aside and told her I got a call from our daughter, Allie, and we were meeting her for dinner at a local restaurant.

"Allie called you?" She pulled out her phone and reviewed her messages. "Why would she call you?"

It was a reasonable question since our daughters usually only called me when they had car or lock problems. "Don't know. I didn't ask."

She rolled her eyes as she searched through her phone. "Let me call her."

"No. She told me not to tell you. It's supposed to be a surprise."

Liz appeared totally confused, so I ushered her away from the group and into the event room.

"I got an idea," I whispered to her. "It's about the..." I looked from side-to-side. "It's about the murder. Just go with it. Okay?"

"Okay. Got it. You want to wait until everyone's gone before you..."

"Investigate."

She gave me a crooked smile.

Chapter 31

Amanda took Josh, Boston, and Ambrose on the first trip and promised to return in ten minutes. Liz stayed in the kitchen with the rest of the women, so I sat on the porch watching traffic. It seemed like forever before Amanda returned. She stepped out of the SUV and tipped up her sunglasses. Katie, Missy, and Renee soon clambered into the vehicle. I told Amanda that we wouldn't need a ride, so she didn't have to make another trip. She gave us a thumbs up and hopped into the vehicle, waiting at the driveway's end for a break in traffic. Liz and I waved as they backed out, stopping at the nearest red light. The right blinker flicked its intentions and, finally, they were gone.

"What is it you want to do?" Liz asked. "I was enjoying hanging out with my friends. It would have been nice to show them the terrace."

I told her I wanted to find out what happened to Carpenter. Just waiting around and hoping wasn't good enough. "I don't want this hanging over us and over the Lincoln event. We need to try."

"Don't you trust Knutsen?"

"Sure, but he needs witnesses or evidence."

She looked at me for an uncomfortably long time. "Okay. I'll play along. But only if you agree that *trying* is all you can do. You can't bring her back to life, and you can't expect to solve her murder. It's Detective Knutsen and Detective Bailey who handle that. All you can do is try to find something that might help them. Frankly, we found tape residue on the boat which they missed, so we have already helped. Do you agree?"

Arguing with her wouldn't do any good. Particularly since she was right. "Yes, I agree. All we can do is try."

"Good. Okay then. What do you want to do? Do you want to go look at the boat again?"

"No. I want to go to Turville Point."

"Turville Point?"

"It's next to Olin Park. Remember, Knutsen said it was the best place for a person to enter Lake Monona without being picked up by someone's surveillance camera or a city camera." He also mentioned Olbrich Park, but I didn't bring that up.

"Do we drive or walk?"

"Google says it's just under two miles along the Capital City Trail to where Olin and Turville connect. It says it's a forty-minute walk. I'd rather do that, since it mirrors the path the killer may have taken."

Liz shook her head slowly, then went inside and grabbed a bottle of water from the refrigerator.

The trail ran along the lake. Railroad tracks and a busy four-lane road were between us and the path. There was no rail traffic, but it took a few minutes to cross the street.

The path, railroad tracks, and road ran on a thin patch of land which, along with a bridge, separated Lake Monona from Monona Bay. The path continued through Olin Park and past Turville Point.

As we walked, a trio of sailboats coasted nearby while a breeze blew in the unmistakable smell of red algae from the bay. We talked about the boats and the route the *Eloquence* took on the night of Carpenter's murder. My recollection was we had anchored a third to a half mile from shore with the port side facing the Monona Terrace Community and Convention Center. If the boat were still on the lake, we would have been able to see her from the trail.

"You're thinking the killer swam from Turville Point to the boat?" Liz said. "That would be at least a mile and a half. People swim at two to three miles per hour. So that's possible. Maybe they were in scuba gear, like you or Knutsen mentioned. That would make it easy for a competent swimmer."

"Scuba gear might be overkill. If it were me, I'd have a wet suit and fins. That way, I wouldn't have to worry about the air tanks and stuff. Remember, if someone swam to the boat from Turville, they would have to get the equipment and themselves there without being seen. And they'd have to exit without being noticed. If I were the killer, I wouldn't bring a car. There are too many cameras. Too many opportunities to be seen and identified."

"So, you want to assume the killer walked to the park?" Liz tightened her grip on my hand. "Or biked. Maybe they just wore a backpack for the knife and the wet suit and fins."

"Yes. Biking makes sense."

"So, you think this is it?" She took a drink and looked up at the late afternoon sun. "You think the killer swam to the boat rather than it being someone from our group?"

"I'm not counting anyone out, but I think it was the killer who taped something on the toon. My guess is that something was a tracking device."

"If there was a tracking device on the boat, it points away from Katie."

I smiled, knowing my wife didn't want her friend to be a cold-blooded murderer.

Approaching Olin Park, I observed a single pier extending onto the lake. Four boats were attached, and each moved as waves pushed against the shore. We passed a dozen residential buildings within the park's boundaries. I saw at least three more piers as we crossed a bridge that went over a creek.

Instead of continuing on the path, we turned toward the water, pausing in front of the park's boat launch. It took a minute before I spotted a surveillance camera on a light post. I took a photo, and we continued along the lake, staying behind the cluster of trees and bushes that hugged the shore.

Trying to stay as close to the water as possible, we took a small trail which brought us into the Turville Point Conservation Park. I had been on the path several times, and my recollection was that it ran along the shoreline for about a quarter of a mile to Turville Point.

"What are we looking for?" Liz asked.

I stepped off the path, grabbed a tree, and crouched down. "A sign that someone entered or came out of the lake with scuba gear or a wet suit. There might also be evidence of something having been buried."

"I'll tell you if I see scuba gear lying on the shore." Liz put her left foot forward while keeping her right leg straight and resting her hands on her waist. I called it her Miss Greece pose, because it reminded me of the pose women used in beauty contest swimsuit competitions. Liz's mother, who was born in Greece, used to stand the same way when she was angry. "How far do we have to go?"

"Not much further." I waved her forward and started down the shoreline while she stayed on the path. Keeping away from the water was necessary for her.

"This seems...futile," Liz said after a few minutes. She was staring at her phone. "Notice I didn't say a mean word like stupid or idiotic."

"Thanks," I said without turning toward her. There was movement ahead of us, followed by the murmur of voices.

Liz and I exchanged glances. I hopped off a rock and onto the path, pausing when I spotted the first of two City of Madison Police officers.

Chapter 32

The female officers looked young, but they both recognized me. The taller of the two even called me by name, explaining she had worked with me in the spring. She said I had replaced a line of locks at a horse show at the nearby Alliant Energy Center.

Following introductions, they asked if we were regulars on the path and if we were there on Tuesday evening. Apparently, they were looking for the same thing as us. One of them held a partially filled trash bag. Something inside it was oval-shaped, which caught my attention.

"Is that a U-lock in there?" I pointed at the bag.

The taller officer chuckled. "That's right. I forgot for a second that you're a locksmith."

"That I am."

"You're right that it's some sort of lock. There are also three unmatched gloves, a hat, and a few socks. The lock's a half oval." The officers exchanged glances, and she stuck a gloved hand into the bag, pulling out a black lock. "Looks reasonably new."

I leaned forward, verifying it was a U-lock, perhaps a foot long. Sportneer was the brand. Probably made of steel and zinc. "It's a bicycle lock. Did you find a key?"

"Nope." She flipped the base. "It's unlocked."

"Where'd you find it?"

"Nearby," the other officer said, pointing toward the lake. "Just west of Turville Point, at the shore's tree line."

"Do you mind if I look at the keyhole?" I asked. "I won't touch it." She nodded, so I leaned in. There were plenty of scratches, which told me the lock was not new.

After a brief discussion, they said they needed to head to the station to turn in their evidence and change shoes.

"See, it isn't just me," I said after the officers had moved on. "The cops had the same idea, and they actually found something."

Liz shook her head. "A lock? So what?"

"It may be a clue."

"You're saying that the lock they found relates to the murder? What are the odds of that?"

"Fifty-fifty."

"No way."

"U-locks are for bikes, and they found it right around where someone would go into the water while avoiding cameras. Why else would you lock up a bike near the shore unless you're going into the water?"

"Maybe you're going fishing."

"Have you ever seen anyone fishing along this part of the shore? There's too much algae."

"No. But I've never seen a person go into the water from here either." She motioned toward the departing police officers. "Even if you're right and the killer used it, what good would it do? Do you expect to find fingerprints on it?"

"Doubtful, but you never know."

"They should check, but it won't do any good. It's just another futile thing the cops have to do."

Deciding not to argue, we continued along the trail. Rather than searching the same area that the two women had just searched, I stayed with Liz on the path. Finally, we got to Turville Point. We made our way to the shoreline and gazed across the lake. The convention center and the Wisconsin State Capitol were in the distance.

"Let's head to the parking lot," I said after admiring the view.

"You're giving up?"

"They already searched the area I was interested in. Everything past this point is wooded, but the houses on the other side of the bay have cameras aimed at the other side of Turville Point. If someone swam to the boat, they would use the part they already covered, since it's the area where there's the least camera coverage."

She nodded her agreement, and we walked quietly on the trail, exiting near a parking lot between the two parks. Liz stopped, sitting on the curb at the end of the lot. After finishing the water, we took off our shoes and socks and did a tick check. Not surprisingly, Liz was clean, but we found something crawling on one of my socks. We moved about thirty feet and sat again.

Looking to the south, I spotted rooftops near the park. "See the buildings behind the trees?" I asked. "They're hotels, both of which are MB clients." I was referring to MB Lock & Security. "They have full set-ups, including cameras."

"Don't you think Knutsen would have already reviewed their security footage?"

"Yeah." I nodded, staring at the buildings. "The trail goes in front of the hotels. I'm sure cameras cover it. If it was someone who swam from Turville Point, they might show up on those tapes on Tuesday evening or night. If they didn't drive, they're probably walking or biking on the trail. The problem is that the MPD doesn't know who to look for. Even if they see the same person going through once in each direction, what good would it do? At most, it tells them if it's a man or a woman."

Liz didn't comment, so I leaned my head down and the realization came to me. I admitted to myself that, unless fingerprints were on that lock and they matched with a suspect, there was likely no evidence that someone had gone into the lake at Turville Point. Perhaps I knew it was a futile search, but I had to try. At least I had done that.

We put our shoes on and started back to the B&B. As we got to the trail, a runner came toward us. She had thin arms and ran like Kermit the Frog.

Liz tugged lightly on my hand. "Have you read anything on the internet about the murder? I saw a story show up on my Yahoo! feed."

"More national press, huh?"

"The article included a picture of Carpenter in a swimsuit."

"Aha," I said. "That explains it."

"Today's *Wisconsin State Journal* story implies that the investigation's at a dead end. They quote Detective Bailey. She says they're awaiting the results of the medical examination. It sounds like the police are of the same mind as you; they realize the murder will remain unsolved since there's no hope of new witnesses and little chance of new forensic evidence. Unless they find prints on that lock, the medical examiner is their last chance."

"When is the forensic report due?" I doubted the report would provide game-changing evidence.

"The paper said they were hoping to have a preliminary report today. Maybe they'll have an update yet tonight."

I nodded and, as we walked, I thought about how the police investigation would move forward. If the bicycle lock and the video evidence came up empty, the best thing they could do was to search for motive by digging into people's backgrounds. It was possible that one of the group had a connection to Carpenter that we were not aware of. Or perhaps there was someone they hadn't yet identified who had a motive. Maybe one of her social media followers was a psychopath.

Walking between the bay and the lake, we decided to stop for a bite at the Echo Tap, since it was nearby. As we waited for our food, I pulled out my phone and wrote a few notes. I went through the suspects I was aware of, deciding there were six people or groups of people who had a motive. I entered thoughts on each of them but passed over Renee and Abby as they had no motive and no prior history with Carpenter. In addition, the only opportunity each had to kill her was during the relay race. And, if one of them had done so, they would not have won.

> Josh
> Only has a motive if Carpenter was having an affair with someone else. No evidence to support that.
> Had the best opportunity to kill her. He could have hidden the knife on the boat. Also, he could have put the duct tape on

the boat's toon to make it look like someone had attached either the knife or a tracking device.

Amanda
No obvious motive, as she seems to have checked out of her marriage to Josh. Though Josh's family has money, he doesn't, and a divorce would not significantly impact her monetary situation.
As a Marine, she probably has the physical ability to swim to the boat. Like Josh, she could have put the duct tape and the tracking device on the toon. A neighbor spotted her at her house shortly after sunset, which is supported by her car and phone records.

Ambrose and Boston
Ambrose dated Carpenter, but it's a weak motive as there's no evidence that he was a spurned lover. Perhaps she had some secret about him and was blackmailing him. Don't see any other way he would have benefited from Carpenter's death.
Ambrose could have hidden the knife in his long shorts. If he killed Carpenter, Boston would have seen it. If one of them did it, they would have had to have put the tape on the toon at the marina or after they got into the water.

Caleb and Jenn Iacomini
Revenge is one motive, as Carpenter gave their wine a crappy review. Even if one of them was crazy enough to kill over the review, would the other cover for them? There's always the possibility that she knew something about one or both of them and was blackmailing them. Seems unlikely, but not impossible.

Caleb could have hidden the knife under his shirt or lifejacket. If one of them killed Carpenter, the other saw it. As with Ambrose and Boston, if they did it, they would have had to put tape on at the marina or after getting into the lake. Unless, of course, the tape was only a coincidence and didn't relate to the murder.

Leonardo "Buzz" Dalbesio
Spurned lovers always have a motive, though we have no evidence that he wanted her dead. There doesn't appear to be a custody battle, and he doesn't have a financial motive for killing her, barring the blackmail idea.

Physically fit, so if he can swim, he could have made it to the boat. To do this, he would have had to have somehow snuck into the marina and taped the tracking device to the boat. He has an alibi based on his girlfriend, which is supported by his phone's GPS.

Katie and Missy
No known motive, though Katie knew Carpenter prior to the event.
Both were in the water, so theoretically, either could have done it, though only Missy had a good opportunity to sneak the knife onto the boat and into the water. As with Ambrose and Boston, the killer would have had to have put the tape on the toon at the marina or after getting into the water.

None of it was satisfying.

"Are your notes about the motives or the alibis?" Liz asked as I closed the app and stuffed the phone in my pocket.

"Both. Multiple people have motives, but they are weak. That's what bothers me most."

"What bothers me," Liz said, "is the seventy-two that Carpenter gave to Fusion Rock."

It was tempting to roll my eyes, but I held off. "What about it bothers you?"

She shook her head. "It makes no sense. None. It's a solid wine and, from what I've read, she was a good critic. Why did she give it such an awful review? She either tasted something the rest of us didn't, or there was some other reason."

"Yes," I said, running my tongue across my lips. "Maybe there was a reason." I was suddenly interested in a wine review. "Maybe there's an underlying secret, like Knutsen suggested.

A reason someone wanted Carpenter dead. A reason we don't yet understand."

Chapter 33

We ordered the food to go, but instead of carrying it to the B&B, we sat on a bench outside the restaurant. A couple about our age whirled past on roller blades as I passed a grilled chicken sandwich to Liz. Mine was a spicy chicken sandwich, and the first bite left me looking for something to drink. Unfortunately, Liz's water bottle was empty, and I was too tired to go back into the restaurant for tap water. Instead, I mixed in a few French fries before taking another bite.

"You're thinking Carpenter had something against the Iacominis?" Liz said.

"It's an idea. I mean, you're the expert. If you can't figure out why she would have given such an awful review, that's inexplicable. I don't like inexplicable."

"Won't the police..." She paused as she finished chewing. "Won't the police be looking into Carpenter's background and those of the people who were on the boat? If there's a reason she didn't like them, shouldn't they find it?"

"Those would be steps you'd think they'd take. The problem is, they aren't focusing on the Iacominis any more than the rest of the people who were on the boat trip. I wish we knew more about her and our winery owners. Did Katie tell you anything about Carpenter's background?"

"You know she's from Chicago and met Josh on the Jersey Shore back when they were college age, right? The newspaper articles say she's thirty-four years old, so that would have been maybe fifteen years ago that they met. Her daughter starts kindergarten this fall, so she's probably five. Let's say she got married six to eight years ago."

"What else?"

"She has her vlog. And she's been a critic for a bit, so there is probably a good online trail. I looked at her website on Wednesday, but some of the site has been taken down. Oh." She stopped eating and patted my arm. "Katie also mentioned that Carpenter was once a victim of sexual harassment. Apparently, it had a big impact on her."

This was news to me. "Did she tell you what happened?"

"No. She was just talking about how Carpenter was always concerned about her vlog, since she knew some people thought she was taking advantage of her looks. She told Katie about being harassed to illustrate that there was a bad side to being in the public eye."

"Unfortunately, I'm not surprised that a vlogger whose appearance is intertwined with her message would get hassled."

"Katie said it wasn't some random fan, but someone in the industry. I wish I were at the library. If so, I might figure out what happened." The Madison Public Library had subscriptions to scores of databases, including historical newspapers and city directories.

"What would you do if you were at the library?" I asked. "How would you research her background and find out something about her being harassed?"

"It's unlikely I would find anything unless it resulted in a court case. However, if we suspect it was Caleb who hassled her, then I would focus on whether they knew each other or crossed paths. First, I'd have to identify her. I don't know her maiden name, so I'd start with her ex-husband." She shoved a green bean into her mouth and continued talking. "There can't be many Leonardo Dalbesios in the country, let alone in the Chicago area. Hopefully, I'd find either a marriage announcement in a newspaper or a marriage record. That would give me her maiden name and possibly her parents' names. Once I had those, I could probably get her date of birth. Then I would trace where she lived and worked."

"There also can't be too many Caleb Iacominis in Wisconsin. That sounds Greek," I said.

She laughed and shook her head. "It isn't Greek. To me, the name sounds Italian. But you're right, it's not a common name, so there probably won't be tons."

"What would you do next?"

"I'd figure out if the two ever lived near each other and where they worked. I'd also look to see if both their names show up in the same newspaper articles or if one of them got arrested or something. Finally, I'd cross-reference the festivals that each judged."

"Good idea."

She nodded. "I'd also look into Caleb's wife. Do you want me to call Betty? She's probably home already. Unless she's got something going, she could probably log on from home and search. Either that, or we could make our way over to the downtown library tomorrow. It's only a fifteen-minute walk from the B&B."

Betty had worked for Liz a dozen years earlier. She'd do whatever search Liz asked her to do. "Call her. I would like to know tonight if there's any obvious connection between Carpenter and either of the Iacominis."

She sat the chicken sandwich on her lap and texted Betty, asking her to call. She showed me the message and asked if I wanted to add anything. I told her to say it's a "minor emergency." She added it and Betty called her within thirty seconds. After a five-minute conversation, Liz sent another text with the information she had on Carpenter and the Iacominis.

"How long will it take her to dig into them?" I asked.

"A few hours. The hard part is that we don't know Carpenter's or Jenn's maiden names. Jenn might be the hardest to trace, especially if her maiden name turns out to be Smith or something like that. Obviously, she could come up with something hot really quick. Say, for instance, there's an article in a Chicago newspaper saying that Caleb and Carpenter were working together as wine critics. If she finds that, she'll contact us right away. Or if they judged the same wine competition. Though I'm not sure how easy it is to come up with those listings."

After taking the last bite of my sandwich, my mouth was an inferno. I drowned the remaining fries in ketchup and slurped them down. There was nothing to do but go back to the B&B and wait. We stuck wrappers and used napkins into a trash can.

While it wasn't progress or evidence, it could lead somewhere, so I felt a surge of energy. Stretching my arms above my head, I noticed a bicycle leaning against a no parking sign. A combination Master Lock hung from a security cable. I flipped the lock over, noting that the keyhole looked unmarked. That wasn't surprising, since the owner probably only unlocked it using the combination.

My mind shot back to the shed behind the Larson Place B&B. It had been bothering me, and suddenly I knew why. I dropped the lock, and it banged into the bike's crank arm.

"Cy," Liz said. "What is it?"

"The shed lock is brand new. I'm sure of it."

"Not the shed lock again. So what?"

The blue sky above was clear, as were my thoughts. "Earlier, Josh reminded me that some of the critics, including Carpenter, arrived on Monday night. Monday night might be the key."

"Monday night? I don't get it."

"We might not prove who killed Carpenter on Tuesday night, but we might be able to prove who had *tried* to kill her on Monday night."

"Tried to kill her?"

"Yes." I nodded slowly.

Chapter 34

I felt like running to the Larson Place, but I wasn't about to suggest it, so I speed-walked, pulling Liz along. She asked me to explain what the rush was, but I felt as if I had captured a butterfly in my hands and if I talked, it would escape. Fortunately, she knew me well enough to play along.

When we arrived, I leaned into the foyer and called out several names. No one responded. The rest of the group were apparently still out. I asked Liz to keep an eye out for them while I got a few things ready.

She didn't say a word, but her eyes said enough. Stepping into the fireplace room, she stared outside.

I held a finger in the air, implying I'd tell her in one minute. Grabbing her phone, I ran upstairs to our room. The dead bolt opened, and I took the brace off the window that had a screen. After unlocking the window, I opened it and took off the screen, setting it on the floor next to the bed. I closed the window and hurried downstairs, taking two steps at a time.

She was sitting in front of the unlit fireplace. "Cy, this is getting annoying. What's it about?"

"The lock." I pulled her up and handed over her phone. She followed me to the front door. We rushed down the steps, crossed the grass, and turned onto the driveway. "Like I said, it's new."

She shook my hand away. "So?"

"Do you remember when Knutsen had me pick it?" The shed came into view, so I turned and waited for her. "He said the owner told him it was a Yale."

"I'll repeat. So?"

The padlock seemed to draw me to it. Next thing I knew, the silver, black, and blue lock was in my hand. "What do you see?" I asked, waiting until she came closer. "It isn't a Yale; it's a Master Lock."

Her eyes widened. "Do you want me to say it again?"

For a moment, I struggled to find words to explain my thoughts. "Look at the keyhole."

"Cy!" I thought her eyes were wide before, but now they were almost round. "You know I struggle with this. I'm trying to focus, but it's hard. I can see the keyhole, but it doesn't look different from any other lock."

"Sorry. I know. Just trying to underline that it is brand new." My heart was thumping. "When I picked her on Wednesday, it was the first time anyone had ever picked her. I'm willing to go even further and to say it hasn't been opened with the key more than a few times, if ever. When someone puts in a key, it rarely goes directly into the hole. Instead, it bounces and scrapes along the entryway, which leaves marks."

"You already told me that it's a new lock." She switched to her Miss Greece stance. "So what?"

"I'm also sure that the ladder inside the shed was used recently. But how could someone access the ladder when the shed was locked?"

"They had the key. So, someone *has* opened it before."

"The owners say they have both keys to the shed's lock, and they have been out of town for two weeks." I pulled out my kit and laid it on the concrete slab below the doorway. "I think someone cut through the owner's Yale lock. This person didn't want anyone to realize that they had accessed the shed, so they put a new one on it. A Master Lock. I think this happened on Monday night or early Tuesday morning."

There was still plenty of sunlight, so I didn't worry about a flashlight. Instead, I slid in the turning tool and then the pick. I'd been inside the keyhole before, and I knew the feel of her entryway and my mind saw the pins and could feel the springs. After a few seconds, she opened, and the body of the lock dropped. I smiled and glanced back at Liz. She was looking to the side. Apparently, a pair of fluttering birds was more interesting than me opening a lock. I set it on the ground and pulled up the shed door.

"What are you doing?"

"To test my theory, I'm going to use the ladder to get onto the roof. I want to make sure a single person could deploy it without major difficulty."

"You think this happened on Monday night? Couldn't the owners or their handyman have been up there? Maybe the handyman had to go on the roof and the owners were already on this trip, so he broke the lock and replaced it?"

"A handyman would have access to the house and could get onto the roof through the third-story windows. Why would he bother using a ladder?"

She didn't respond, so I pointed at the ladder resting against the side of the shed as I slid on a pair of gloves which were in the corner. The ladder was held up by two curved pegs which were nailed to the wooden structure. It was fully compressed, made of orange fiberglass, and had silver rungs. Dirt was on the bottom legs, so I took a photo. I slid the phone into my pocket and counted twelve pairs of rungs.

Crouching down, I reached between the sixth and seventh pair and rested a beam on my shoulder. I grunted as the weight transferred from the pegs to my body. My legs pushed into a standing position, but the ladder teetered forward. I crouched and extended my arm until the ladder stabilized. Then I asked Liz to go over to the driveway, and I carried it out of the shed.

"Cy, this is foolish. You might drop it and break a window."

It probably was stupid, as a single person deploying a twenty- or twenty-four-foot ladder was never easy. But I had experience with them, and I thought I could do it without too much difficulty. Walking toward the house with the ladder, I aimed for a spot between a huge back window and the house's edge. Large windows were expensive, so I had to keep the device away from the glass. As I got about ten feet from the house, I flipped my hips and threw the top of the ladder into the air. When it was vertical, I wrapped my legs around the beam and used the rope to extend the device. Once fully extended, I leaned it toward the house until it rested against the second-floor gutters.

"Easy-peasy," I said.

Liz shook her head. "Bull. Even I could see you were struggling."

"Struggling or not, I did it."

The ladder had pads at the bottom of each beam. This was ideal for setting up on concrete or hard flooring, but they sometimes slipped on grass, so I lifted it slightly, and flipped the pads. With the pads turned sideways, I hopped on the bottom rung, pushing the beams into the soft ground.

Then I looked for the two indentions I had noted earlier. The morning rainstorm made the search difficult, but I found a spot only six inches to the left of the ladder, and a second one exactly twenty inches to its right.

I motioned Liz over, telling her to stand on the bottom rung once I started climbing.

She nodded her agreement. "Then what?"

"Then I'm going to go into our room."

"Good. And then you can tell me why it matters."

Chapter 35

It was a good-quality ladder, and it felt solid as I climbed. Once I was on the seventh rung, Liz stepped on, stabilizing the beams. Sixteen steps up, my head was even with the gutter. I examined the metal, hoping to see evidence of the rails having leaned against the roof at an earlier date. There was a spot about six inches over, but it was far from distinct, so I continued up, reaching a hand onto the asphalt roof tiles. After one last rung, I stepped onto the roof, crouching until I got comfortable with the pitch.

"Okay!" I called to Liz. "Move away. Go back to the driveway."

She stepped off and marched away. At the asphalt's edge, she stopped and turned around. "Now what?"

"I'm going to push the ladder to the ground."

"What?"

"I'm going to push it into the grass. There's enough space that it will fall to the side of the shed. I can either do it from here or wait and do it from the ground."

"You're kidding! How are you going to get down?"

"Through our window."

I wedged a foot against the edging and placed my right hand on the ladder's top rung. It would need a good shove to ensure it would fall away from the house. But I needed to make sure I didn't slip or push too heavily against the gutter. "Here we go," I said as I shoved. Teetering slightly, the ladder landed with a swish and a thud as it settled on the high grass. "I'll meet you in our room!"

Liz didn't look happy about it, but she started down the driveway as I climbed on all fours to the third-floor siding. It was not a steep pitch, but I took it slow.

Four third-story windows faced the back of the house. Two belonged to our room and two to Ambrose's. The bathroom window faced the side and wasn't accessible from the roof, nor were the hallway windows since they faced the road.

I was closest to our windows, which was good since I wanted to enter through the second one. I went up straight, then sideways, my hand gliding along the siding. Once at the window, I placed my case on the roof and grabbed a long, flat pick. Slipping it between the window and the frame, I leaned on it, causing the frame to lift an inch. Squeezing a finger underneath, I lifted until the frame fully extended. As I got ready to enter, the door's deadbolt clanged open followed by the creaking of the hinges.

I was aiming to be inside before Liz, but didn't quite make it. "Hello, husband," she said as I crawled in, headfirst. "What happened? Now both our windows are missing screens."

"I took it off a few minutes ago." I nodded toward the screen lying against the wall. After catching my breath, I wiped sweat from my forehead and sat on the bed.

"So, what is this all about?" She sat next to me. "What are you trying to do, other than make me worried about sleeping here tonight?"

I put a hand on her knee. "Someone broke into this room before we arrived on Tuesday."

"You're sure of that because...?"

"Four things which, by themselves, might mean nothing, but collectively, they make it likely. First, there's the brand-new lock which doesn't match what the owner said was on the shed. Second, there were indentions in the backyard matching the exact width of the ladder. Third, there's the missing screen on the window furthest from the headboard, and finally, the tape residue on the frame of the mirror. Just like with Josh's boat, the tape used in this room left adhesive residue."

"I get your issue with the lock and the ladder," Liz said. "How about the screen? You're saying the robber threw it away or something? That's why the room is missing one?"

"Most likely, the intruder cut through it to gain entry. It would be the simplest thing to do. But they didn't accomplish what they wanted and didn't want anyone to know they'd broken in. Leaving a cutout screen would imply that a break-in occurred, so they took it with them."

"How about the other thing? You said something about tape."

I pointed at the mirror that sat on one wall. "There's tape residue on the frame. It feels fresh. My guess is someone attached a listening device to the frame. At first, I thought it was a camera, but the residue sits on the back end of the frame. A camera would aim upward. It was probably a bug. They probably removed the device after taking off the screen and getting inside." I took pictures of the screen and of the mirror.

"In your mind, these things add up to someone having broken into our room." She nodded her head slowly. "Okay.

I'll buy it as a possibility, but it could be a coincidence. Maybe the break-in happened weeks ago?"

I put my hands in the air as if giving up. "That doesn't explain the ladder or the lock."

"Okay. If so, what did they want? I mean, why would someone break into our room? Are we the killer's actual targets? It can't be that they were trying to rob us. It's not like we brought anything that's worth much."

"The break-in happened on Monday night or early Tuesday morning. When the break-in occurred, no one other than Carpenter and Ambrose would have known this was our room."

"Oh, you're right. This was originally Carpenter's room. Ambrose only changed that on Monday evening. Everyone else would have thought it was her room and not ours."

"Yes," I said, nodding. "The person broke into what they *thought* was Carpenter's room."

Chapter 36

L iz suggested I call Knutsen, but I was hesitant. When we met with him the previous day, he had been far from sold on my argument that someone had broken into the shed. Even if I could convince him that something had happened, I wouldn't be able to prove a connection to Carpenter's death.

My theory was that someone broke into the room on Monday night intent on killing Carpenter. The plan was foiled because she switched rooms with us. If correct, whoever broke in had previously accessed the room. I suspected that because it appeared they had installed a listening device in the room using tape. They also made sure the window was unlocked. But when they broke in expecting to find Carpenter, the room was empty, so they took the listening device and damaged screen with them. They then put the ladder back in the shed and disposed of the Yale lock. Prior to our arrival on Tuesday morning, they replaced it with a Master Lock.

It made sense, but the appearance of a break-in didn't overwhelm Liz, and it probably wouldn't be enough for Knutsen. I wasn't even sure it was enough for me, as it could all be deemed circumstantial.

"If you're right," Liz said, "why not come back on Tuesday night and break into her room on the second floor?"

"Josh didn't fly into Madison until Tuesday morning. Monday night was the only time the killer could count on Carpenter being alone in her room."

She closed her eyes. "If there was a break-in, it couldn't have been Ambrose or Boston."

I nodded in agreement. "Ambrose knew she was changing rooms, so why break into Carpenter's old room, except perhaps to retrieve the listening device? Also, he's got a third-floor room. If he wanted to get inside the other one, he could have gone out his window and into hers. Why bother breaking into the shed? And since Ambrose and Boston were connected at the hip during the swim, one couldn't have killed her without the other seeing it happen. This theory would at least clear those two."

Liz nodded her agreement. "It would leave the Iacominis, Amanda, Carpenter's ex, Katie, Missy, Renee and Abby. It might clear Josh depending on when his flight came in."

"The problem is that some of them had neither motive nor opportunity. I'd exclude Renee and Abby for this reason, as they never met Carpenter before the tasting, and I don't think they had the opportunity to kill her while in the water. I might feel different if they lost the race against Katie and Missy, but they didn't. As for Missy, she may have had the opportunity, but she also hadn't met Carpenter prior to Monday night."

She nodded. "Plus, Josh, Renee, Abby and Missy didn't arrive at the B&B until Tuesday morning."

I nodded. "Of the suspects we haven't excluded, only Katie was at the B&B on Monday night."

"Katie is no killer," Liz announced.

"I don't think she is the killer," I said, "since she doesn't have a motive. But we can't ignore the possibility." Liz and Katie had developed a friendship over the past few days. It appeared to be a relationship based on similar interests and mentalities, but it struck me as odd that Katie would seek to bond with a person who was nearly twenty years her senior. "Has Katie been in our room at all? Have you invited her to our room for anything?"

"Me?" Her eyes searched the room. "No. I don't think she's even been on the third floor other than one time when the downstairs bathroom had a line and we came up. Besides, didn't you say there are cameras in the shared areas?"

"Yes." I tried to think of the location of the two cameras on the staircase. "Assuming they were working, they should pick up anyone going between floors, though I don't know if the police collected footage from inside the B&B since the murder happened on the lake."

"Boston told me they got video from inside the house for Monday and Tuesday," Liz said. "Missy freaked out and was concerned that there might be cameras in the bedrooms, but Boston said there's a total of six only in common areas. I assume the police wanted to see the footage in case Carpenter got into a fight with someone, which might show motive for the incident."

"Okay. Makes sense." I thought about how Katie could get outside the house from the second floor without being on camera. "I think you're right. The cops can check if she left the house. The only exception would be if she used a rope or something to go out through the window. Though climbing out her window seems silly since she has a front-facing room. It's the room where I found the heart attack victim. There's traffic on Wilson Street, even during the middle of the night. And don't forget, the Dane County Courthouse is across the street and the sheriff's and the MPD's offices are nearby. There's a ton of cop traffic on the street."

"Assuming Betty finds nothing on the Iacominis, isn't Carpenter's ex-husband the best suspect?" Liz asked. "Katie said he's a jerk."

"You'd think so, but Knutsen says he has an alibi for Tuesday evening."

"Okay. Then the Iacominis could have driven here on Monday night and broken in. Even so, what's different about Monday night compared to Tuesday night? We can't even prove someone broke in on Monday and if we did, we wouldn't know who."

"Nowadays, cell phone locators, Wi-Fi access, and surveillance cameras are a detective's best friends. If there's a murder, the cops figure out exactly where their suspects' phones were during the time of a killing, and they track Wi-Fi usage and video footage. This killer is smart, so he or she was careful to hide his or her activities." I put my finger in the air like I was a prosecutor coming to a startling conclusion. "But after trying and failing to kill Carpenter on Monday night, would the person have been so careful? Most people wouldn't think twice about replacing a Yale with a Master Lock, but..."

"Most people, thankfully, are not lock freaks."

I gave her a dirty look before continuing. "Yes, most people are not lock *aficionados*. The person might assume that no one would even know they broke into this room or why they broke in. They may have also been careless when disposing of the screen and the broken lock and careless when heading home on Monday night." I thought about the conversations I had with Detective Schuster regarding our phones and about the form I signed. "Do you remember what access we gave them for our phones? They probably asked for the same thing for everyone."

"The form gave them the okay for Tuesday's records," Liz replied.

"All of Tuesday?" I asked. She nodded. "Then that's probably what they requested from everyone."

Liz looked puzzled. "You sound disappointed."

"Assuming the person broke in after midnight on Monday night, it would have been Tuesday. If Carpenter's ex, Amanda, the Iacominis, or Josh had phone records implying they were downtown any time on Tuesday morning, the cops would have that information. You'd think that would have come up, as they would have wanted an explanation."

"Maybe they did and Knutsen just didn't tell us. You guys may be friends, but he doesn't tell you everything about an investigation."

"Knutsen was totally uninterested in my suggestion about a break-in at the house." I patted my hand against the wall. "If he knew that, say, Carpenter's ex was near this building at two o'clock in the morning on Tuesday, he would have been interested in my break-in theory. That tells me that none of the phone records they reviewed showed anyone being near the Larson Place early Tuesday morning except those who you'd expect. That would be Boston, Ambrose, and Katie."

"Let me guess. You're suggesting that, if your theory's correct, it had to be Katie?"

That was the direction it was going, but twenty-five years of marriage had taught me that, while honesty was important, so was tact. "I'm not sure what to think," I said. "Fortunately, we have a way we can determine if we should be concerned about Katie."

"What?" She leaned into her Miss Greece pose. "Should we just talk to her? Maybe she can prove she's innocent?"

I held a hand in front of her as if surrendering. "If it was Katie, the video will pick up her coming downstairs after midnight on Monday night. If not, the only possibility is she used a rope or a ladder to get in and out of her second-floor window. But she would have had to dispose of it as well as the screen, the lock, and the tools. If I'm her, I don't take the screen far. I might hide it in the shed. Or I might just leave it at the house and walk a few blocks to dispose of the other stuff. Just as likely, I'd dispose of them in the same spot. My guess is we'll be able to find the screen, since the killer won't think it's something anyone would look for."

"So, you want us to search for the screen?"

"Yes."

"If we find it along with a rope, then it doesn't look good for Katie."

I stepped closer, but didn't touch her since she was still in her Miss Greece pose. "Yes, but I don't think she did it. If we locate the screen but don't find a rope, it points away from her."

"Okay." She relaxed her pose. "Let's look for the screen."

Chapter 37

My goal was to search for the screen while keeping an eye out for the other items. A damaged screen, even if it had been broken down, was bulky and difficult to hide. Unless the person had a vehicle, they wouldn't take it a long distance. Katie had flown in from California and took a taxi to the B&B, so she had no vehicle.

I was unsure if the smart door locks recorded when a door opened from the inside. If not, the person who broke into the room could have easily accessed the entire third floor without fear of being detected. That included the bathroom and the hallway. And since the attic entrance was in a shared area, they could have accessed it as well.

The attic entrance was directly above the automatic vacuum cleaner. Standing on a chair, I reached for the scuttle hole and dust fluttered down, implying no one had been in the attic for months, if not years. I slid the cover back in the entryway and jumped off the chair.

The downstairs was next. Liz pointed out a camera that would pick up anyone going into the basement, so we ignored it and went outside. I reopened the shed and searched. After ten minutes, we were at the point of giving up. A fence sat on one side of the yard. Behind it was a commercial building that included a law office. Directly behind the backyard was a small apartment building and to the other side and across the driveway, another house.

The commercial building and apartments had dumpsters, but they also had cameras, and I suspected the killer was smart enough to stay away from them. The other option was the neighboring house. It was a run-down wooden structure, much like the Larson Place before it was renovated. But I didn't see any outside trash bins.

Looking across the driveway, I spotted the neighbor's shed. Going to the edge of the property, I peered at the latch. A padlock held it shut, so it wasn't an easy target. I could have picked it in minutes, but the last thing we needed was to get arrested for breaking into a neighbor's shed.

"Let's hang it up," Liz said with a glance at the B&B. "I'm tired from the walk and people will be back soon. Let's put the ladder away. Remember, they might not like the idea of us sticking our noses into this." Her voice turned to a whisper, and she stepped closer. "Especially the killer."

She was right. I compressed the ladder while it was on the ground and returned it to its spot inside the shed. Once the door was down and locked, Liz started for the house. There was, however, one other place I wanted to search.

"Before going inside, I want to check the route from here to the Capital City Trail," I said. My thought was that, if the person who broke in wasn't staying at the Larson Place, they could have come via bicycle. Though there were many ways to approach the house, the trail made sense.

She told me she was going inside, but I could finish the search on my own. Saying I would be back within ten minutes, I jogged to the front of the house and walked a block before turning onto the dead-end road which approached the railroad tracks.

The rail line ran parallel to the trail. The area around the tracks seemed a suitable spot to dump a screen, since brush and high grass dominated one side. I walked parallel to the tracks beside a short brick wall that appeared to be there to control erosion. I picked up a stick while I walked, which I used for peering beside and underneath bushes.

Going eastward, I poked into the bushes with my stick, spotting beer cans, paper bags, empty liquor bottles, and a syringe. People on the other side of the road, walking along the trail, looked suspiciously at me. A passenger in a passing car shook her head as she stared me down.

There was no sidewalk where I was searching and no foot traffic. Poking between bushes, I spotted something metallic. With the aid of my stick, I pulled the branches apart, revealing the edges of a window screen. The mesh had been pulled off, and the edges were twisted into a clump. Pulling the bushes back further, I spotted the mesh and pulled it out with the branch. A wide oval hole was cut into it.

"Holy shit!"

My initial giddiness didn't last. Instead, I started a more complete search. Not only was I looking for rope, but also for a bolt cutter, as the intruder would have needed something to cut through the Yale lock. If they had picked it rather than cutting it, they would have just used the same lock after they put the ladder back in the shed.

Several minutes later, I texted Liz so she would know why I was late. She replied, telling me that Ambrose and Boston had returned, but the others were still out. Her text said she told them I took my daughter shopping. She wrote, "Ha, ha!"

afterward. I smiled when I read it, since she knew I would never take my daughter shopping.

After a few more minutes, I gave up, deciding to let the police continue the search. Convincing them that a search was necessary would be the next challenge. I leaned against the rock wall and called Knutsen. He was at home, eating a late dinner with his wife. We talked, and I listened to him slurp spaghetti and curse when he got sauce on his shirt. Even when swearing, he sounded even-keeled.

He finally agreed to see the screen, and he wanted me to walk him through my idea tomorrow morning. His preference was for me to not touch anything, but to wait nearby until a City of Madison Police officer arrived. He said he would call and get back to me if there was a problem.

The sun had already set when an officer parked his cruiser on the dead-end road. I waited until he crossed the small path that led from the road to the tracks.

After pointing out the screen to the officer, I showed him a picture of its match from our room and texted it to him and Knutsen. I said I thought the suspect also had bolt cutters, a utility knife, a cut Yale lock, and possibly a rope.

The officer nodded as I spoke, but it was apparent that his intention was to collect the screen and get out of there. He had a large plastic wrap and, while wearing gloves, he pulled the bent frame out of the bushes and wrapped it. Then he stuck the mesh alongside it. I walked with him as he carried the package to his vehicle, sticking it inside the trunk. As I finished my statement, Knutsen called. He said he had talked to Bailey, and she wanted us to meet at her office at seven in the morning.

"It's your chance to convince us that this potential prior-night break-in is worth following up on," Knutsen said.

That wouldn't be difficult if, as I suspected, their investigation had ground to a halt. "Do you know anything about a bicycle lock some of your officers found along the shore near Turville Point?"

"No," he said after a pause. "How do you know about what my officers are doing when I don't?"

I laughed. "It's probably nothing. Liz and I ran into two officers, and I could see they had found a lock. I knew them from an earlier job, so they weren't afraid to talk to me."

"If we got prints off it and matched them with one of your group, I think I would have heard about it. Do you think it's important?"

"If there were no matches, then it might not do us any good. Any news from the autopsy?"

Knutsen laughed. "You really want to be a cop, don't you?"

"Nah. Anything crazy, like her being pregnant or drugged or something?"

"No." He paused. "Just between you and me, the preliminary report showed alcohol, as well as a small amount of cannabis, which wasn't a surprise since we found some in her room. Otherwise, it just confirmed that her throat was cut, leading her to bleed out in moments. It doesn't lead us anywhere new."

Which was why they were interested in my story.

Chapter 38

Returning to the Larson Place, I found Katie and Boston sitting in the front room by the fireplace. The window was open, and their hair lifted with each gust of wind. Both women had a glass of wine on the floor beside them and were holding e-readers. Katie looked up at me and volunteered that Liz had gone to bed. Heading up the stairs, I downloaded the B&B's security app and waited in the hallway for it to load. Once completed, I registered and held my phone to the door. The deadbolt clicked, and I pushed, but the door held tight.

"Is that you, Cy?" Liz called.

"Who else?"

"Just a second."

She had set the door jammer, and it took a full minute before she gave me the okay and I went inside. She was in shorts and a T-shirt, and auburn hair hung over her eyes. I told her about the police officer picking up the screen.

"Just got off the phone with Betty," she said.

"Any news?"

"Nothing startling, but a few interesting things. She was able to track Carpenter and Caleb Iacomini. Jenn Iacomini was more of a challenge since her maiden name is Anderson."

"What did she learn?"

She pulled out her phone. "Caleb is fifty-two. He's from Syracuse and attended school in New York where he studied journalism. During summers in college, he worked at a vineyard. After more than a decade in New York City, he worked for a magazine in Chicago while also being part-owner of a wine bar."

"Chicago, huh," I said. "This would have been when Carpenter was there?"

"Yes, though after eight years he moved to Milwaukee. A few years later, he met Jenn. Soon afterward, he purchased a share of Fierce Heart Winery, and they married. It only took a year before they had a controlling interest in the vineyard."

"Did Carpenter ever work for the same magazine as Caleb?"

"No. She has been in the wine industry since college. First, she sold wine for a distributor in Chicago, then worked as a sommelier while freelancing as a critic. Betty didn't find any direct connection between the two, but the geography is promising. It's likely that people in the industry would cross paths at some point."

"Yeah," I said, "but it's a sizeable area. It's not exactly a smoking gun."

"There is, however, one other interesting thing. Remember, I gave her Katie's and Missy's names as well? Betty did some searches on them. She couldn't find anything on Missy, except her writing. I had told her where she graduated from college, where she was from, and where I thought she lives. It's like she doesn't exist."

"What do you think that means?" I asked.

"Betty says Missy LeBrun definitely did not graduate from the University of Nevada-Las Vegas's Sommelier Academy."

I joined her on the bed. "What could that mean? Knutsen has interviewed her. Is she providing fake credentials or is she using a fake name?" The idea of her being in witness protection came to me, but it sounded too stupid to say out loud. "Perhaps I should just ask Knutsen. He has to know who she really is."

She nodded her agreement, and we talked for a few more minutes, recounting things Missy had said or done. Liz then started her own internet searches, pulling up multiple newspaper articles and reviews written by Missy.

"This is a waste of time," she said. "Why don't I go down and ask Boston and Katie? Boston collected my social security number, address, and everything and saw my driver's license and I-9. She has to have seen the same for Missy. I'll just tell her I have a friend who graduated from UNLV's Sommelier Academy around the same time as Missy or something like that. I can ask if she noticed exactly what year she graduated."

Liz asking questions made me nervous, but it would be good to know if Missy's background was real. If it wasn't, we needed to find out who she really was and if she had a motive for killing Carpenter. "Okay," I said. "Missy is probably in her room. I'll walk down to the second floor and keep watch. Don't do it if she's around."

She nodded, and we crept down the stairs, turning the light on at the second-floor landing. Liz continued down, and I sat on the step, watching for signs of movement from the four rooms. In the distance, I heard muttering, and soon Liz returned, waving me up the stairs.

"What's the word?" I whispered, as we went into our room and closed the door.

"I'm an idiot." She frowned. "It's a pen name. I should have thought of that."

"A pen name? Wine critics do that? What's her real name?"

"Missy Brown. She told Boston that she thought Missy LeBrun sounded more interesting."

A chuckle slipped out of my lips. "Suppose it does."

"Foolish of me not to think of it," Liz said, shaking her head. "I've not been in this game that long. I knew some critics used pen names, but I never met one who did."

"Okay then. The cops must have done background on her and the college students, but it appears that no motive has come up. Unless she was afraid that Carpenter would expose her true identity as Missy Brown."

We both laughed and eventually pulled out our phones. Liz sent Betty a text with Missy's updated information and we sat on the bed for half an hour, surfing the internet and playing games on the devices. At ten thirty, she announced it was time for bed. After a final bathroom visit, I did my nightly security routine, and she crawled under the covers, turning onto her side. Pulling in tight, I wrapped my left arm around her waist, resting my hand below her breasts.

"I'm going to meet with Knutsen and Bailey tomorrow." I paused as my nose pushed her hair away from her neck. "Seven o'clock at the sheriff's office building."

"So, they think you're onto something with the Monday night break-in?"

"I wouldn't go that far. They are probably stuck. Like we were saying, it's going to be difficult to prove who killed Carpenter. Too many people had the opportunity and too many have a motive, no matter how silly. And while we've been assuming it's someone she knows, there's always the chance it was one of her followers or some psycho who saw her online. Even though a number of us were in the vicinity, there's no evidence to hook anyone with the murder. It's going to be hard for them to close this out. The screen provides evidence, which suggests there's another option."

"At least they're willing to listen."

"That's about it."

"What if you convince them? Then what?"

"They should search video surveillance cameras for anywhere from ten at night on Monday to four in the morning on Tuesday. That won't make them happy, but it makes sense. They'll also take another look at the internal cameras. We think they already have the footage for both Monday and Tuesday. They'll just have to focus on the period when everyone should be asleep. The good thing is that, when reviewing external cameras, they'll be able to compare people and vehicles that show up on early Tuesday morning footage with those who show up on Tuesday just before and after the murder. It provides them with more data points."

Liz turned toward me. "Do you want me to come along when you meet with them?"

"Yes, if you don't mind. But it's okay if you choose to get some extra sleep instead."

"No, I'll go." I released my grip as she turned onto her back. She smiled and looked into my eyes, though I doubted she could even see me in the darkness. "This time, I'll be *your* plus one."

I stared into her brown eyes, then I kissed her lips and my hand slid along her hip. Her stomach felt warm, and I pulled her tight.

Chapter 39

We were ten minutes late for our seven o'clock appointment. A deputy met us at the entryway. Instead of bringing us to an interview room, he took us past numerous offices, leaving us in a room with a series of cubicles, one of which appeared to be Detective Bailey's. It was the first time I'd seen her since she had shown up at the front door on Wednesday morning.

Bailey called Knutsen before offering us coffee and water. She sat us in two spiny office chairs which barely fit within her space. Her cubicle walls were five feet high and empty except for a calendar and a framed award.

"Why don't we get started?" Bailey said. Her voice was even squeakier than I remembered. I decided she'd be a great voice actor since she could play an adolescent for years. "Detective Knutsen should be here momentarily and..." she pointed at Schuster, who was leaning against the cubicle. "There's Cam."

I walked the detectives through my theory about a Monday night or early Tuesday morning break-in. I talked about the lock, the screen, the ladder, and the tape residue. Knutsen soon joined the meeting, sporting a newly shaven head.

"The reason I'm entertaining this," Bailey said, "is we're dead in the water right now." She looked at Liz and then back at me. "Sorry, that was not an intentional pun."

We both nodded, and I motioned for her to continue.

"If your theory about a Monday night break-in is correct, forensics may come up with something on the window screen or in your room. Has anyone from your group besides you two been inside the room?"

I looked at Liz and said, "No. But on Monday night, when it was Carpenter's room, she may have been inside."

"The number of prints we'll have in the room will make things problematic. It's the nature of a hotel or a B&B room. Detective Schuster and some of our techs will spend the morning going through the video evidence. We already have footage from inside the B&B. Hopefully, we'll spot something of interest."

"I suggest you check out any cameras along the Capital City Trail, particularly those at the three hotels on John Nolen Drive. The ones across from the Alliant Energy Center." I glanced up at Knutsen. "The screen was left just off the railroad tracks that are across the road from the trail. If the killer wasn't a person on the boat, which is what I suspect, he or she went into the water at Turville Point and swam to the boat."

"It will take time to access private cameras," Bailey said. "We just went through an extensive process for Tuesday night, so we'll go back and ask for early Tuesday morning. We'll do it, but people will be pissed, so they may drag their feet."

"MB Security manages the cameras for two of the three hotels near Turville Point. I'm sure I could have it to you within the hour."

"Sure." Bailey looked at Knutsen. "Why not?"

"That would be great," he replied.

"If there was an earlier attempt," Bailey said, "it might allow us to focus on a smaller group of suspects. There were nine people in the water on Tuesday night and a handful of them have a motive to kill her, though some motives seem weak."

Liz leaned forward and raised a finger. "Do you know anything about Carpenter accusing someone in the wine industry of sexual harassment? We're wondering if that could hint at a motive."

Bailey locked eyes with Schuster.

"She filed a complaint about a dozen years ago against a male superior while working for some place called Central Wine Distributors," Schuster said. "We looked into it, and the man she complained about is now sixty-one, if I recall correctly. He lives in Sarasota, Florida. His wife verified he was in Florida on Tuesday."

"Darn," Liz said. "We thought that sexual harassment thing might explain why she had something against the Iacominis."

I jumped into an explanation of how Liz was perplexed by Carpenter's review of Fusion Rock. Liz nodded fervently as I spoke. The detectives didn't seem convinced, but Bailey asked Schuster to look further into any connections between Carpenter and the owners of Fierce Heart Winery.

Knutsen cleared his throat and raised his hand. "Before doing that, I should tell you that, when I interviewed Jennifer Iacomini, she shared a story about having words with Carpenter last fall."

"Words?" Bailey said. "Tell me more."

"There was a grape stomping festival at their winery. They regularly invite wine critics and Carpenter showed. It seems

Jenn thought Carpenter was flirting with Caleb. This led to a minor altercation."

"Why hadn't I heard about this?" Bailey asked, eyeing Schuster.

"It's also in Caleb's statement," Schuster said. "I didn't see it as particularly damning, so my report didn't highlight it."

Knutsen nodded. "That was my read as well. Caleb said his wife had had too much to drink that day. He thought she over-reacted. While Josh wasn't present at the altercation, Cam talked to him about it. He said Carpenter was a touchy person. He said many people viewed it as flirting, but he says it's how she was and it meant nothing."

"Okay," Bailey said. "Still, it's good to know about. It could be important."

"I'll follow up with the three of them," Schuster said.

"Good," Bailey replied. "But I'd like to be the one who speaks with Josh. He's the one I worry most about. That's what makes me disinclined to consider Mr. Bartholomew's break-in theory. It would exclude Josh, since he had landed in Madison on Tuesday morning. We verified that his plane disembarked shortly after four a.m. It seems unlikely that he could have gotten to the Larson Place before dawn."

"You view Josh as the primary suspect?" It was not a surprise, but I wanted to hear her argument. "What do you see as his motive? It seems to me he loved Carpenter. Why would he want to kill her?"

"Love and hate are emotions that sometimes cross." Bailey exchanged glances with her colleagues. "The nature of this murder, killing someone by slicing their throat." Her voice cracked, and she swallowed. "It betrays emotions toward

Miss Dalbesio. Deep, passionate emotions. Did you know Carpenter had recently ended the affair with Josh?"

"Yes." I looked at Liz and then back at Bailey. "Josh said she was pressuring him to divorce. He implied, however, that the relationship with Carpenter would continue. Apparently, he had filed for separation from his wife. Filing for divorce was the next step."

Bailey pointed a pencil at me. "That's what he says, but we don't know what Ms. Dalbesio was thinking. Only three people appear to have known that Josh and Carpenter were having problems. First, there is Carpenter's ex-husband, Leonardo. He claims she told him she was ending the relationship. Second, we have Ambrose Houser, who says Carpenter told him she was," she made air quotes, "pausing the relationship. Finally, there's Josh. His wife says she didn't know about the claims, so she can't clarify anything."

"You believe Leonardo over Josh?" I asked.

"I don't know who to believe." She raised her eyebrows. "Do you know who Carpenter spent Sunday night with?"

"No idea."

"Leonardo Dalbesio."

"Seriously?" I said.

"Yes." She tapped the pencil against her desk. "Carpenter drove to Madison on Sunday with their daughter, Maddie. Leonardo arrived on Sunday, and they took her sightseeing. Leonardo claims they shared a room but slept in separate beds. This is consistent with the daughter who says she slept with her mother in one bed, while her father was in the other."

"So, they took their daughter sightseeing and after staying the night, he drove the daughter back to Chicago?"

"That's the gist of it. It implies that the fracture in Josh and Carpenter's relationship might have been more significant than he claims."

We sat silently for a few moments, and I tried to decide whether Josh could have been lying this whole time.

"How about his wife, Amanda," Liz said. "Couldn't the same sort of emotions apply to the jilted wife? Doesn't she have as good a motive as Josh?"

"Maybe," Bailey said. "But you'd think those emotions would go more to the husband who is cheating on her than to his mistress. I still say that the nature of the killing lines up most closely with a jilted lover such as Josh. The view we have is that Josh and Amanda had drifted apart. They claim to still care for each other, but they are no longer intimate. They were both having affairs. I can't see her killing his mistress in a fit of passion."

"How else would you kill someone in that situation?" I paused, expecting an answer, but everyone stared at me, so I continued. "Remember, I was on the boat. To have killed her without being seen or heard, the killer had to do it when Carpenter was isolated. He or she had to make it quick. I'm no expert, but I don't think strangulation would be fast enough, especially since she was wearing a lifejacket. There would have at least been splashing."

"What are you suggesting?" Bailey asked.

"It might not have been a killing of passion. Slicing the throat might have been necessary to make it quick and to avoid being seen. Also, let's not forget about the bicycle lock. That might end up being important."

"What bicycle lock?" Bailey asked.

"MPD found one at the shore near Turville Point," I replied. "It's a Sportneer U Lock."

"Why does that matter?"

"It's not the most common brand," I said, "and it's not a combination lock, like most bicycle locks. If someone in our suspect group has a Sportneer key, there's a good chance it relates to that lock."

"You're suggesting someone inadvertently left the lock there?"

I nodded.

"If that's the case, wouldn't they get rid of the key? Why keep it if it could incriminate them?"

"They probably did," I replied, "but most key bicycle locks are sold with two or three keys. Those extra keys tend to end up in a junk drawer. People often forget about them."

"Why would they bring an extra key to the B&B?"

"Guess I wasn't thinking of the B&B." I looked at the off-white floor, then looked Bailey in the eye. "I was thinking of searching a different house."

"Cy, you think you know who the killer is, don't you?" Knutsen said.

"Yeah." I glanced at Liz and then at Knutsen. "I think I know who the killer is."

Chapter 40

I expected Bailey to tell me about how I should leave murder investigations to the professionals, but she and the other detectives let me talk. It was good to be listened to, but it was as if they thought I would spill out a fully developed theory which would solve the murder of Carpenter Dalbesio and provide enough evidence to put the killer away. While I didn't have a complete theory, I had a sense of the people I had met over the past few days and an idea of what may have happened.

"The killer was in Madison on Monday and Tuesday night. That excludes Josh. And Ambrose and Boston could access the third-floor window without using a ladder, so I don't think they were involved. Also, the killer had to know which room Carpenter was assigned. And they had to know ahead of time."

"Sure," Bailey muttered.

"Josh knew what room she would be in. He told me so. I can't see her sharing that information with our other suspects, except perhaps her ex-husband. Liz and I certainly didn't know which room anyone else was in until we arrived."

The detectives exchanged glances. "We examined her phone," Bailey said. "You're right that she told Josh which room she was assigned. It was a text back in June. He replied and provided his room number. I'm not aware of her sharing her room assignment with anyone else," Bailey said. "It doesn't mean she didn't tell someone verbally."

"We can't know for sure, but there's no reason at this point to believe that Katie, the Iacominis, Missy, or the students knew which room Carpenter would be in."

"That leaves Josh and the ex," Knutsen said. "But you're saying it couldn't have been Josh? Does that mean you're accusing Leonardo Dalbesio?"

"You're forgetting Amanda Peterson," I replied.

"Josh's wife?" Bailey said, pointing the pencil at me again.

I nodded. "Is it hard for someone to get a look at their spouse's phone? I don't think so. Liz and I, for instance, know each other's passwords. She can get into mine if she needs to, and vice versa."

"Okay." Bailey nodded her head. "Go on."

"Carpenter was having an affair with Amanda's husband. She's a US Marine and would have had the strength to deploy a twenty-four-foot ladder on her own. Someone mentioned that she usually goes on the swim outings that accompany Ambrose's wine tastings, so she must be able to swim. She could have swum from the shore to the boat and killed Carpenter. My guess is Amanda intended to kill her on Monday night. She had scouted the Larson Place for Ambrose and was familiar with the house. Josh and Amanda had checked out the house a few weeks earlier before the tasting as well. At that point, she could have installed a recording device in the room."

"Why bug the room?" Bailey asked. "If someone wanted to kill Carpenter in her room at the Larson Place, it would be good to know she went to bed. But if it were me, I'd put a camera outside the room."

I cleared my throat to buy time to organize my thoughts. "She wanted to know not only when Carpenter was in the room, but when she was asleep. Also, she knew she could remove the device after killing her. If she had hidden a camera in a common area, she wouldn't have been able to retrieve it without going into the hall. If she left a camera in the hallway, your lot would find it."

Bailey tried to comment, but her voice creaked. She coughed before continuing. "In your theory, how was she going to kill Carpenter on Monday night? Was she going to cut her throat?"

"Don't know. Maybe she would just suffocate her, since that would be the easiest and most efficient. Or perhaps she was going to make it look like a robbery. But her plan fell apart when Carpenter moved from her third-floor room to a second-floor room."

"You're saying she cut the screen to get in," Knutsen said. "How about the window? Was she just assuming it would be unlocked?"

"The room is hot and stuffy. I can tell you, since I've been there the last few nights. Both windows were unlocked when Liz and I showed up, and the one with the screen was open. My guess is the owners leave it open during the summer so it doesn't get stifling. There wasn't a guarantee, but Amanda probably assumed it would be unlocked if not open."

"Okay," Knutsen said. "Why break in if Carpenter wasn't in the room?"

"The room faces the back of the house, and it's pitch dark. She knew the light was off and no noise was coming from inside. Perhaps she broke in and was surprised to find the room empty. Either that, or she knew it was empty, but wanted to remove the listening device. She didn't know what room Carpenter had moved to, but even if she did, it faces the road and it's not easily accessible without being seen."

"How about Tuesday night?" Bailey put down the pen, pulled out lip gloss, and rolled it along her lower lip. It made her seem disinterested, but I suspected it was an act. "Do you think she winged the killing on the lake?"

"More likely, it was her backup plan. Either that or she already had a tracker and everything she needed to get onto the lake. Since the first attempt didn't work, she put the tracker on the *Eloquence* and snorkeled or swam out to the boat. Before killing her, she took the tracker off and dropped it into the lake." I patted Liz's thigh. "That is the noise my wife heard."

Bailey's lips pushed together as she dropped the gloss into her purse. "You're suggesting she cut Carpenter's throat and then just swam ashore?"

"Suppose so. Detective Knutsen said he thought Turville Point and Olbrich Park were the best launch points to enter and exit the lake without being seen or caught on camera. I figure it was Turville Point, since it's nearer to Amanda's house and where Josh's boat docks. She probably cut Carpenter's throat, pulled her under, and unclasped the lifejacket. She swam underwater to the other side of the boat, leaving the jacket, then headed for shore."

Bailey looked up at the other detectives before locking eyes with me. "Keep in mind that a witness saw her just after sunset. Also, her cell phone was at her house all evening, as was her car."

"What exactly did this witness see?" I asked.

Knutsen cleared his throat before responding. "It was a Mrs. McPherson. She is a widow who lives across the street. Says she saw Amanda's silhouette moving inside the house."

"Sounds weak," I muttered.

"Maybe," Knutsen replied. "But it's persuasive when combined with the car and the cell phone records."

"Couldn't she have left the phone at home and biked to the lake?" I asked.

Knutsen rolled his eyes, but didn't respond.

"What's her motive?" Bailey asked. "Both she and Josh paint a picture of a marriage that has cooled into a friendship. Why kill Carpenter? Does she hate her that much?"

"I don't think this was about hate or jealousy. I think greed was the motive."

"Greed?" Liz said, almost to herself.

"Have you heard about Josh's mother?" I asked. "She's loaded and is extremely ill. Josh had been visiting her in Nantucket."

"Yes." Bailey's voice sounded impatient and even more child-like. "And?"

"Josh had already filed for a separation and was working with a lawyer. He was going to divorce Amanda and marry Carpenter. How would the mother's death have impacted things if it happened before the divorce finalized?" Liz and the three detectives gave me a blank stare. "There was no pre-nuptial agreement. If the mother died before they divorced, Josh would suddenly be flush with cash. Amanda would get her share in any divorce. But if they divorced before the mother's death, she only splits their house and some minor savings. She doesn't get any of the inheritance."

"Cy," Liz said after a long pause. "Inheritances flow outside marriage." I gave her a confused look, so she continued. "If Josh inherited a million or even ten million dollars from his mother, it would be separate property and need not be divided during a divorce, so long as he kept it in his name and didn't combine it with Amanda's money."

"Really?" I sounded as deflated as I felt.

"Yes, really," Knutsen said. "Also, there's a fundamental problem with your theory about Amanda leaving her home. Even if you want to argue that the witness was incorrect, there's still her phone. The problem is that it moved during the evening. I don't recall the details, but it moved within the house shortly before eight, and then again at nine, which is consistent with her statement. Phones don't move on their own."

I remembered him mentioning this, but details were fuzzy, and my mind was still struggling with Liz's explanation of how inheritances worked in a divorce. "Where did Amanda go that night?"

"Nowhere," Bailey said. "She was just moving around in the house. She said she was reading, and all she did was go to the bathroom a few times before finally going to bed."

My gaze jumped between the three detectives. "Cell phones track movement within a house?"

"Sometimes." Bailey giggled. "It's amazing what phones can tell us. They tell us whether they were on or off. If on, we can almost always identify the device's location within a few hundred yards. It can get much more precise depending on what apps are loaded and how the phone's settings are managed. Sometimes, they tell us if the phone moved just a few meters and exactly when. They tell us when they use Wi-Fi.

It can be exceedingly useful. Leonardo Dalbesio is in a similar situation. His phone was at his home on Tuesday night, but we can see he moved around within his apartment. The only difference is that he wasn't alone, as his girlfriend was with him."

"Amanda was having an affair, right?" I asked. "Could this guy have been at her house, moving her phone?"

"Nope," Bailey replied. "He was at a conference in Chicago. We verified that."

Everyone was staring at me. I wanted to argue, but I could see it was useless.

Knutsen patted my shoulder. "Cy, you may be onto something about Monday night, but it's probably not Amanda unless there was someone else involved with her in committing the murder. We certainly will review footage from late Monday and early Tuesday. Maybe we will come up with something."

"If we end up sold on your break-in theory," Bailey said, "it might force us to focus more on Leonardo Dalbesio's alibi. It's possible his girlfriend lied. He may have left his phone at their apartment and she moved it around a few times. It might explain things. We'd also re-interview the woman who saw Amanda that night."

"Guess you're not going to search Amanda's house for the Sportneer key?" I asked.

"We don't have probable cause to request a warrant," Bailey replied. "Not even close."

I wanted to get out of there. The motive I had settled on had disappeared and, as Knutsen said, phones don't move on their own. I cleared my throat again, but the second delay didn't bring in a new argument. "Let me re-think things."

"Don't worry about re-thinking anything." Bailey turned to her computer, which had gone black. "That's our job. We'll be following up on your idea about a Tuesday morning break-in. There is a good chance we will search the shed, your room, and the rooftop. The owners already gave us permission to search the shed, and you can allow us to search your room. Hopefully, the owners will give us permission to search the property. If not, or if we have trouble getting a response from them, we'll request a search warrant. Unless something goes wrong, we'll be over yet this morning."

I checked the time on my phone and thought about how their arrival would end the day's tasting. As I understood, the last two sessions were set for nine and eleven. We'd finish at twelve-thirty and would have to be out of the building by two in the afternoon. It was hard to know what the police search would do to the timeline.

"If you do search based on my theory," I said. "Any chance you could let at least the first testing happen before you bust in?" I explained the timeline.

"Sure, we'll wait until after your first session." Bailey chuckled and shook her head. "I don't really care about timing, so long as we arrive before everyone leaves." She looked at Knutsen, who nodded his agreement, and then at Schuster. "Okay. If we decide to search the B&B, we'll show up after ten thirty, but before you leave at two. Does that make sense?"

Liz and I nodded before making our way out of the office.

Chapter 41

The police were acting on my theory about someone breaking into the B&B. They took my ideas seriously and were considering them in their investigation. I should have felt that I'd done all I could to find out what happened to Carpenter. But I didn't. Instead, I felt foolish.

"Why didn't you tell me about your inheritance idea?" Liz asked as we walked outside. "I would have told you it was wrong, and you wouldn't have had to embarrass yourself."

"The idea just kind of came to me. It seemed like a good argument. It was just..."

"Wrong." Liz patted my hand. "Don't worry about it, Hun. And thanks for talking them into letting us finish today's first flight. Tasting will be tough, though. Every breath you take reminds me of the spicy chicken sandwich you had last night. I should have told you to get a plain one."

I paused at the intersection, my right hand holding her tight. It was something I had grown used to doing, even though it wasn't necessary in the daylight. "I know this is important to you. Who knows how Ambrose would manage things if he had to cancel two sessions?"

"If we don't get to the last one, he can probably add a session to the Nebraska event," she said. "Either that, or Boston can come up with a different place to do it. The only issue will be Katie, since she flies out today."

The Larson Place looked as it did on the day we showed up for the first tasting. Once the outer door clicked, we stepped inside. Ambrose waved as he crossed the foyer and headed into the kitchen. We went upstairs and relaxed in our room for a few minutes before joining a group in the kitchen.

Bagels and donuts were available again, but this time, there was no sparkling wine. As I finished my second plain bagel, the doorbell rang. Liz and I exchanged glances. Then I made my way to the door, fully expecting that our police detectives had changed their minds and had come early.

Instead, I found Caleb and Jenn Iacomini standing on the porch, smiling. Caleb was holding a bottle of liquor in one hand. He asked to see Liz, and he stood nervously, as if he were picking her up for a date. I backed up and motioned for them to come inside. It seemed like a bad idea to allow two more prime suspects into the house, but what else could I do?

The couple followed me down the hallway and into the kitchen. They shook hands with Boston and Ambrose and waved to the rest. Liz was leaning against the oven, so I pulled her over. When she recognized Caleb, a smile slid onto her face, and they shook hands. It was her natural smile. I realized he had promised to bring her a bottle of Fierce Heart's reserve bourbon. She faced the event room and held the bottle high, evaluating the color.

He glanced at his wife. "We weren't sure whether we should bring it, considering all that's happened. But we have a meeting in town with our insurance agent, so we decided to drop by."

Liz nodded and thanked him. "I'm looking forward to trying it."

Caleb examined the bagels and the donuts, but didn't grab one. Ambrose commented on the bottle's design, so I tapped Jenn's shoulder and motioned for her to step aside.

"Yes," she said. I don't think she knew my name.

"Question for you." I steered her away from the event room. "We were talking about this review that Carpenter had of one of your wines. Fusion Rock, I think it's called."

Jenn's eyes widened, and she seemed to fall backward as she backed away. "Not that again."

"My wife and I don't get it. What did Carpenter have against you guys?"

She peered around me, then retreated through the hallway and into the fireplace room, her heels clicking with each step. "That's my fault," she whispered.

"Your fault?" I leaned down, so we were eye-to-eye. "What do you mean?"

"Carpenter visited the winery last September, I think. Yes, it was during our grape stomping festival. Anyway, Caleb gave her two bottles of Fusion Rock so she could review it. She and I, however, had a spat. I hate to speak ill of the dead, but Carpenter was a flirt, and she was giving Caleb more attention than I liked. Silly, I know, but anyway, I let her have it. After calming down, I apologized. It was still daytime, so we sat outside, and she was good about it, explaining how she realized she was sometimes too handsy with people. In the end, we opened one of the two bottles of Fusion Rock and shared a few glasses before she took an Uber back to Madison."

"That doesn't sound like a big deal."

"It wasn't. But it meant that she only had one bottle for tasting. Apparently, when she opened it a month or two later, it had cork taint." Her eyebrows shot up, and she nodded as if she expected me to know what cork taint was.

"That's why the wine graded poorly?" I asked. "It had cork taint?"

"Not quite." She let out a large breath, as if trying to calm herself. "Carpenter would not grade a tainted bottle, so she called and requested a replacement. Caleb was traveling, and we were out of Fusion Rock at the winery, which was unusual. We were scheduled to bottle in a few days, but I was in town, so I bought one at a nearby grocery store, boxed it up and sent it to her. You see, Caleb is the one who handles this type of thing and, though I should have known better, I wanted to help. I thought it would be fine to get a bottle from a store. Normally, I would have just had Caleb handle it, but I didn't want to bring up the argument I had with Carpenter again."

"It was a sore spot?" I didn't know where this story was going.

"Yes, so I took care of it myself and forgot about it until Carpenter's review came out. Caleb was furious. A few days later, he called her, and found out the bottle she had tasted had not been hand delivered by him but had been shipped from a grocery store." Jenn wiped a tear from her eye. "It was the ultimate faux pas. It's not the way wineries provide wine to critics. I should have known that, but somehow, I didn't."

"The shipping made the wine go bad?"

"Liquor stores and grocery stores are inconsistent in how they treat wine. Some will leave them standing next to a window where they get sunlight and everything. This can have a negative impact. Something about the bottle was off."

"Caleb assumed Carpenter got a bad bottle?" I suggested. "That's the gist of it?"

"Yes. He said for all we know it may have been sitting on a shelf in the sunlight for five years. Fortunately, Carpenter agreed to re-test. She did so last week, and Fusion Rock came in at a respectable eighty-nine. She included it on her website with a note that she would do a vlog illustrating the importance of proper shipping and storage of wine. Caleb was thankful, as was I, since I felt so bad about the rating. It's a pisser she never got to the vlog, but at least she published the revised rating."

Caleb was calling Jenn's name, so she joined him in the kitchen. A few minutes later, the couple wished everyone good luck and headed toward the front door. I followed them out.

Sitting on the porch, I searched for Carpenter's website. While her vlog was down, her wine ratings were still available. I located the eighty-nine rating for Fusion Rock. The review ended with a comment about the earlier rating of seventy-two and the promise of an upcoming vlog on why the change occurred. It was just as Jenn had claimed.

It seemed our suspect pool's motives were getting weaker rather than stronger.

Chapter 42

A flight of sparkling wines comprised the morning session. It went smoothly, and the light was good, so Liz didn't struggle with identifying colors or noting viscosity. When Boston summarized ratings, there were few disagreements, and the discussion lacked the vigor of earlier sessions. My sense was that the weight of the week's events had overwhelmed the group. Everyone was ready to go home and move past the event.

When we finished, I meandered to the front room, peering out the window while Liz helped clean. I expected the police to arrive at any moment, though I didn't know if they would come on foot or in a high-tech van filled with forensic equipment and testing materials.

After a few minutes, I leaned against the wall, pulled out my phone, and played solitaire. As I lost, someone came up beside me. It was Josh.

"Who you waiting for?" he asked.

"No one," I lied. "Just watching traffic. How about yourself?"

"Amanda. She just went to get the SUV."

I was surprised since I hadn't seen her leave. "Doesn't she have to clean?"

"Boston let her leave for a few minutes so she can bring up our SUV. She'll be back to help prep for the last session. They mostly need her for pre-work. Decanting, labeling, organizing, and stuff like that."

"How are you doing?" I asked, looking out the window.

"About the same. They say time heals all wounds." He let out a spatter of a laugh. "Let's hope that's true. Not only do I have Carpenter to think about, but there's also my mom."

"How is your mother? I hear she's sick."

He nodded and took a few moments before replying. "The doctor thinks three months to a year, which is better than we had expected. My bigger concern is making these last months bearable for her. She's in considerable pain."

"That's too bad. Sorry. Is that why you're unsure whether you'll be able to attend the rest of Ambrose's tastings?"

He tucked his hands into his armpits and stared out the window. "Now that I'm moving back to Nantucket, I'm less concerned. I'm going to stay at the house where I grew up." He glanced at me. "It's just as well, since Amanda and I could use some space from each other."

"Are you still going to file for divorce? Or does Carpenter's passing change things?"

"I don't know. I might give it one more chance. Before, it was a done deal since I was in love with Carpenter. Geez, I was going to propose to her as soon as the divorce was complete. Now, things are different. It's not as if she's really done anything wrong."

"Amanda, you mean?" Perhaps he didn't know about her affairs.

He nodded. "Being physically separated for a few months might bring something back to our relationship, and maybe it will help her. She used to be such an independent person. When we first met, she didn't need anyone. She was the toughest and most self-assured woman. Now, for some reason, she needs me. Needs my friendship. Maybe living separately will bring back her independent streak, or maybe it will bring back a spark in our relationship. Or maybe it will make it easier when...if we divorce."

"What does your mother think about all this? Has it been tough on her?"

"Mom's not a hundred percent there mentally. She knew we had issues, but I've put off telling her we're separating. If I do file for divorce, though, I will have to tell her. It will be hard. Amanda, you see, gets along better with my mom than I do. While my dad came from money, my mom didn't. I think she sees herself in Amanda, which makes her protective. My biggest concern was always that Amanda would tell Mom about Carpenter. Now I'll likely have to tell her myself."

"Your mother's health," I said. "Does that impact anything with the divorce or its timing?"

He gave me a look, as if the question crossed a line. "Of course not."

"Sorry if the question was inappropriate."

He sighed. "I understand why you're asking. The police also asked, and I told them the truth." His voice trailed off, and he pulled out his phone. "That reminds me. I should check. I'm waiting for information from my Mom's..." He stepped away and leaned against the fireplace.

Glancing out the window, I spotted a police vehicle, but it drove past aimlessly. When I looked up, Josh was shaking his head and his face was white, as if the blood had been drawn out.

"What is it?" I asked. "Is something wrong?"

"No, no," he said, talking more to his phone than to me. "Sorry." He turned his attention to me. "I had asked my lawyer to verify how I understood something about my mom."

"Did something happen to her? Is she okay?"

"Yes, it's not about her health. It's legal stuff. Things about her..." He paused, as if struggling to decide how or whether he should talk to me about the thing which had obviously upset him. "It's about her estate, you see. Kind of what you asked."

I nodded, as if I knew exactly what he was referring to.

"The police wanted to know about her will, which I thought I knew enough about to tell them. I also contacted her lawyer to verify my understanding of it. He just got back to me, and there is a surprise."

"A surprise?"

"I told the detectives that I'm the sole beneficiary of my mom's estate." He stepped closer, and his voice dropped to a whisper. "I may need to talk to the police again as it's more complicated than I thought."

"You can tell me if you like. I'll keep it between us."

There was a long pause. "Maybe talking about it is a good idea," he said. "I don't want anyone to think I lied."

"What is this *complication*?"

"I am the sole beneficiary of her estate, but there's also a trust my mom and her lawyer created, which I knew about but obviously didn't understand. It seems Mom's investment accounts transfer on death to the trust. I will receive eighty percent of the trust, but my wife receives twenty percent. If we were divorced, the entire amount goes to me. But if we're still married when Mom dies, Amanda gets twenty percent."

"Twenty percent?" The wheels in my head spun. That could be a significant amount to a teacher's assistant and reservist who grew up poor. "You're saying this twenty percent goes directly to her if you're still married when your mother dies? Twenty percent of what? A thousand dollars? A million dollars?"

He shook his head slowly. "I suppose the investments are in the ten-million-dollar range. She would get twenty percent of that."

"Wow," I said.

"I know what you're thinking," he said. "I was thinking the same thing. But Amanda doesn't know about the trust. I knew about it, but I guess I didn't understand it. I certainly don't intend to tell her about it. Also, it's only the investment accounts. It doesn't include real estate, art, cars, or boats. That's maybe half of her assets."

"You're sure Amanda doesn't know?"

"I don't think she does." He bit his lip, and his eyes looked upward. "About a year ago, my mom and her lawyer gave me a briefing on her estate plan. The lawyer went through the will, the trust, her investments, bank accounts, and real estate. A lot of stuff transfers on death to keep it outside probate, but it's a bunch of legal stuff. He also sent me an email with the details, but I guess I didn't really understand things. Either way, he instructed me to tell no one else, saying it was only between him, my mom, and me."

"There's no way she could have found out? Might your mom have told her, or could she be reading your emails?"

"Anything, I suppose, is possible." He rubbed his eyes. "You see, the last time we were there, Mom was declining." The pace of his words slowed. "Amanda sat with her several times, including when I met with the lawyer. It's possible Mom said something, even though her lawyer instructed her not to."

"If the police find out, they will undoubtedly have more questions for her."

He looked at me, and I could see confusion or fear in his eyes. "Even if she found out somehow, it couldn't have been her. She was at home when...when things happened. Detective Bailey said it's cut and dry. She couldn't have done it." He forced out a laugh, but it was more of a cry.

"I heard there was a neighbor who saw her sometime shortly after sunset. A Mrs. Mc...something."

"Mrs. McPherson." He snorted. "I wouldn't put too much weight on anything she said. Either way, it's the other stuff. Amanda's phone, for instance. Bailey says she was at home. She had to be."

"Why wouldn't you trust what Mrs. McPherson said? Do you think she would lie?"

"No, she wouldn't lie. It's just that her eyesight is far from twenty-twenty. Once, I took out the trash wearing only khaki shorts, and she thought I was naked. Maybe she saw something. It's possible, I guess. That's why they remain focused on me as their number one suspect."

"This is all past my pay grade," I said, shaking my head. "But one thing I know is that you didn't kill Carpenter." The words came out without thought, as I was still wrapping my head around the motive Josh had just shared. "You couldn't have."

Josh's mouth was open as if he was about to reply, but he paused, wiped his eyes, and pointed out the window. "Speaking of Amanda, here she is."

A black SUV pulled into the driveway. My first thought was that she would have to move her vehicle when the police arrived. Then I looked back at the velvet chair, the fireplace, and the vacuum cleaner inside the house.

Suddenly, I knew everything.

Chapter 43

Knowing what happened doesn't mean everything immediately made sense. But I now knew who had murdered Carpenter. I knew how she was killed, and I knew why.

I remembered the keys Josh had handed me as I backed up his boat. "Do you and Amanda own bikes?" I asked.

"Bikes? Sure. We are big bikers. Why?"

I had wanted to ask him this question earlier, but had hesitated, thinking there could still be a chance that he planted both the tape on the boat and the bicycle lock. "Do you own bike locks?"

"Sure."

"Is one of them a Sportneer U Lock?"

He took a moment before responding. "One's a combo lock, and one's got a key. The keyed one is shaped like a U, or maybe a racetrack, but I don't remember the brand."

"Where do you keep the keys?"

"Cy, what's this about?"

"It's just an idea I got about the murder," I mumbled. "Me being a locksmith and all means it involves locks."

He let out a slight chuckle. "Amanda and I each have a key. If there's an extra, it's probably in our desk drawer."

Before I could ask another question, he pulled his keys from his pant pockets. They were the same keys I had seen when backing his truck into the Yahara River. One with a square frame caught my attention. I recognized it as the style of key Sportneer used. "I bet that's the bike lock key," I said.

He nodded, then stared at me for a moment before sticking the keys into his pocket and walking toward the foyer. The front door swung open, and I heard Amanda's voice. She still wore her black and white uniform but had added a Milwaukee Brewers baseball cap. I imagined a knife in her hand, and I saw her killing Carpenter Dalbesio. Boston waved, and the Petersons walked down the hallway toward the kitchen. I followed, spotting Liz at the table.

"Five minutes," Boston called out. "Remember, we've got a lot of cleaning to do afterward, and we need to be out by two, so everyone be ready to help when we are done tasting."

Amanda tossed her cap onto the counter and joined Boston. Renee set a flight of glasses at our table while Liz wiped the counter. I rushed forward and put a hand on my wife's shoulder.

She twisted toward me, wide-eyed. "Jesus, Cy! You scared me to death."

Grabbing both her shoulders, I leaned so close that our noses touched. "I know Amanda did it. And I know how and why. I am sure."

"She did what?" Her eyes widened. "Oh, that."

I let go of her, then took her hand and pulled her through the kitchen and into the hallway. Letting go, she followed me into the front room. No one was in sight, but I listened for footsteps coming from the kitchen.

"Josh says his mother's investments go to a trust, of which twenty percent goes to his wife. I guess this doesn't go through probate, so though he is the sole beneficiary of the will, Amanda will own twenty percent of the trust provided they are married when his mother passes. He doesn't think Amanda knows about it but admits he could be wrong."

Her voice was little more than a whisper. "How much are her investments?"

"He estimated ten million dollars. Twenty percent of that..."

"Is two million dollars."

I nodded and pulled her toward the fireplace. "Josh and Amanda own a Sportneer U Lock. Josh has a key."

"Is that the brand of the one the police found along the shore?"

"Yes, Sportneer is a common bike lock brand, but not nearly as common as Master Lock or several others. What are the odds that they own one?"

"Interesting," she whispered.

"The other thing you'll bring up is her alibi. Josh mentioned that the woman who saw her that night has awful eyesight. He doesn't put a lot of faith in her testimony, but was swayed by the other part of it. Remember, Knutsen said her phone and car were home early Tuesday morning and Tuesday evening? The cops say her phone moved within the house that evening, so they infer she had to be there because..."

"Because phones don't move on their own."

"Right." I pointed at the robotic vacuum, which sat silently beside the fireplace. "Suppose she taped the phone to one of those at her house? Maybe it's programmable, so she could have it run at certain times?"

She stared at the vacuum. "It would look like the person was walking around in the house."

"Yes. Don't newer vacuums allow for programming like that?"

"Ours does, though I've never used it." She put an arm around my shoulder. "They also have a memory; meaning, if it wasn't destroyed, Knutsen could probably determine exactly when it ran."

I thought about our vacuum. Liz had an app on her phone that controlled it. "Is the memory in the phone app or the vacuum itself?"

Lifting her glasses, she rubbed the base of her nose. "When I got rid of my parent's automatic vacuum, I not only had to delete the app from my dad's phone, but the manual suggested that, for data security purposes, I do a factory reset. That wouldn't be necessary unless there's a memory in the vacuum itself."

I kissed her on the lips as a sense of relief came over me. Not only did I know who killed Carpenter, but I might be able to prove it. "The cops already have her phone's GPS data. My guess is that the times when the vacuum ran on Tuesday morning and Tuesday evening will align perfectly with the times when her phone moved within the house."

"Holy cow." She laughed and her head shook. "That might work, assuming they have a vacuum or there's a record of her buying one. And it has a memory."

Liz had a good point. I had assumed Amanda used her own vacuum, but she could have bought one with cash and disposed of it after the murder. Before I could get out another thought, Ambrose's booming baritone interrupted, and Liz stepped into the hallway. I pulled out my phone and texted

Knutsen, telling him I thought Josh had the key to the lock they had found near Turville Point.

Ambrose called my name, so I knew they were waiting for me. I stuck my phone in my pocket and rushed into the event room.

Sitting at our table, my mind raced. I imagined scenarios and considered how we could present our argument to the police. As I told Liz that the first two entries were deep pink, it occurred to me that the best approach might be to start with Josh's key. If it opened the lock, it would make my argument easier. I could suggest that Knutsen and Bailey dig into the automatic vacuum. They could determine if Amanda had recently purchased one and ask Josh if they already owned one. They might even have enough information to get a search warrant.

If the key didn't work, it might be a hard sell, but I thought about Josh and about how he had spoken of his own suspicions. Perhaps it would be easier to convince him than the police.

After finishing the color grades, I had nothing to do but wait and watch my wife spit into her red cup. The good news was that it was the last flight of the event and, despite having ten entries to judge, everyone moved fast. The bad news was that the clock seemed to have slowed. Staring forward, I saw Amanda leaning against the counter. Her phone was in front of her, and I wondered what she was doing. Was she playing a game? Researching? Checking emails? What does someone do when they think they've gotten away with murder?

Ambrose's last speech was poignant and surprisingly short. Boston, Amanda, and Renee passed out extra glasses for everyone. It included red wine which, according to Ambrose, was the entry Carpenter gave the highest grade during her one day of tasting. The servers poured for themselves and even for me. As I held up the medium ruby liquid, I saw Amanda standing next to Josh, holding her own glass. I wanted to throw the wine in her face, but it would be a bad look, and she would probably pummel me.

After a toast to Carpenter, people hugged, and Katie came over to our table. She gave me a quick, one-handed hug, then embraced Liz. I hurried to Josh. He was shaking Ambrose's hand. As they separated, I grabbed Josh's elbow and pulled him closer.

"I know who did it." We locked eyes. "Meet me by the fireplace."

"You're serious?" he said.

"Definitely."

After she finished hugging two more of the young women, I grabbed Liz and meandered through the kitchen. We were soon in the fireplace room, and moments later, Josh poked his head around the corner. I motioned for him to come closer and pointed at the vacuum.

"Do you have an automatic or robotic vacuum at home?" I asked.

Liz moved toward the foyer, presumably getting ready to be our lookout. A blind lookout was better than no lookout.

"Yes, we have one." Josh nodded his head. "Why?"

"Is it programmable so it can run at specific times?"

"Yes, I think so."

I explained my theory about how Amanda could have taped her phone to the vacuum. I told him about the lock the police had found and about the break-in on the night before the murder. He seemed confused as I explained. Dampness was in his eyes. As I finished, I could see he knew I was right. Glancing back at the foyer, I saw Liz's arm wrapped around the entryway. It appeared she was talking to someone.

"You think they can access the memory from our vacuum?" Josh touched the one sitting by the fireplace. "If so...could that shoot down or verify her alibi? And if you're right, could that prove it?"

"It would be damning to her alibi," I said. "Do you have the app on your phone?"

"Me? No. Amanda does."

I noticed movement out of the corner of my eye and saw Amanda in the entryway. She looked at Josh and me. I saw concern in her eyes. Then her gaze moved from Josh to the vacuum and then to Liz. I was sure she suspected something.

For a moment, I thought she was going to approach us and join in the conversation. Perhaps she would gauge her husband's attitude and determine if he suspected her. Instead, she turned and walked out the front door. I went to the window and saw the SUV's door swing open. The engine roared to life.

"Where is she going?" Josh asked as we stared out the window. "She didn't hear us talking about the vacuum, did she?"

"I don't think so," Liz said. "But you two were looking at it as you spoke and Josh, you looked upset. I think she may have figured out what you were talking about."

"If that's the case, she could head to your home so she can destroy the vacuum, or at least its memory." I stared at Josh as Amanda backed into traffic. A pair of horns blared.

"Is that possible?" he asked. No one answered. "We should call the police."

I pointed at an approaching police cruiser. "They're already here."

Chapter 44

The Dane County Sheriff's Office cruiser's lights flipped on before it got to the Larson Place. The SUV stopped just before the driveway. A van marked with the City of Madison Police Department logo followed. It pulled past the SUV and backed into the driveway. A third marked police vehicle completed the caravan. If they had shown up two minutes earlier, Amanda wouldn't have been able to back out of the driveway, and we wouldn't be worried about where she was going and what she was doing.

Bailey, Schuster, and a uniformed sheriff's deputy got out of the SUV while Knutsen and an MPD officer exited the cruiser. The van had pulled further into the driveway, so it was beside the house. I imagined a handful of people wearing funny uniforms and surgical gloves, but I didn't bother to look.

Josh, Liz, and I clambered down the steps. I let go of Liz's hand and rushed to Knutsen. "Amanda Peterson just left," I said. "We should go after her. Josh says his wife is a beneficiary of some of his mom's investments. She gets twenty percent, so long as they're still married. That means she has a motive for wanting Carpenter dead. Something other than jealousy."

Knutsen turned toward Josh, who was standing in front of the police car. "What is he talking about? I thought you said you were the sole beneficiary of the will."

"Technically, that's correct," Josh replied. "But I contacted my mom's lawyer to verify the details. He sent me an email as a heads-up."

"And?"

"It seemed I didn't really understand my mother's estate." He provided a long-winded explanation of the trust and of his mother's investments.

Bailey and Schuster joined us, and I laid out my theory. Josh nodded as I spoke and added a few comments. Liz chimed in, explaining that Amanda may have inferred Josh and my conversation about the automatic vacuum cleaner.

"What amount of money are we talking about?" Bailey asked. "How much would go to this trust?"

"Afraid I don't really know," Josh said. "It probably approaches eight figures."

Bailey and Knutsen looked at each other. I could see them counting digits.

"You're suggesting Amanda killed Carpenter to delay a divorce?" Knutsen looked at Josh. "Is that what you think too? She would get money upon your mother's death if she was still married to you?"

"Yes." He slapped a fist into his hand. "I didn't want to believe it. What an idiot!" He turned to me. "The fact that she couldn't have been there. I hung on to that belief. But now? I saw her expression before she took off. She did it, and she'll do what she can to destroy any evidence. She's not one to give up."

"Did you bring the bicycle lock?" I asked Knutsen.

There were murmurs as Knutsen walked back to his vehicle and pulled out the black lock. It was inside a clear plastic bag, and he put on gloves before pulling it out. "You said you have a key?"

I looked at Josh. "Give him your keys."

He handed them over without delay. "It's the black, square one," I said.

Passing traffic was the only sound as Knutsen held the key up, then stuck it into the bicycle lock. It turned. "This is it," he said.

Bailey took two quick breaths and stared at Josh. "Do you have an automatic vacuum, like Cy suggested?" He nodded. "Is it still at you and your wife's house?"

"Yes. Unless she used a different one or bought a replacement." Tears rolled down his cheek. "We need to stop her! If she did it, if she killed poor Carpenter, she can't get away with it."

"You think she's going home to wipe the memory?" Bailey turned to me. "Is that even possible?"

Liz leaned between us. "The data is likely on the vacuum itself, but it's also transferred to the phone app, which collects the data. Some of that then gets shared with the company, though I don't know if there's anything personally identifiable."

"What's that mean?" Bailey's eyes darted between Liz and me. "Can she destroy it or not?"

"She can certainly delete information on the app," Liz replied, "but she probably needs to do a factory reset to delete data from the vacuum itself. She may not know how to do that. There's a good chance she'll just delete the app and physically destroy the vacuum or its chip."

"She will try to destroy it one way or another." Josh was shaking and rage was in his voice. "I know her. She's not about to give up the life she wants. If she can't figure out how to destroy it from the app, she'll go home and destroy the vacuum. She'll claim she rushed out because of some bullshit reason. Maybe she'll say she was mad that I suspected her."

"Let's head to her house," Bailey said while looking at Knutsen. Then she turned to Josh. "Will you come with us? We can go into your house with your permission. Having you with us makes that approval clear, particularly if Amanda is there."

"Yes. Let's go."

"Cy, you and Liz come along as well," Bailey said. "You seem to know more about these vacuums than we do, and we don't have time to research."

Bailey put Schuster in charge of the team at the Larson Place, which was necessary since everyone had joined us outside. Knutsen put the lock in the SUV's trunk and ushered Josh, Liz and me into the back seat. The two detectives then went into a discussion about whether they should take one vehicle or two.

"We don't have time for this!" Josh yelled. "We need to beat her to our place, or at least get there before she can destroy the thing."

"Calm down, sir," Knutsen said. "We have your address. The west district will have units there within two minutes. Either way, they'll be at the house well before us and before Amanda."

"Sorry." His chest heaved. "I wasn't thinking."

Bailey and Knutsen talked about whether the primary goal should be to apprehend Amanda or to protect the vacuum.

Since she might use her phone to delete the vacuum's memory, they prioritized apprehending her. They agreed to keep the MPD officers hidden, so Knutsen instructed dispatch to send two units without sirens to the street directly behind Josh and Amanda's house. The officers would wait in the backyard and detain anyone trying to enter the house.

After calling dispatch, the siren turned on. Soon we were roaring down Madison's West Beltline Highway at eighty miles per hour. As we drove, Bailey quizzed Liz on vacuums and called someone on her team. Unfortunately, Josh didn't have the app on his phone, so they didn't know which make or model they were dealing with.

"What if she destroys the memory?" I asked.

Liz leaned forward. "Even if she does, the vacuum company may collect and keep enough data to show when it cleaned. No telling how much information these devices collect on us and what they share."

"Let's hope we don't have to find out," Bailey said. Even when discussing police work, she sounded like a teenager. She stopped as a call came on the radio announcing that a black SUV was pulling into the driveway and the garage door was raising.

"I don't like the idea of your officers coming up to her in a confined space like the garage," Josh said. "She's a Marine who served two tours in Afghanistan. She's not one to be messed with. If she feels threatened, she might do something stupid."

Bailey nodded, and Knutsen told the officers on the radio to wait for them before contacting the suspect. Knutsen then asked for two additional units. As we entered Josh's neighborhood, the siren went silent. After turning onto their street, the cruiser pulled to the side of the road. Josh said we were about seven houses from his home.

Before exiting the vehicle, Knutsen twisted his neck and looked me in the eye. "You three wait here. Hopefully, we'll get near the house without her noticing us. We will just pretend we're civilians walking around in the neighborhood."

The door slammed, and the detectives crossed the road and started down the sidewalk.

"They don't look like any civilians I've seen around here," Josh said. Sirens were in the distance.

The two detectives were near the house when the garage door raised. Even from seven houses away, I saw the SUV in the garage with its back gate open. Then someone appeared behind the vehicle holding a bicycle. "What the hell is she doing?" I muttered.

"She's taking her bike," Josh said. "She's putting it in the SUV."

As she placed the bicycle into the back of the vehicle, Knutsen and Bailey approached. The uniformed officers joined them, leaving Amanda standing at the edge of the garage surrounded by four cops.

Josh leaned toward me, and I smelled wine on his breath. "They got her." He rushed out of the vehicle, leaving the door hanging open.

Liz and I looked at each other, then hopped out. We watched as Josh ran toward his house. Bailey turned toward him as he stopped at the edge of the sidewalk, calling his wife a murderer and every swear word I could imagine.

Chapter 45

Bailey, accompanied by two Dane County Sheriff's deputies, took Amanda downtown for questioning. Liz and I stayed with Josh until more deputies arrived. One, a stocky man wearing sunglasses, brought Josh inside the house, keeping him away from the bystanders crowding the area. We returned to Knutsen's vehicle and watched as a pair of City of Madison police officers taped off the property.

Shortly afterward, a trio of local news station vans arrived. The temperature in the cruiser was rising, so we got out and sat on the hood. A dark-haired reporter, who I recognized from television, descended on us. I pulled Liz off the car, and we walked up the street, ducking under the police tape. An officer stopped us, but when we mentioned Knutsen, he passed us off to another officer, who had us sit on the back porch's wicker chairs.

After ten minutes, Knutsen joined us, sitting in the remaining chair. He tapped my knee. "Our techies at the office just finished going through the video footage that MB sent us."

"And?"

"We think we pick Amanda up on the path on Tuesday. I don't remember the exact times, but we see a woman going downtown at around two in the morning. An hour or an hour and a half later we see her heading toward her house. On Tuesday evening she goes downtown again. This is the best sighting since there's still light. She must have gone home a different way, as we didn't pick her up after the murder. With enough effort, we'll find her heading home."

"You're clear it's her you're picking up on camera?"

"The person on tape is a female in a black helmet riding a red Trek bicycle. There is a U-lock attached to the bike. The rider is in a gray hoodie, which is tied tight. Our techies say they can't swear it's Amanda, but they say the bike is likely a match with the red Trek Domane AL 4 we found in Josh and Amanda's garage. The lock helps, and there's also a black bike helmet."

I smiled and patted Liz's knee.

"The evidence is adding up," she said.

"Yes, it is," Knutsen replied. "We rushed the bike, helmet, and lock to the lab guys. My guess is they'll find evidence on the helmet that whoever wore it recently was also in Lake Monona. The bike might produce evidence as well. As to the vacuum, she deleted the app, but didn't do a factory reset. Bailey's people are working with some folks to access that information."

"So, the video evidence, the lock, and the vacuum give you a strong circumstantial case, right?" Liz said.

"Yeah. We still don't have anyone who saw her kill Carpenter, and it's doubtful anyone will come forward. We are, however, going to interview the man she was having an affair with. It's possible he knows something."

"Let's hope."

"It would be helpful if you two went through what you think happened again. A summary to cement things for me."

"Sure," I said, with a nod to Liz. "We can only speculate on how things started, but my guess is Amanda always figured she would get at least a share of Josh's family fortune. At some point, she probably found out details. Perhaps Josh's mother told her about the trust, or maybe she found the email from the lawyer to Josh which included specifics."

Liz tapped my knee. "So, she knew that, in order to share in the fortune, she had to stay married."

"Right. And at some point, Carpenter became a threat. She was forcing Josh to divorce, and Amanda was worried the divorce would occur before his mother died."

Knutsen shook his head. "Why didn't she just kill the mother?"

"That might have been more efficient," I replied, "but she would have been an obvious suspect. Besides, she got along with the old lady. Maybe she preferred killing Carpenter."

"One thing bothers me," Liz said. "Couldn't Amanda have dragged out the divorce until after Josh's mom passed? I mean, contested divorces can drag. Why kill Carpenter?"

"She could have tried to do that," I said. "But Josh was going to talk with his mother about it. It's just a guess, but Amanda may have assumed that, if he filed for divorce, the mother would adjust the trust, cutting her out immediately."

"At some point, she decided to kill Carpenter," Knutsen suggested, "to ensure she would share in the mother's estate."

"Yes," I said. "Plans for the Madison tasting had been in place for a while. Amanda likely focused on it as her opportunity. She knew she would be a suspect, so she needed an alibi, something that would prove that she couldn't have been involved in the murder. I don't know if she had already had affairs at this point or if she instigated one or more to minimize her apparent motive. Either way, she knew that Ambrose's wine tastings always involved swimming or boat rides, and she assumed Josh would offer to take everyone out on his boat."

"I hate boats," Knutsen said.

I shook my head and laughed. "Okay. Glad you weren't on board. Either way, Amanda probably didn't know what room people would be in until Ambrose assigned them about a month before the event." I looked at Liz. "That's when everyone got a text or an email with their room information."

"Yes," Liz said. "My notice came through exactly a month before the event."

"Carpenter shared her room information with Josh via text or email. I forget which. Amanda probably went into his phone and saw the room assignments."

"Okay," Knutsen said. "Why bother with the house break-in if she had already planned to kill her on the lake?"

"The boat trip was weather-dependent. When rooms were assigned, I'm guessing she saw an opportunity. She realized Carpenter would be alone on Monday night and her room faced the back of the house. A night attack at the B&B could look like a botched robbery. Maybe she thought that would keep the focus away from her. Her only issue was to make sure Carpenter was asleep when she broke in. To mitigate that risk, she put a listening device in the room, sticking it to a mirror with some sort of adhesive."

Liz patted my arm. "How did she get the listening device into the room?"

"Josh told me that he and Amanda checked on the property a few weeks before the event. He said someone walked them through the place. I don't know who it was, but my guess is they didn't watch them too closely, and she slipped the device behind the mirror."

"Okay." Knutsen wrote in his notepad. "What do you think happened on the night Amanda broke into the B&B?"

"Amanda had bought a few things ahead of time. She must have had a burner phone and a bolt cutter, both of which she bought out of town with cash, just as she purchased the listening device, the knife, and the tracker. She still, however, planned to use her own bicycle and helmet. Didn't see those as risks."

"Which may lead to her downfall," Knutsen said.

I shrugged my shoulders, implying he might be right. "On Tuesday morning, she biked in, taking the Capital City Trail since it minimized cameras and interactions with other people. She probably parked the bike nearby and walked to the house while carrying the bolt cutters and, perhaps, a knife. Standing in the backyard and using an app on her burner phone, she would have been able to hear that there was no sound in the room. There was no other activity in the house, so she assumed Carpenter was asleep in bed. Using the cutters, she opened the shed and accessed the ladder."

"She probably had experience with ladders since she deployed it by herself in the dark. If something had, however, gone wrong, she could have just run away. The cops would have assumed it was a robber. But she successfully deployed it and got to the roof. The window furthest from the head of the bed was probably unlocked and open, so she cut a hole in the screen. Reaching through, she took it off and climbed inside. There was, however, a problem."

"The bed was empty," Knutsen said.

"Yep." I chuckled. "She must have had a fit. But she was smart enough to improvise. Taking the listening device and the screen with her, she crawled onto the roof and closed the window. She climbed down the ladder, but must have had some trouble retracting it, so she just pushed it into the grass and then retracted it and placed it in the shed."

"Do you figure she was wearing gloves this whole time?" Knutsen asked.

I nodded my agreement. "The only problem was the lock. It and the missing screen were obvious clues that someone had broken into or tried to break into the house. Rather than just leaving the shed unlocked, she bought a padlock and put it on the shed later in the morning."

"The Master Lock," Knutsen said.

Once again, I nodded. "Maybe that's all that was available, or maybe she thought it wouldn't matter. Before heading home, she hid the screen and probably the bolt cutters near the railroad tracks which run near the Capital City Trail. She then rode home, returning the same way she had arrived. She assumed no one would know that someone had tried to kill Carpenter on Tuesday morning, so she was less cautious."

"Too bad she didn't stop while she was ahead," Liz said.

"In her mind, she wasn't ahead." Liz rolled her eyes, but I continued. "I think we know what she did on Tuesday night. After leaving dinner, she drove home and got her vacuum ready. It was programmable, so she set it to run when she would be gone. My guess is she did the same thing on Monday night."

"What about the witness?" Knutsen stuck a finger in the air. "The woman who saw her moving around inside the house on Tuesday evening? Did she see something, or was she mistaken?"

"My guess is Amanda had bought motion-activated lights and set them in areas where the vacuum would move. This wouldn't explain the neighbor seeing a silhouette of a person, but the change in lighting would make it appear that someone was moving inside. She probably wasn't banking on a witness, but the neighbor lady saw lights turning on and off and inferred she was moving inside the house."

"Meanwhile, she biked to the lake," Knutsen said.

"Yeah. Using the same route, the same bike, and the same burner phone. The only difference is she brought a wet suit or at least fins. She didn't want to lock her bike to a bike rack. Maybe she was worried someone would remember it, or maybe she was worried that it would get ripped off since it's an expensive, high-quality bicycle."

"So, she locked it to a tree near the shore," Liz said.

"Yes. She may have had a change of clothes there as well. She simply swam out to the boat, got rid of the tracking device, then cut Carpenter's throat. The tracker is probably on the bottom of the lake, along with the phone. My guess is she had the phone in a waterproof container but threw it into the lake after the killing. When she got to shore, she ran into a problem."

Knutsen and Liz exchanged glances but said nothing.

"After getting dressed, she unlocked the bike and rushed back home. In her excitement, she must have left the lock. Perhaps she realized it, or it might not have dawned on her until she got home. The lock is jet black, so it would have been hard to see in the dark."

"So, she rode home without the lock," Liz said.

"Yeah," I replied. "She probably threw away her key and figured there was no way anyone would connect the lock with her since she had wiped it free of fingerprints before departing and wore gloves when she touched it."

"Did she bike home on a different route?" Knutsen asked. "Is that why we didn't pick her up coming home?"

"That's a good guess," I replied. "She knew the police would review camera footage on Tuesday evening and Tuesday night. It might be safer to not be seen twice on the same camera."

"And then she just went home and slept in her bed," Liz said.

Knutsen and I nodded in agreement.

Chapter 46

Knutsen packed Liz and me into a police car and drove us to the Larson Place. He said a Dane County Sheriff's deputy took Josh to the Public Safety Building while Amanda was at the Dane County Jail being held on obstruction of justice charges.

The vehicle that Schuster and Bailey had arrived in hours earlier was still in the B&B's driveway. Knutsen parked behind it, and Ambrose and Boston came outside. They were relieved, not because they saw us, but because they probably realized that Knutsen's arrival would allow their departure.

Schuster soon joined us, and they ushered everyone into the kitchen. Missy came down the stairs last, holding a bottle of soda. We sat around the table while the detectives provided a brief update. A few people asked about how Josh was handling the news.

"He's pissed as hell at Amanda," I said. "I think he blames himself for not knowing what she was capable of."

"Amanda seemed intense," Missy said, without showing emotion, "but I didn't sense the level of it." She looked at Knutsen. "What's next? Does she go to jail?"

"The sheriff's office is holding her on obstruction. They'll analyze the evidence and determine if they have enough to charge her with first-degree murder." He rubbed his bald head. "My guess is they have enough, though much of the evidence is circumstantial. Hopefully, she'll confess. If not, there will be a trial and it's likely that all or some of you will be called as witnesses."

A few people muttered questions at the same time, so Liz raised her hand. Knutsen pointed at her, and everyone looked her way. "How about the trust that lists Amanda as a beneficiary? Will she still get that money?"

"My guess is that, if Josh's mother is still of sound mind, she will change the beneficiary. If not, Josh will need to get power of attorney. While he is presumably going to fast-track a divorce, there's a chance Amanda could still inherit if the mother dies before they make changes."

"That wouldn't be, like, fair," Missy said.

Knutsen chuckled before tossing a lifesaver into his mouth. "Welcome to my world."

"I suspect they can get changes made quickly," Liz said. "She's got money, so undoubtedly, she has an excellent attorney. She may have liked Amanda, but I can't imagine her wanting a murderer to inherit."

After a few more questions, Knutsen and Schuster verified that everyone had provided statements. They then gave permission for people to leave town. Liz and I collected our luggage, and I left our bags on the porch.

Renee was the first to leave the B&B. After collecting a business card from Liz—I didn't even know my wife had business cards—she headed toward the Capitol Square. Missy was the next out, noting she had a three-hour drive to Eau Claire. She gave us semi-hugs and trudged toward the nearby parking ramp wearing a backpack and carrying a duffle bag.

Katie was the only one of the group planning to fly out. She had already missed her flight, so she said she would book a hotel room for the night and fly out in the morning. Liz invited her to stay the night at our house, volunteering me to drive her to the airport. She agreed, so she brought her luggage onto the porch, ready to go home with us.

Ambrose and Boston stood on the steps as Liz, Katie, and I walked down the sidewalk. We waved to Knutsen and Schuster as they shuttered the building.

"I really appreciate you letting me stay at your place tonight," Katie said as we waited at the intersection.

"No problem," Liz said. She paused, shaking her head. "I have a load of messages from the kids. Allie was the first to figure out that we were at a murder scene." She locked eyes on me. "There are nine texts from Kayla, twelve from Allie, and four from Brandy. Let me send them a quick note so they know everything's okay."

I looked at my phone. There were two messages from Brandy, one from Kayla, and none from Allie. That's how it always was. They almost always went to their mother; I was the "other" parent.

"Allie is waiting at home," she said, squinting at her phone.

"I'd love to meet her," Katie said.

Once across the road, Liz patted Katie's shoulder. "This will certainly be a trip to remember, won't it?"

"Yes, it will." Katie grabbed Liz's waist. "And we're going to be in Nebraska together next month. If you're interested, I'll hook you up with a few of the better wine competitions. I could show you around San Francisco or Portland. It would be fun."

"That sounds great. So long as my husband is okay with going?"

I gave a thumbs-up.

Liz laughed. "No hesitation?"

"No hesitation," I said. She needed me, and I had done what was necessary for Carpenter and the rest of the group. Not only had we tried to figure out what happened to her, but we had succeeded. If I ever saw her daughter, I could look her in the eye. Maybe I would drop to one knee and tell her I knew her mother. I could tell Maddie how beautiful and talented her mother had been. I could tell her that her mother had typed her name every time she opened her phone.

It wasn't much, but it was something.

Epilogue

A t eight in the morning, Liz announced she was ready. Our daughter Allie took the large bag, and I took the suitcase. The garage door was open. I grasped the SUV's back gate, and it raised. We threw the bags into the trunk. Liz also had two small containers, but she wanted them inside the vehicle.

Assuming a few stops, Liz figured the drive to Lincoln would take less than eight hours. The trip didn't excite me, but I had to admit that I was looking forward to seeing Katie and Boston. Unfortunately, Josh wouldn't attend, as his mother died two days earlier and he was busy with funeral preparations.

Josh said the doctors were surprised that she gave in so soon. The good news was his mother's lawyer had changed the trust several weeks before her passing, so the entire trust would go to him. The ironic thing was that his mother died earlier than the doctors had expected. If Amanda hadn't murdered Carpenter Dalbesio, she would have received roughly two million dollars.

Three weeks earlier, Liz and I went to Naperville for Carpenter's funeral. Josh was there, as were Ambrose, Boston, and Leonardo Dalbesio. None of us sat with the family, but Josh cried more than anyone in the church. Once the funeral was over, he left for a nearby hotel, saying he'd be flying to Nantucket in the morning.

For the past month, Josh and Amanda Peterson's house was empty. He left the keys with me so I could check on things at least weekly. I didn't ask for payment, but I assumed the newly rich Josh would make it worth my time.

It took several weeks before Dane County charged Amanda with first-degree intentional homicide. Knutsen told me he expected some sort of deal between the county and Amanda, and he expected it would involve her pleading guilty to murder.

Before leaving for Lincoln, our middle daughter, Allie, joined us in the garage. I handed her the keys to our house and to Josh's house. Her job was to check on both at least once while we were gone. She didn't ask for payment, but she had recently voiced an interest in getting into the wine industry, just like her mother. Something told me we'd come back to a house that was missing a few bottles of wine.

After backing out of the driveway, we waved goodbye. Liz then sent a text to our youngest daughter. She was still in La Crosse, Wisconsin, where she would start her sophomore year.

All our children were worried about their mother going to the tasting, particularly since there had been a murder at the last one. Our oldest daughter, Kayla, pulled me aside a week before and reminded me that my job was to make sure her mother was safe.

"Yeah," I told her. "I'll be with her the whole time. And we won't go on any boat outings." It was an easy promise to make, since Ambrose and Boston's event plans kept us away from all bodies of water. His tradition of swims and boat rides during wine tastings was apparently over.

"Mom really appreciates you, you know? She knows you get restless following her around."

"I don't mind being her date. I will bring my kit and a dozen locks to play with. It's my entertainment."

She rolled her eyes. "Dad, it's good that you are so easily entertained."

Acknowledgements

Thanks to all who supported me in writing this book. Special thanks to Dannielle Breen, Dianna Breen, Dan Birrenkott, Matt Breen, Sue Krumenauer, Bradley Bryant, Kelsey Breen, and Dave Greenwell.

About the Author

Paul Breen plays guitar poorly and spends far too much time on genealogy. A native of Columbus, Ohio, Paul grew up in Madison, Wisconsin, and worked at the University of Wisconsin-Madison. Paul enjoys running, biking, music, sports, history, and visiting brewpubs. He lives with his wife and family in Madison.

www.ingramcontent.com/pod-product-compliance
Lightning Source LLC
Chambersburg PA
CBHW020356110726
47899CB00006B/1743